Bring Home the Ghost

K. Follis Cheatham

Bring Home the Ghost

Harcourt Brace Jovanovich
New York and London

Requests for permission to make copies of
any part of the work should be mailed to:
Permissions, Harcourt Brace Jovanovich, Inc.,
757 Third Avenue, New York, New York 10017.

Printed in the United States of America

Library of Congress Cataloging in Publication Data

Cheatham, Karyn Follis, 1943–
Bring home the ghost.

Bibliography: p.
SUMMARY: Traces the adventures of two boys,
one the slave of the other, in the first half of
the 19th century as they grow to manhood on an
Alabama plantation, experience its devastation,
and move west to find a freer way of life.
[1. Slavery in the United States—Fiction.
2. Friendship—Fiction.   3. Plantation life—
Alabama—Fiction.   4. The West—Fiction]   I. Title.
PZ7.C399Br   [Fic]   80–7981
ISBN 0–15–212485–3

First edition

B C D E

Contents

3-1

I

All You Can Count On

1

August, 1827.
*A swell of blue-black smoke columned up from the creek
bank and hung over the fruit trees against the pale sky.
Soon the entire grove was covered with the thick, acrid
cloud.*

*"Cane fire, Masta Cobb! Masta Tolin's done gone down
to it already!" a buxom black woman called as she ran to
the white man by the stone fence.*

*Willis Cobb let the handles of the sledge fall from his
fingers and hurried toward the billowing black smoke.
"Tolin," he muttered huskily. He could see his twelve-
year-old son riding his horse through the orchard toward
the canebrake. Willis ran between the cotton plants. His
heavy work shoes thumped loudly on the reddish earth. A
flatbed wagon rumbled down the work road and two black
men jumped off with shovels. Their running figures were
lost in the smoke.*

*"Tolin!" Willis's shout was barely heard over the roar of
the fire. "Tolin!" Occasionally Willis could see the men
tossing lumps of dirt on the fire as it crept along the dry
grass toward the orchard. "Tolin!"*

*A blue-roan horse skittered out of the dense smoke and
fled in terror along the road to the stable. The stirrups
flopped crazily from the saddle on its back. Willis ran to*

where his son's horse had emerged. The heat singed his heavy blond eyebrows and made the backs of his hand tingle.

"Masta Cobb, no!" A thick black hand pulled on his arm. It was Jake. "Don't go in there!"

Everyone backed away as the fire rumbled and crackled. A four-foot-wide trench had been dug between the cane and the orchard. It was clear of grass and twigs; the fire would burn out. The orchard trees nearest the trench were covered with soot and appeared withered, but they would live.

"Masta Cobb! Here! Come quick!" Seth's angular frame bent over something as he called.

In the trench, not more than fifty feet away, were two bodies. The smoke was lifting when Willis reached them.

"Tolin! Oh, God!" Willis turned one inert figure over and pulled it to his chest as if it were a cloth doll.

"Pa?" The voice was weak, and a slender arm reached for the man's neck.

"Oh, son! Are you hurt? Why did you ride down here?"

"They was needin' help, Pa. Fire was movin' fast."

"I saw your horse . . . I thought . . ."

" 'Twas Jason that done it, Pa. He saved me. That horse threw me and Jason pulled me out."

Willis glanced for the first time at the figure that was beside them.

The roan horse was back. It snorted and stamped to a stop on the road. Seth grabbed the bridle as its rider dismounted.

"Tolin! Oh, Tolin!" Nancy Cobb rushed over to the man and boy. Her face was wan and strained.

"He's all right, Nancy," Willis reassured his wife as she caressed their son. "You shouldn't have ridden down here."

"No broken bones? He's not burned anywhere? When I saw his horse come flying up to the stable—" She cried into her gray skirt, trying to calm her fears. How much more pain would this Alabama land bring her? she wondered.

4

How much? Her first son, Aaron, had been killed the month they arrived from North Carolina. Fourteen, he had been. And Priscilla—so lovely—dead of a fever before she was three. There were the two miscarriages, and now this.

"Jason done it. He pulled me out," Tolin said again as his father helped him to the wagon.

Jason forced himself to a sitting position. A young black woman dabbed at his soot-streaked face with the hem of her skirt. She didn't speak, but she comforted him with motherly pats.

"Jason?" Nancy Cobb looked at the boy with tears in her eyes. "Thank you for our son, Jason. Are you hurt?"

"No, ma'am." Jason struggled to stand. His eyelids fluttered slightly and he pressed his dusty toes into the earth to steady himself. He was tall for ten years old and a trifle thin. His brown arms and legs were bony protrusions from under his clothes. He held his left arm close to his side.

"You are hurt," Nancy said suddenly. She knelt by the boy and lifted his arm. The faded blue shirt was scorched, and hung in black tatters down his left side. An ugly burn was already blistering across his shoulder and back. "Willis, the boy is badly burned. He needs careful tending."

"We've got salve for burns. I'll send some out to the quarters this evening."

"Willis!" Nancy turned abruptly to where he sat on the wagon seat with Tolin. Her blue eyes snapped a warning to him, and he knew not to argue.

"Put him in the back of the wagon," he said with a sigh. Then he spoke to the Negroes. "You all get back to work."

Willis helped his wife onto the wagon seat as the boy staggered to the back. Seth tied the roan to the wagon, and Willis slapped the mules to action.

Soon the land seemed peaceful. A cardinal darted through the orchard and surveyed the blackened canebrake. The sound of the hoes began again as the slaves chopped away between the cotton rows. The wagon clattered up the road toward the house.

5

I didn't know if I should get in that wagon or not, even though Miz Cobb told me to. I looked to Skalley to see if I should. She nodded at me, brushed a speck of ash from my cheek, and then went back to her hoein'. I pulled myself onto the wagon bed, and my back and arm hurt so I could hardly see. Mistuh Tolin, he turned and grinned at me from between his folks. His face was still blacked up, and there was soot in his light brown hair, but his eyes—they was blue eyes like his ma's—they shone all happy and nice.

"Zeus got skittish," Mistuh Tolin started sayin'.

"You don't ever ride a horse into a fire, son. And a cane fire! The smell alone is enough to make them bolt."

"Yes, sir. I tried to run out after the horse, but the smoke choked me down. I hit my head on something. I remember seein' Jason over me, pullin' me, before I passed out."

I passed out then myself. I heard Miz Cobb sayin' somethin' about bravery, then I just keeled over. When I came to, I was layin' on my right side on a cot in the pantry of the Cobbs' big frame house. I could smell hot bread, and turnip salad. My mouth got all watery and I tried to sit up, but the pain was on me like the fire was still burnin' on my back.

"Now, whatchu think you a-doin'?" Mattie looked down at me, her brown face smilin' from over her white apron, then she disappeared into the kitchen.

I laid real still and the burnin' eased. I looked down at myself as best I could. Things was different about me. I was wearin' a shirt of Mistuh Tolin's and a pair of his pants. My arm and shoulder was bandaged up good, and my scalp felt tingly where my head had been washed.

"Mattie," I called soft. "Where's Skalley?"

Mattie come back to me with a big biscuit in her hand. She helped me to sit, and then gave me the biscuit. "Skalley's down in the quarters where she's suppose to be. Now, whatchu want with Skalley when you got these fine folks here to care for you?"

I didn't say nothin'—just bit into the biscuit. It had been

two years since my mama died of a fever. Skalley was sixteen then, and didn't have no children of her own, so Mistuh Cobb give me to her to keep till I was growed. Skalley couldn't talk—she was borned that way—but her and me, we got a lot of meanin' to each other.

"They's a-talkin' in there 'bout you," Mattie said low as she brought me a plate of greens and side meat. I steadied the plate on my knees and hunched into eatin'. I had to close my eyes at times against the pain, but the food was worth it. "Miz Cobb, she want to manumit you." I looked up at Mattie, curious, while I chewed. "That's fancy talk for *free*. She says you done saved her boy and Massa Cobb ought to let you be free." Mattie chuckled. "Ain't gonna happen, though. Massa Cobb ain't gonna let a youngun like you go free. He don't see you ten years old like Miz Nancy do. He see you twenty and workin' his fields twice as hard."

I finished eatin' and stared at the plate while my stomach rolled half-full in me.

"You want some more? Sure you do. Miz Cobb tell me to give you whatever you wants." Mattie took my plate and strolled back into the kitchen hummin' to herself. She left the door open and I could hear voices from the dinin' room.

"Well, Pa? You still haven't said nothin' about Jason," Mistuh Tolin was sayin'. "Will you manumute—"

"Manu*mit*," his ma corrected.

"Will you give him freedom? He'll still be workin' here. He don't have nowhere else to go."

"He *doesn't*," Miz Cobb corrected again.

"Tolin, son. There's one thing you have to get clear. That boy is a slave. True, he saved your life, but it was no different than he should have done, seein' that he belongs to this here plantation."

"You didn't pay nothin' for him," Mistuh Tolin argued. "His ma was carryin' him from that carpenter that built our house. You told me that."

"His daddy was a slave, and so will he be. That's final! If everybody went around setting loose their slaves when they did something good . . . No sense to it! Do you turn loose a horse because he wins you a race? No! He's just doing what's expected."

"Willis! I don't like that talk," Miz Cobb said real strong. "A man is not a horse!"

Mattie gave me my plate and went out, closin' the door behind her.

Manumit. That was a strange word. Why couldn't the white folks just say what they was meanin': set a slave to freedom? I wondered what freedom was like.

"They's done a-talkin'," Mattie said as she came back and dropped another biscuit on my plate. "Done eatin' too. Looks like I'm gonna be stuck with you around for a while." I looked at her real quick while I commenced on the biscuit. "You ain't bein' freed, but you's bein' took by little massa for his own boy."

Mattie walked out. I wasn't sure what anything meant, but my stomach was full for the first time in a long time, and if things was to continue that way I wasn't gonna complain.

2

I was two weeks up in that house, and Miz Nancy Cobb herself would come and change the bandages on my shoulder. She kept the burn all greased up with some mixture of butter and weeds that smelled real bad and drew flies somethin' fierce. My shoulder hurt a lot, too, when she took off the old wrappin's, and I'd grit my teeth to keep from cryin'. Even so, I really liked the times she'd come, 'cause she smelled sweet and talked friendly, and her eyes was always smilin'. Mistuh Tolin would come with her most times, and his ma would make him take up a book and read to me. He acted like he really wanted to, but soon as she left he'd put the book away and tell me how many turtles he flipped over at the crick, and who was doin' what in the quarters.

"Jake was tellin' stories last night," he said one afternoon. "All about the time him and my granddaddy were in the Revolutionary War."

"What's that?"

"The war at the ocean—with the British. My granddaddy was at the battle of King's Mountain, and Jake carried his powder and shot. Ain't you heard him tell that?"

"Oh, sure! But I likes it best when he talks about comin' west to Alabama. All about the injun fights and settlin' of the land."

"Yeah." He got quiet, and I remembered Bitty sayin' that his brother, Aaron, got killed then. He was struck down by an Indian tomahawk. I'd heard Mistuh Cobb talk about it, too. Neither Mistuh Tolin nor me was born then.

"You remember that story about Jake meetin' the mountain cat on the trail?" he said of a sudden.

"In the thunderstorm? And how he reached in that cat's big mouth when it roared?"

"Yeah! And grabbed its tail and yanked it inside out!"

We was laughin' over the story and Mattie come to the door frownin' at us. "Your pa's comin', Massa Tolin," she said real quiet. Mistuh Tolin pulled out the book his ma had left with him.

"Tolin! What in tarnation are you doing in here?" Mistuh Cobb's voice sounded mad. "It's the end of the week. Go put out the rations for the folks in the quarters."

"But Mama told me to read to Jason."

"You aren't no schoolmarm. Put the book down. We got nine workin' slaves on this place and they aren't gonna tend their own rations. Now get to it!"

"Yes, sir." Mistuh Tolin backed out of the room.

"And give an extra measure of sorghum all around— except to Bill. He's been slack as usual." Mistuh Cobb looked down at me. "I'm movin' you out to the cabin with Jake and Bitty, you hear? Want you back to working, too. Can't be feedin' you a peck of meal a week when you ain't working."

"Half a peck, suh," I told him.

"What?" He glared at me.

"Just half-peck is all I get. I won't be eleven till early November. But I could eat a full peck if you give it!"

"Um." He scratched his jaw and walked out.

I don't think he'd gone three paces when Mattie come rushin' in. "What's the matter witchu, boy, talkin' like that?" She sorta whispered at me and grabbed hold of my ear between her strong fingers. "Don't chu know how to act around white folks? All that laughin' and carryin' on with little massa." She pulled me off the cot by my ear and started grabbin' up my things. Her voice got louder. "If you're gonna be up here by the house you got a few things to learn! You don't speak 'less spoke to, and don't act like you know too much about *nothin'!*" She stuffed the sheet from the cot in my good arm. "Talkin' out to Massa Cobb that way. I never heard the like! Remember, the onlyest thing he's interested in from you is good work. That's why you's bein' fed—not to give him no back talk about his rations. He give us salt pork and rice, and chickens to raise, and seed for gardens—and you come along squawlin' about half a peck of meal. You hear what I'm sayin', Jason?"

"Yes'm." I was still rubbin' my pinched ear on my shoulder.

"Now, you get on out to the cabin. Lord help us. Maybe Jake and Bitty can get you some sense. I never!" And she shooed me out the door.

I felt sorta sad leavin' that house, not 'cause it meant I'd be goin' back to work, but 'cause I knowed it was the house my pa had built and I sorta felt close to him, bein' in the house like that. I never knowed my pa, Marcus, but my ma sure talked proud about him.

I turned around and backed toward the fence by the stable path so I could look at the house some more. It sure was pretty.

"I hope you got eyes in the back of your head."

Jake's voice scared me and I turned around quick. "No, suh." I had nearly run into him. "Mattie—she say I'm movin' in with you." Jake wasn't tall, but he was broad and thick all through the shoulders like a plow mule. His hair was almost white, but his arms was tough with muscles like a young person's.

"I hear tell that." He got a grin on his wide face and put his big hand on my good shoulder. "I also hears you got a lot to learn."

"Yes, suh." I hung my head and remembered how Mattie had just scolded me.

"A lot to learn about smithin'!"

I looked up fast. "About blacksmithin'?"

"Yep. If'n you're to be little masta's man, you got to learn a trade."

"Yes, suh!" And I followed Jake to my new quarters with him and Bitty in the old Cobb cabin.

First thing Jake taught me was the ways of the stable. I curried and fed the horses; checked them for flies; cleaned and oiled tack. I especially took care of Mistuh Tolin's roan horse, Zeus. After another three weeks I was tendin' the bellows at the large, three-sided brick forge where Jake made the iron hot enough to shape into axes and froes. I got my first pair of brogans then to protect my feet from the hot coals that sometimes spilled on the floor.

That forge stood as wide as I was tall with places in one side to set in the anvils. Jake had four different hammers, chisels, and six pair of tongs hangin' on the wall beside the forge. I worked the treadle that hooked to the bellows and kept the air blowin' on the coals so the fire would stay hot. Jake could make that metal ring with his hammerin' blows, and sometimes we'd get a rhythm started: my bellows goin' *whoosh!*, his hammer goin' *ring! Whoosh, ring! Whoosh, ring!* Jake had a special song to go with that rhythm.

> Hammer come down *(whoosh, ring!)*
> Hammer come down *(whoosh, ring!)*
> Hit that iron make a mighty good soun'.
> Heat up the iron *(whoosh, ring!)*
> Make it glow red *(whoosh, ring!)*
> Pound ten froes 'fore I go to bed.
> Stoke up the fire
> Take up the tong
> Iron's my life and I'll hammer it strong.
> Hammer come down *(whoosh, ring!)*
> Hammer come down *(whoosh, ring!)*
> Hit that iron make a mighty good soun'.

Then he'd take that heated-up metal when it was all shaped the way he wanted and stick it in a tub of water to cool it down. The steam would hiss up in our faces and the smell would scratch my throat. I always backed off real quick 'cause too much heat made my shoulder hurt where the burns was. Seems like I could feel them burns even when the sunshine was strong.

My movin' in with Jake and Bitty meant I didn't hardly ever go to the fields no more. I worked in the stable and ran errands to and from the house for the growed folks. I slept in front of Jake's hearth and ate with him and Bitty, not down in the quarters with Skalley. I worried some about her bein' alone, but I'd no cause to. Kusa moved his mattress to Skalley's cabin in a week's time of my bein' gone. Skalley was the youngest female on the place, 'ceptin' Mattie; and Mattie and Horace come together.

I took to sneakin' extra food out to Skalley and Kusa. I'd take a piece of pork from the springhouse near the kitchen, or some extra meal when I could get to the porch bin. After two weeks Mattie found out. She whupped me good with a rug beater, and told Mistuh Cobb I was stealin'. He threatened to send me back to the fields full time, but Jake come to my aid.

"He's got a strong arm, Masta Cobb. Gonna need a new man at the forge some day soon, suh. I's done hammered lots of plow blades—don't know how many more. He needs be taught all the things so's he can be a good man for Masta Tolin. So's he can stand beside him like I done with you, suh."

Mistuh Tolin was there that day, and he backed off from his pa a bit and grinned at me. He come around later while I was at the hay rack.

"Jake sure can talk good!" he said. "I'll bet he's the only black man my pa'll give a listen to."

"Sure seems like it." I forked some hay over the fence to the mules.

13

"You think Jake will tell some stories down in the quarters tonight?"

"Dunno. You gonna come if he does?"

"Yep. You give me a lantern sign. You know, wave it in a big circle, and I'll come."

"Your pa better not catch you!"

"He don't care, so long as I got my work done for him."

"Tolin!" Miz Cobb's voice was callin' from the house. "Tolin!"

"Got to go. Ma wants me to finish my lessons before I have to go to market with Pa. And I think I *would* rather read the *Odyssey* than stand all day in a stupid cotton lot."

I wondered what an odyssey was while I watched him run off to the house, then I thought about the cotton lot. I didn't even know what one looked like. I'd never been off the plantation 'ceptin' for revivals held up the road on the church grounds. Sometimes I'd think about cities like Montgomery, or Columbus, Georgia. Mattie and Horace had lived in Mobile and New Orleans before they come to Cobb's. They knew all about livin' in fine stone houses, and carriages and fancy balls. They'd tell about it sometimes in the evenin' talkin' in the quarters. I always liked to hear about those far-off places, and any kind of travelin' sounded good to me.

"It's like this ol' place was fresh to farmin'. Rocks keep a-poppin' up," Bill grumbled a few nights later. Seth was playin' mournful sounds on his mouth harp and everybody was easin' out of the work day. "You'd never figure a plow has bit into that land every year for twelve," Bill went on.

"Thirteen," Bitty said quick. "Masta done brought us here before this was named the state of Alabama. Settlin' us down right in the end of that injun war."

"Injuns?" Carrie said, all big-eyed. She was seven and the next oldest youngun on the place besides me.

"Creeks, baby," Margaret said to her. "Like runs the store out by the river. I told you."

"It was 1814," Kusa said. He was African. Sometimes he'd say strange words he remembered from his before life. "This one was tiny." He patted Skalley's leg and they smiled at each other. "I had to carry her some in them mountains."

"Where was Jason?" Carrie asked over the dirt she had heaped in front of her.

"Lord, child, Jason wasn't born yet!"

"I got started when that house was bein' built," I bragged.

"Yes sir, that Marcus come down from Montgomery to build a house, and ended up with a wife and a boy baby on the way by the time he was through," Jake said with a grin.

Margaret chuckled and laid aside her needlework. "Why, I never saw two folks take to each other like Marcus and Jason's ma. Oh, Lord, how they did go on over each other."

"You remember how he kept braggin' up how he was savin' his money to be free? 'Hirin' out for my freedom money,' he'd say."

"Um! An' you see what come of it," Jake said in a warnin' voice. "The Taits sold him down to Mississippi in '18 when Marcus weren't but fifty dollars short of the price. They just sold him off."

We was all real quiet, 'cause didn't nobody like to think of gettin' sold off. I chucked another piece of wood on the fire and wondered if my pa ever got his freedom, or if he just kept workin' and workin'—all for nothin'.

"Land is all you can count on," Seth said. "Love it and it love you back."

"That's right. You don't got much to complain about, Bill," Judith said.

Bill sighed and rested his head on her leg.

"This plantation can yield better'n fifty acres easy. We got a good place," Judith went on.

"And we's lucky, I think, to belong to a workin' man.

15

That's the only reason I stay around here, 'cause Masta Cobb works out there in the fields with us," Kusa said. "Why, I bet he hauled more rocks than you did today, Bill."

"Masta Cobb ain't content less'n he gots his hands in the soil, sure enough," Bill admitted. "But what you mean, Kusa, that's the only reason you stays around? Where you a-figure to be goin'?"

"Freedom."

Jake frowned. "Don't go talkin' that nonsense, Kusa."

"I was free once. I gonna be that way again. This here ain't so bad with the Cobbs, but come a time when it change—or when he talk like to sell me off—"

"And whatcha gonna do?" Mattie snorted.

"I don't like to think none about that day," Seth said. "But it could come. We're down to plantin' only thirty-two acres of cotton, and Masta Cobb likes to work with the stock more than the fields. You see that new trottin' mare he bought for the buggy? Now if he was to go to raisin' horses or sheep—well, could be he'd no need for this big a crew."

"He always got to have somebody to scythe the fields. Livestock gotta eat more than jest grass," Jake said.

"Or he can buy it, sure enough, from a grain man. One just settled out toward the river."

"He's too much of a workin' man for that," Bitty said. "And Miz Nancy Cobb ain't about to let us go nowheres. You know how she carried on when Massa wanted to sell Jason and his ma."

Bitty had told me a lot how Mama was so took with my pa, Marcus, that she wouldn't hitch up with nobody else after he was gone. Mistuh Cobb was wantin' all his females to breed for him and so he tried to sell me and Mama off in '20. Miz Cobb wouldn't let him. Seems she couldn't stand to part with none of her folks she'd brought from Carolina.

"Miz Cobb might have some maladies, but she's still got fire in her eye when she gets her mind set to somethin',"

16

Mattie said. "Like the way she is with that boy of hers. Bound and determined he's gonna know more than just plantin' crops. Has him readin' over those books at all hours."

"She's drawin' him from his pa," Horace said.

"He's the only thing she's got in this land that hasn't died and gone from her," Bitty declared. "It's only natural. You hold on to that what gives you strength."

I looked up the long hill to where the big house was snug on its stone foundation. A few lights glowed in the windows, and I wondered if those folks sat around and talked like we did. Did they wish they was someplace else doin' different things? I sure enough knew Mistuh Tolin did. Horace was right. His ma's hate for the plantation was growin' in him, too.

The lights went off at the house, and like it was a signal, the talkin' stopped. We all went to our sleepin' quarters, quiet and tired. Pretty soon there wasn't nothin' but the crickets and the treehoppers to be heard. I wondered if Mistuh Tolin was listenin' to them like I was; then I went to sleep.

3

I turned eleven sometime in the first part of November, and winter had barely set in before I was tryin' to swing a hammer on orange-hot iron to make new hoe blades. I got handy with the whetstone, too, and Jake turned all the honin' work over to me.

There was other stuff I learned, too, and not always 'cause I wanted to neither. One mornin' Mistuh Tolin and me was playin' out what he called the Battle of Thebes, and Mistuh Tolin fell into a sluice pen after pretendin' it was a moat. We was both laughin' about it, and he was shiverin' from bein' wet. His ma got upset and rushed him into the house for a bath. Then Mattie caught hold of my ear.

"You let him get all messed up that way? You ain't got the sense God gave a goose!"

"We was just playin'!" I tried to squirm away from her, but couldn't. "And he done it to hisself."

"You don't *play* with no white boy. You *belongs* to him. He might laugh with you now, but tomorrow he might think it funnier to whip you!" She marched me to the stable and shoved me toward Jake. "This boy's headin' us all for trouble!" And she told what had happened, makin' it sound like it was my fault Mistuh Tolin got dirty.

Jake didn't say nothin' till after Mattie had stomped back over to the house. "She had trouble before like this. That's why she get so upset," he said. "She got on real well with the folks she belonged to before, but one day she broke some fine dishes, and the mistress there took after her with a dog chain. Horace, he was gardener for them, he come to her aid, and they was both sold off. That's how they come to Cobb's."

"Just for some little ol' dishes?"

"She was funnin' when she should have been sober. Somethin' you better remember. There's times to hustle and times to hang back." He nodded a bit and patted my shoulder. "You learn their moods by watchin' and listenin'. Like you and little masta. It's good he spend time with you like he do, but jest remember what it's all about. You gots to know him as well as you know yourself."

"We just have fun together, that's all. Ain't nobody hereabouts our ages to play with."

"It ain't fun, boy! You learn! And don't go thinkin' that little white boy is any different than other white folks!"

"Yes, suh." But I couldn't true believe that the laughin' times Mistuh Tolin and me spent together wasn't nice for both of us.

There was a night after the fall harvest when the Cobbs had company and I was by the stables watchin' the people come. Jake and the carriage drivers was smilin' and noddin' while they handled the horses and helped the white folks. They'd laugh a little if it seemed to be right, or walk off with their eyes down when it was necessary. My ma had always taught me to be proud of myself, that's why she said I was to say Mistuh and not Masta. My pa taught her that. She said he said that a man's eyes should be lookin' out, not down, otherwise he'd always be walkin' in circles. When we was all in the quarters everybody held their heads up. I sure didn't like seein' Jake shufflin' like he done that night around the white folks.

Even so, I found myself bein' careful of my actions. What happened to Mattie and Horace kept runnin' through my thoughts and I got quiet and started listenin' more. Maybe Mistuh Tolin *was* the same as other white folks, but he didn't seem to change none. He'd slip out to the stables while his ma was asleep (she slept a lot, 'cause her health was failin'). Mistuh Cobb wasn't much for Mistuh Tolin studyin' books anyway, so he never said nothin' about it.

"Jason, when you get done with your work let's go back to the crick," Mistuh Tolin would say sometimes, all grinnin' while he spoke.

Jake would make my work light and I'd take off with Mistuh Tolin. We'd fish and snoop around the brush. Mistuh Tolin talked all the time about what he liked and didn't like, and how he wished there would be a school near, 'cause he couldn't wait to go. He also grumbled about his pa and havin' to learn how to keep track of the plantin' and crops; or which little lady he smiled at in church one Sunday and how he didn't believe in hell.

"Do you believe in hell, Jason?" I just shrugged. "I sure enough don't—unless it's right here and now like you bein' colored and me livin' on this damn plantation." He pulled a piece of bark off a spruce tree and pitched it into the crick. "You don't say much anymore, Jason. Like you couldn't talk at all."

"Guess that's from all the time I was livin' with Skalley," I said slow.

"You haven't lived with Skalley for nearly six months! And you used to be different anyways. Now you're actin' like everybody else. All quiet."

We watched a frog leap from the water. I slapped at a mosquito.

"I need you to talk to me, damn it!" Mistuh Tolin turned sudden. "There ain't a body I can talk to around here that talks back from my age. I thought you was gonna be different."

I could feel him gettin' mad and I worried on what to do. "Well, suh. Me and you do talk about the horses at the stables, and how mean or dumb they are."

20

"Oh, Jason!" He kicked a stone into the crick.

"What do you want to talk about, Mistuh Tolin? Crops? Fishin'?"

"No! I don't want to talk about crops or horses or fishin'. I— Oh, hell!" He ran through the bushes toward the house.

I went back real slow, scared I'd get whupped for makin' him mad, but I didn't.

I didn't see too much of Mistuh Tolin after that, and when he did come to the stables it was just to get his horse or to give some orders to Jake or me. He took to his book-studyin' real hard, too. I kept learnin' my job and gettin' stronger. I figured the good times was over for Mistuh Tolin and me. I wondered if I had kept actin' like my old self that he would have still been friendly. It worried me some about the changes that had happened, and more than that, I missed his company.

"Jason, saddle up Zeus for me," Mistuh Tolin ordered one morning. It was late spring, nine months after the cane fire.

"Yes, suh." I worked fast, seein' him tense and in a hurry.

"When my pa comes in, you tell him I went to fetch the doctor for Ma," he said as he sat the saddle.

I looked up to the house that had been quiet for so many days. The curtains in the upstairs room was drawn, and Mattie was scarce ever seen except to shout out orders for Jake and me to do. If Mistuh Tolin was goin' all the way to the river settlement for the doctor, Miz Cobb was real sick, especially with him goin' without his pa's say-so.

By the time Mistuh Tolin and the doctor got back that evening Mistuh Cobb had been called in from the field by Mattie. When I took the doctor's horse—it was lathered from the fast ride from the settlement—Miz Nancy Cobb had passed out of our lives. Mistuh Tolin's face twisted and strained to hold back tears when he found out. I got busy with the horses, and all the field work had stopped. Skalley was cryin', as was all the other women. Jake was cryin', too.

21

Mistuh Tolin disappeared and nobody seemed to miss him until almost dark.

"Tolin!" Mistuh Cobb's voice sounded like a cannon shot. "Jason, where's Tolin?" I looked at him all big-eyed. Mistuh Cobb peered into the stable and saw the roan horse, then looked back at me. "You find him, boy! You find him and bring him home!"

"Yes, suh."

I took off toward the gristmill—back to where we used to go fishin' near the woods. I figured to start there and work around past the orchard and then into the hills by the pasture.

"Mistuh Tolin!" I called. "Your pa wants you home. Mistuh Tolin!"

I found him straightaway. He was right there where we had been when we last went out together. "Mistuh Tolin." I puffed to a stop. "Your pa's worryin' for you." I looked around. He had taken an axe to all the trees. He had felled the little ones and girdled the big ones. He stood there with that axe in his hand and stared at me. I backed away. He looked kind of crazy and I didn't know what he'd do.

Suddenly he slumped to the ground and cried. It was heavy, painful sobs that came from him. I knew what he was feelin'. It hadn't been that long since my mama died. I sat down beside him and when the tears was gone from him we talked. I didn't feel no shame in speakin' out, and we talked about our mamas and how good they had been. We talked about not havin' any brothers or sisters to cry with us. We talked about all the times when little joys was with us and no one would listen.

That was the beginning and, more than any other time, I know *that* talkin' changed my life.

4

They buried Miz Cobb up in the graveyard behind the house next to the graves of her younguns that had gone before her. Mistuh Cobb cried. Mistuh Tolin was stone somber. That night before I went to bed I was wishin' I could do somethin' to give some comfort. I stood by the fence around the house and stared into the quietness. Mistuh Tolin come to the window of his room. I waved. He waved back.

Every evenin' for two weeks I stood by the fence before goin' to the cabin. Mistuh Tolin would come to his window. We'd wave to each other, and that's all I saw of him 'cause Mistuh Cobb made Mistuh Tolin stay with him while he holed up in that house like a marsh rat in a bog. Jake could talk to him. Mattie was there to care for the house and fix the meals, but Mistuh Cobb didn't want to see no one.

After a week of mournin' and layin' back Seth took over runnin' the fields since it was a time of plenty hoe work.

Bill didn't like it none. "Can't see no reason for us to work without his say-so."

"We don't work, they's no crops. They's no crops, he got no need for us. You want to be sold off somewheres to git run by a horse-ridin' overseer? That ain't for me!" Seth said.

Most folks felt like Seth, and they started hoein' the fields. I stayed up at the stable to run messages and keep an eye on the younguns.

"Ain't gonna make no difference," Bill complained one night. "If he wants us gone, don't make no never-mind to him what we been doin'!"

"You don't know Masta Cobb," Jake said. "He's a fair man. I know him, and I knowed his pa before him. Fair. Mighty fair."

Jake seemed to be right. Mistuh Cobb come out after nearly three weeks, and Mistuh Tolin was with him. Jake and me saddled their horses and I could see Mistuh Cobb eyein' the way things was kept up. They rode off through the quarters and out the top-crick road to where the big plantin' was. When they come back Mistuh Cobb took Mistuh Tolin straight back to the house, but that evenin' he had Mistuh Tolin get out a smoked pork shoulder and some coffee for everyone.

I stood by the fence that night, but instead of wavin', Mistuh Tolin ran out to where I was.

"I was afraid you wouldn't be here tonight since you saw me already today," he said.

I shifted uncomfortably and smiled a bit. "Maybe things'll get back to normal now that your pa's up and about."

"I don't know." He put his hands on the fence between us and I could see his fingers squeezin' the picket posts. "He says it's all up to me now. Jason, he wants me to run this place!" He drew in a shaky breath. "I tried to get Jake to talk to him, but even that didn't do no good."

"Maybe he'll come to hisself pretty soon. 'Specially after ridin' around today."

Mistuh Tolin looked back to the house. "I hope so. I sure hope so."

But Mistuh Cobb didn't come to hisself. In fact, at the end of the month he disappeared for nearly a week and Mistuh Tolin had to take the big wagon to the settlement for supplies all by hisself. Mattie helped him make up the order. When Mistuh Cobb showed up again he was trailin' two new horses, and started makin' plans for a bigger stable. Mistuh Tolin tried to talk to him, but his pa just kept on with the horses.

"You're a big boy now, Aaron," he said.

"I'm not Aaron!" Mistuh Tolin raged.

Mistuh Cobb stared at him. "No. No, you're not." He sorta dropped what he was doin' and walked to the house.

"I can't do it!" Mistuh Tolin yelled after him, but his pa kept on walkin'. "I don't want to do it," he said more quiet.

"Looks like you're gonna have to try, Masta Tolin," Jake said gentle. He patted Mistuh Tolin's shoulder. "Just for a while till he's feelin' better."

The time stretched out, and months went by. Mistuh Cobb was hardly ever in the fields and would go off for days to trade or race horses. He even trained me to ride for him, and I got to go to little towns, and to Eufaula. I even went to Dothan once and we was gone for four whole days! Mistuh Tolin didn't like it none, and worried about his pa and all the plantation work. Mattie and Horace helped him plan rations and supplies, and Seth kept charge of the fields, but I could see him gettin' thin and tired-eyed. That took some of the joy outta my travelin'.

"He's sendin' me to Mobile next week with the cotton," Mistuh Tolin said in September. We was stumpin' through the woods and Mistuh Tolin was carryin' an old flintlock pistol. He took aim at a crow's nest and fired. The dry twigs scattered and fell as his shot hit. "What do I know about crops, or cotton—grades of lint? Seth's gotta go with me. And another thing," he kept on while he reloaded, "I've been studying to go to normal school—to be a teacher. That's what my ma wanted. How can I go to school when he's sending me around the state to learn about cotton?" He shot into an old stump.

"Wish I could go to Mobile," I sorta dreamed out loud.

"You!" Mistuh Tolin rammed another wad into the gun.

"You have to ride races for my pa in Montgomery next week! Stupid horses. And you better be sure to win, too. I think he's bet a bunch of money on those races."

He sounded mad and different than his other talkin'.

"Yes, suh. I'll win," I said quick.

And I did win, too, but the money never come home. It all went to pay for a stud horse, and the stable got bigger.

"It's not ever going to be like it was before," Mistuh Tolin said when he got back from Mobile and saw the new horse. He gave a hard, tired sigh and looked around at everything like he was seein' it all for the first time. When he walked back to the house his steps was long and slow.

The light glowed in his room late that night, and from then on it didn't seem he complained too much at all—at least not to me. But I'd hear him arguin' plenty with his pa. One time in particular was the next spring, 1829, after Mistuh Tolin and Seth come back from a buyin' trip to Huntsville. Mistuh Tolin had a copy of a paper called *The Appeal*, put out by folks up North against slavery. His pa didn't like it none.

"You can't run a plantation without slaves," Mistuh Cobb declared.

"You can hire help. Same as up North!"

"Profits are slim enough as it is without payin' for work you can get nearly for free."

"It's not right owning people."

"You're soundin' more like your mother every day, Tolin. I loved her dearly, but she never understood economics. Now get out of here, and God help you if I ever see that newspaper around here again!"

Mistuh Tolin stomped out and grabbed my arm. He tromped us up the hill to the woods behind the graveyard, scowlin' all the way.

"You know, Jason? I don't care what my pa thinks. This paper has some important stuff in it. Look at it." He handed me the paper he had been grippin' real tight.

I took it and looked at the brownish ink marks, then up

at him. His eyes was dark mad. His face flushed and he snatched the paper back.

"It's not right!" he yelled while rippin' up the pages. "We're barely two years different in age and you can't even read that!"

His eyes got big and he grabbed up one of the torn pages. "I'm always talking about being a teacher. Well, I'm gonna teach you to read, Jason. We'll start right now!"

"Me?" My heart was poundin'.

"Why not? See. This is a J, and here's an A." He showed me the marks on the paper that made the letters of my name. "I've even got a book all about a Jason. Jason and the Golden Fleece. Come on! Let's get it!"

"But, Mistuh Tolin, I never heard of no slaved person able to read."

"Don't you want to learn?"

I seemed to have trouble gettin' my breath I was so excited. "Oh, yes, suh!"

"All right, then. We'll do it!"

And he started that very afternoon readin' me the words: " '. . . and Jason reliant on God, threw down his saffron mantle and stepped to work. Flame by craft of strange witch maiden, harmed him not. Gripping plow, he bent the necks of the oxen under . . .' "

By the end of that week I had learned the letters, and was strugglin' with the words on sight. Mistuh Tolin gave me a charcoal and foolscap, and had me printin' up letters and words over and over in the back of the tack room. The more I learned, the more I wanted to learn.

Jake found the papers one day and got real mad. "What you mean, Masta Tolin? Your daddy don't hold with this, and you know it!"

"I certainly don't see the harm."

"Oh, no? Well, you tell me that when your daddy sells Jason down to N'Orleans! Readin' niggers don't stay with any one masta too long—not in these parts!" He threw the papers into the forge fire.

That night Mistuh Tolin told Jake we was gonna do some night fishin'. He took me down to the crick by the hog run where he had a big lantern and paper and books already hid.

"My ma wanted it this way. I know she did," he said, real serious.

Seems like he was bound to go against his pa—always doin' it in the name of his ma.

Me, I didn't care, 'cause I was learnin' fast, and for several months I kept that book about Jason in the straw of my mattress and I'd practice readin' when Jake and Bitty was asleep.

"It's our place now," Margaret said that summer. I was near thirteen years old. "If we got good food and enough clothes it's 'cause of what we put out," she said.

"Masta Tolin, he's doin' a fine job and we'll never starve, but he don't have his heart to cotton. Masta Cobb, he don't care no more about nothin'," Horace said.

"He cares about his horses, sure enough," I said. Everybody nodded to that.

"He's gonna sell us off one of these days," Bill muttered.

"No. I don't think so. Miz Nancy won't let him," Bitty said.

"Ain't no Miz Nancy Cobb to protect us now!"

"Sure they is," Mattie said as she turned the butter churn. "She's still up there in that house. I hears him talkin' to her sometime. Margaret's right. The place is ours. We got to get good crops so's to keep eatin' right."

"You all is crazy, sure enough," Bill said.

The talk might have sounded crazy, but it seemed to be true. Folks bent their backs into the work. I even got into the fields sometimes if there was a need. Mistuh Cobb had stopped takin' me to ride his horses 'cause I was gettin' so big, and he trained one of Seth and Margaret's boys to take my place. Of course I had my smithin' to learn, and there was lots of times when Mistuh Tolin just took me off with him to talk or to practice my readin'.

Yet for all the work everybody put in durin' the next few years the plantation didn't seem to get ahead. Weevils got in the cotton one year, and then rot killed off fifteen acres the next. There was sickness in the quarters the followin' spring and the plantin' was late and that made the harvest late, and so the price Mistuh Tolin got at the markets was small. It didn't bother Mistuh Tolin none, 'cause he was just concerned with breakin' even and stayin' ahead of the debts, but Mistuh Cobb always hollered about him bein' a poor planter.

"Now, if Aaron was here . . ." he always began; and Mistuh Tolin would walk out.

On top of that Mistuh Cobb kept buyin' and tradin' horses. He pulled Kusa out of the fields to help build on to the stable, and to help me break the new horses. I got pretty good at that, but Kusa didn't have the patience. Mistuh Cobb took a ridin' quirt to Kusa one day 'cause he thought Kusa was bein' too rough with a new mare. Kusa took the blows and didn't say nothin', but everyone knew he was hurt more in the brain than the back. That was the only time I remember any of us gettin' beat by Mistuh Cobb, and that old man seemed to feel bad about it, too. He gave Skalley some extra cloth the next week for no reason, but Kusa didn't forget what happened.

That was when I was still thirteen—in '31; and not too long after that we got hollerin' news from other bondsmen that a black man made hisself up an army in Virginia and was settin' the slave folks free.

"Nat Turner is his name, and they say he wants to make up a settlement of free black folks." Horace was the one that relayed it to us. He had heard it when he was at the settlement with Mistuh Tolin.

The thought of a free black settlement made me tingle all over. I could imagine it sorta like we had it at Cobb's—workin' hard at the crops and other jobs, but all for ourselves. I didn't know where Virginia was, but I wondered if Nat Turner might get down our way. Freedom! Just like that!

"Sounds crazy to me," Bill mumbled.

"Sure enough. Ain't no way any black man can get his-self an army," Bitty chided.

"Onlyest way is with the help of others," Kusa said quiet.

I watched Skalley grab tight on his arm. The youngest of their three babies was still nursin'. She looked to me, and I saw fear in her eyes, but I didn't know what to do.

Next mornin' Kusa was gone. Skalley was red-eyed and poor-lookin'. She come to me at the stable and cried some more.

News come to us three days later that the fightin' was over in Virginia and nothin' left but a passel of dead folks —mostly Negroes. Bitty had been right: couldn't no black man fight against the whites and win. I started thinkin' that freedom was just a dream. Like the white folks talk about heaven, so it was for the blacks—thinkin' about freedom.

Mistuh Tolin didn't like it at all when his pa declared Kusa a runaway and set the law after him, but they never got no chance to lash him like Mistuh Cobb ordered. Word come in two weeks that Kusa was shot by the Georgia militia near Jenkinsburg, Georgia. He bled to death in the wagon that was bringin' him back. We buried him in the graveyard up behind the house with everybody else.

Since Skalley never talked, it was hard for most folks to see that she got quieter, but she did.

5

The plantin' kept sufferin' for us at Cobb's. Don't know the reasons, 'cause other folks was doin' well—especially planter Caulborne. Word was he shipped more than two hundred bales of cotton a year. Of course he had a lot more land than Mistuh Cobb, and he had a big farm and house near where the settlement was growin'. I had first seen his spread when I was twelve and racin' horses for Mistuh Cobb. White folks envied that plantation a lot, but us in the Cobb quarters didn't think much of it at all.

Caulborne had a whip-carryin' overseer (Mistuh Cobb called him white trash) to work his thirty-five male field hands. The quarters for those bondsmen and their families was wooden barracks with dirt floors, not sturdy brick cabins with laid-in floors like we had. That's how come his place got affected by the whoopin' cough so bad in the winter of '32. He lost six slave children that year. But his crops come in good, and that was all he seemed to care about.

When I was fifteen, in '33, Mistuh Tolin took me to Montgomery so's I could learn the farrier trade—that's horse-shoein' and all. It would have been a nice trip 'cept Mistuh Tolin was so worried about what his pa was doin' while we was gone.

Mistuh Cobb was at the stables when we got back ten

days later, and so was Carrie. She run to us before we was out of the saddle, and told us Bill had been sold off, to planter Caulborne.

Mistuh Tolin stomped to his pa and started hollerin'. "You sold Bill to Caulborne? What the hell for? Another of those damn thoroughbred horses, or to pay off some gambling?"

"Don't use that tone with me, Tolin." Mistuh Cobb's voice sounded tired and I figured Mistuh Tolin was right about those gamblin' debts.

"Maybe you forget the promise you made my mother, that we do not *sell* our people. Maybe you forget that you put me in charge of this damn plantation and I had all the debt repayment well worked out. Maybe—"

"Maybe you forget that I'm your father!" The old anger was back in Mistuh Cobb's voice, and Mistuh Tolin stopped short. "There was no reason to keep that Bill around. He was doing no work at all. You weren't hard enough on him. That overseer of Caulborne's will see that he earns his keep."

"What about Judith and their children?"

"What about them? It's not like I'd sent him off to another state. They'll see him at socials, and the way those damn Baptist circuit riders keep comin' through, there'll be so many tent revivals we won't get work out of anyone!"

"Those revivals are about the only times these people get any levity in their lives. You begrudge them that, too? Don't tell me you're afraid for them to have some religion?"

"Is that what you call it? All that hellfire and brimstone preaching? You see to it that they don't go too often. There's one next week, and I want them at no more until this fall."

"You're as bad as all these other folks down here. Afraid the Negroes might understand what they're hearing and find out that they've got rights—like not being sold and traded as so much chattel."

"Shut up, Tolin! Don't talk like that with your boy standing right behind you!" Mistuh Cobb frowned at me, and Mistuh Tolin swung around. His eyes was nearly black with rage, and he looked a whole lot older than seventeen.

"Go on, Jason," he said quietly. I could see him breathin' hard. "Put my things away and then go to Judith. Tell her . . . tell her I'm sorry. Tell her about the tent revival next week."

I left quick. I could see it wasn't a time to hang back.

We went to three revivals that year and saw Bill all times but the last. Seems he didn't work hard enough for Mistuh Caulborne's overseer neither; he got whipped bad, then Caulborne sold him to a contractor that was buildin' roads over near Bogalusa, Louisiana. We never heard no word about him after that.

There was more slave tradin' got done that year, but the next time it went the other way. I was workin' in the smithy the day Mistuh Cobb come in with two real fine trotter horses and this little girl. She was twelve years old, skinny, and half-covered with sores. Mistuh Cobb had traded one of his brood mares and seventy-five dollars to a Georgia man to get them all. Mistuh Tolin started to rage.

"All right!" his pa roared. "I know I said no more live-stock, but they're good stock and . . ." He scratched his jaw and looked at the raggedy girl. "That man meant no good for this child. Look at her."

"We weren't going to buy any more horses, and definitely no more people!"

"What would you have me do? See her die from disease, or sold for concubinage? I know you think I'm hard, son, but I can't stand to see any living thing abused."

Mistuh Tolin didn't say any more.

"That child's had it rough," Mattie said that night after she had cleaned the girl up. Louisa—that was her name—was gonna stay in the cabin with Mattie and Horace. "Her mother was some poor white up Bowdon way, and she been shifted around all her life. Give to a slaver when she was five, she remembers."

"She's high-toned," Bitty said like a warnin'. "She'd probably be better off down in the cities where there's a place for them types."

"She's mulatto—just half white. Got to be octoroon to dance at the rich folks' balls," Mattie said. "Don't know why you'd want to wish that kind of whorin' life on her anyway."

"What's octoroon?" Carrie asked.

"Havin' no Negro blood in you but from one grandparent," Horace explained.

"She's light enough to be octoroon," Bitty kept on.

Seemed to me they was splittin' hairs and for no benefit. Octoroon or mulatto, they was all still slaved.

Bein' slaved was somethin' I thought on a lot. At Cobb's our life was better than for folks at Caulborne's or other places around, but even there I knew I was different. First off, I could read. I didn't tell nobody that 'cause folks in the quarters would have hollered loud about how it wasn't right—or, at least, how dangerous it was. I knew the danger, so I didn't read 'ceptin' when I was with Mistuh Tolin.

Mistuh Tolin was the other difference. He hardly ever asked much of me outside of usual work for him, and when we talked he treated me like I was the same as him and not his servant. He kept up with his studyin', too, and most of what he learned he was teachin' me, so I knew a bit about history, multiplyin' and dividin', countin' money and such. Most times I felt pretty good about my life, but then somethin' would happen and I remembered how it *really* was.

Goin' to revivals was the worst. Bondsmen from all over would be there with their white folks. I'd hear about mean planters and about who had been sold off. There'd be whisper talk about abolitionists and free black folks up North. I always wondered what free black folks did, and how they felt. I'd heard there was black preachers, too, and figured religion would mean all the more if it came from a black man of God instead of white. But the planters down our way worried that Negro preachers—even if they was slaved—would talk about the wrong things and be like Moses: try to set their people free.

"All white folks want to do is hold us in chains," a man from Peachburg said once.

"Mistuh Tolin treats us real good at Cobb's," I said soft.

He just laughed. "That may be, but your Mistuh Tolin still owns you, and you don't have say about nothin'! Come a time and you'll realize that, too."

That kind of talk always started me worryin' on when Mistuh Tolin was gonna change, and after the revivals I'd be feelin' skittish and unsure of my thinkin'.

There was times, though, that the plantation and slavery wasn't on my mind at all. That was when Mistuh Tolin would get me off with him to hunt. Mistuh Tolin liked to hunt—actually, what he really liked was guns. He could handle a musket real well, and he'd take up that ol' Brown Bess (the same one that was at King's Mountain) and off we'd go. Mistuh Tolin even taught me how to shoot that big muzzleloader, and I got good at it. I could prime ball, cotton, and powder and have it up to fire a true shot in less than a minute.

At night Mistuh Tolin would lay back and dream out loud about a regular farm that grew more than cotton and corn, and when he wasn't dreamin' he would pull out a book and read. I'd read, too. Mistuh Tolin would bring the books for me from town. He knew what I liked 'cause he'd see me readin' the headlines in the papers: MISSIONARIES START WEST, or BEAVER MARKET IN ST. LOUIS CLOSES HIGH. The books was printed on rough foolscap paper with drawin's of huge buffalo chargin' across the endless grasslands. They'd tell about the gray granite mountains that towered to the clouds, and about dry brittle land that made men pray for death, and about Indians who shrieked over the hills and killed everyone in sight. The words was wonderful and frightenin' in the same moment, and when I was

35

readin' about that far-away land it was easy to forget all about the plantation and the problems back there.

I loved those times when we was camped out by a little fire. To me that's what freedom had to be like, and I couldn't imagine it any other way.

6

On a day in late January of '36 Mistuh Tolin came ridin' up in a rush. "Jason! We're going to Florida!" he announced as he reined up his sorrel Walker. "I enlisted in the militia."

I sighed heavy and twisted the round bit and pressed the swage down on the red-hot iron.

"Well, suh," Jake said in a bemused voice from where he sat by the door, cleanin' tack. "I don't want to be around when Masta Cobb hears this news."

Mistuh Tolin had been hintin' at joinin' the Florida fightin' for over a month, readin' news articles about the battles and the adventure of bein' in war. It set Mistuh Cobb hot mad 'cause he wanted Mistuh Tolin with him at the plantation. "You always brag up to me what a fighter Aaron was," Mistuh Tolin had hollered at his pa once. "Thought you'd be glad to see me taking a stand." And Mistuh Cobb had scowled and said, "That fightin' was for our land. Our home. Something you don't seem to take much pride in." "I'll take pride in what's deservin', but this sorry lot of crops—" "You're weak, Tolin. You can't run the plantation, and trottin' off to a useless battle won't change that."

"Your pa ain't gonna like it, Mistuh Tolin," I agreed with Jake.

"It doesn't matter," he said with a harsh laugh. "I turned twenty-one last week and I'll be damned if I'm going to sit here and rot any longer while tending his confounded cotton so he can go into debt with horses!"

"You should be takin' a wife, Mistuh Tolin," Jake advised. "Your daddy's gettin' old—needs to see some grandbabies."

"Hush, Jake! You may be able to talk around my pa, but it won't work with me. We're going, Jason. We have to be in Tampa by mid-March." Mistuh Tolin dropped the reins over the rail and walked away in a huff. Jake shook his head and led the sorrel for curryin'. I kept pressin' and twirlin'.

I did all the blacksmithin' now, and Mistuh Cobb was hirin' out my work at the forge so's to earn extra money for better stock feed. I was nineteen. Jake was close to seventy years old—maybe more. Only thing he remembered for sure was that he was nearly growed the year Crispus Atticus went down under British fire.

"I don't know as Mistuh Cobb's gonna let me be goin' to Florida," I said. "He's countin' on money from my forgin'."

"He's got no choice in it," Jake said quietly. I looked to him to continue. "You're Masta Tolin's man—not his. Papers was transferred when you was young—after that cane fire."

"What about those threats you used to give Mistuh Tolin about his pa sellin' me off?"

"Oh, that was real enough for a while. Masta Cobb had rights to do that till little masta come of age."

I studied the nose of the auger I'd just finished and started worryin'. It looked like I was goin' to Florida whether I liked it or not. I couldn't see why he should go down to Florida to fight the Seminole Indians, but Mistuh Tolin had been mighty restless of late. Maybe Jake was right: he needed a wife.

I was thinkin *woman* myself. It wasn't the first time. There was always girls I'd meet at a social or at the revivals.

They'd be dressed out in their best calico prints and eyein' up the men. Sometimes I would get one of them off into the shadows and she'd let me put my hands in warm places that wasn't to be talked about, but this time it was different.

It was always figured that me and Carrie would settle in together, but for the past few months I'd been noticin' Louisa a lot more. She was only fifteen, but had rounded out nice like a woman. Her lips invited closeness, and she knew how to wrap her head in calico so that it made her large dark eyes seem even bigger. When I thought about Louisa it was different than a girl had ever made me feel. I didn't want to just lay with her in the dark; I wanted to be with her all the time. Maybe Mistuh Tolin needed a special woman to make him feel that way.

"Jason, look at this," Mistuh Tolin said that evenin'. He'd come up to my room over the stable where I'd been livin' since I turned eighteen. He held a paper out to me. MILITIA MEETS BATTLE, the headline read.

"It's going to be good. It's going to be exciting! For once I'll feel like I'm doing something worthwhile." Mistuh Tolin strode around the room while I read the account of a skirmish with the Seminoles on the Halifax River. Four men in the militia got killed.

There was another article. I read that one, too, while Mistuh Tolin talked about important decisions and givin' oneself over to a cause. This other article was about how the Indian-Negroes (them was the runaway slaves who was fightin' with the Seminoles—some say they started the war!) was the hardest, meanest fighters ever, and that it was the duty of every American to take up arms to put down the rebellion before it spread to the plantations and started riots among the slaves.

"You should get yourself a wife, suh. I hear *that* can be plenty excitin'." I shoved my shirttail in my pants and hoped he would leave soon so I could go down to the quarters.

"You're beginning to sound like Jake. That's a sure sign

---

we need to be getting away." I didn't say nothin', and he frowned at me. "You want me to leave you alone, don't you?"

"Mistuh Tolin, suh, I want you to do what you've a need to do." I gave him back the newspaper.

"You're getting insolent, Jason." Mistuh Tolin slapped the newspaper against the thigh of his ridin' pants as he walked around the room. "Marvena Caulborne," he stated suddenly. "I'll marry Marvena first thing when we get back from Florida. Does that make you happy?" He stalked out the door and started down the steps. "Go on and find that Louisa girl. I won't bother you any more."

Marvena Caulborne? I wondered as I watched him cross the yard.

I turned out my lamp and went down the steps to go to the quarters. My shirt fitted tight on my broad chest. It was really too small. I had been wearin' Mistuh Tolin's hand-me-downs for most of my years, and I'd caught up with him in growth. Both of us was nearly six feet tall, but I had broadened out from my smith work. I asked in the quarters once if my pa, Marcus, was tall and broad. Skalley nodded he was. Bitty told me I looked just like him—strong-jawed and handsome, she said. I was never too sure about that *handsome* part 'cause my nose stuck out too far and my chin was a bit too long. When Kusa was there he'd told me that showed my ancestors was from high country back in Africa. It didn't matter anyhow.

"What Masta Tolin want with you, anyway?" asked a soft voice. Louisa was peekin' out from the side of the stable, her eyes dancin' and bright.

"Come on over here, girl. You spyin' on me?" I put my arm around her and we started for the quarters. She was warm and smelled like springtime. I slipped my hand under the shawls she was wearin' and pulled her closer.

"I's just waitin' for you. Saw him runnin' up the steps. He have another yellin' session with his pa?"

"What makes you ask that?"

"Anytime him and his daddy argue, or if somethin' goes wrong for him, he's always off to find Jason. Where's Jason? Masta Tolin always want to know."

I slowed us near a thick stand of oak and backed her into the trunk of one. "What you got against Mistuh Tolin that you're talkin' about him that way?" I pulled the cloth wrappin' off her hair and touched the softness.

"I don't got nothin' against him, 'cept he's always takin' you off." I kissed her lips and tried to take her into my arms. "You didn't tell me what he wanted this time."

"Oh, he was tellin' me more about Florida."

"Florida!"

"Yep. We're goin' down there in March so he can fight the Seminoles."

"Oh, Jason, don't go! You don't have to go just 'cause he says so, do you?"

"Well, sure!"

"But supposin' you told him you didn't want to go. What would he do? He might even change his mind. He wouldn't go if he had to go alone."

"What right do I have tellin' him somethin' like that?" I backed off from her. It was finally comin' home that I didn't have no say. "Besides, I ain't never been to Florida before."

"You wants to go!" Her face was rumpled up in a pout. "You's just gonna go off and leave me!"

"I ain't gonna leave you, Louisa." I tried to hug her, but she squirmed away.

"Don't nobody ever want to keep me around, and since you can't get rid of me you're gonna run off!" Then she giggled. "I was just teasin'. How long you gonna be gone?"

"Dunno. A few months." I reached for her again and she let me pull her close and kiss her soft tan face.

"Just a few months. You promise?"

I couldn't promise nothin', I thought, sorta glum. I started on to the quarters. "Mistuh Tolin's talkin' about marryin' Marvena Caulborne when he gets back, so maybe he'll be quick about it."

41

"I don't care what he's plannin', but soon as you get back, I'm movin'," she said as she skipped to keep up with me.

"And where you a-goin'?"

"I'm movin' to that room over the stable to be with my man."

My heart jumped funny and I squeezed her hand. "Is that a promise?"

She nodded. "A promise."

Moonlight was slicin' through the trees by the quarters when we got there. Younguns was still up and the babies was bein' nursed to sleep. Jake was talkin' about the time comin' west when they almost lost a wagon in the Crab Orchard Mountains of Tennessee. Little ones was listenin' with their mouths gapin', and Bitty was puffin' on a corncob pipe while she spun cotton on an old wheel. Seth was whittlin' fish hooks, and there was the good smell of firewood and corn husks in the air.

Louisa and me settled down near Skalley. She was rockin' her youngest, he was five, and I looked at that boy child and grinned. I wondered if Louisa and me was to make a baby how he'd be: tall and broad like me and my pa, or slender and wide-eyed like Louisa. That was somethin' fine to think about. Somethin' mighty fine!

7

It was late March when Mistuh Tolin dragged me off to Florida with him and some of the rowdiest white folks I ever saw. He was in the militia that worked under Colonel Chisolm. They was part of the Second Artillery under command of Colonel William Lindsey, and I dare say those Alabama volunteers didn't like that man one bit. Seemed to me he was a regular sort of man, but he gave some orders that Chisolm's regiment couldn't abide.

Mistuh Tolin's papers signed him up for ninety days, but we spent a good part of that in waitin' for enough other volunteers to show up to make a full regiment. Mistuh Tolin started out enjoyin' the whole mess. He had an air of prestige by comin' into the war with a full-growed bondsman. Most of the men come alone, or with a youngun not more than thirteen. Mistuh Tolin had bought hisself some fine ridin' pants and new boots for the trip, too, so he looked like some of those rich boys who came in from Huntsville or Tuscaloosa. Everyone else was dressed in work clothes or linsey-woolseys.

Mistuh Tolin was carryin' the old muzzleloader from home. Some of the men had flintlocks, but most just had muskets. They almost all had bayonets, either fixed to the rifle barrels or tied to a stick.

When the whole regiment was formed there was seven

hundred and fifty Alabamians. We was all moved up to Fort Brooke, and then the volunteers started for a place called Chocachatti. Colonel Lindsey made the militia pack their own duffles, and that was one more thing the Alabamians added to their dislike of the man. I stayed at Fort Brooke and helped out the smith there.

It was two weeks before I saw Mistuh Tolin again. Two long, scary weeks of loneliness and worry, not knowin' when, or if, he would return. It was a nervous time for more than that reason, too, 'cause folks around the fort kinda suspicioned any strong-lookin' Negro might take off and join the Seminoles. There wasn't too many of us, and we all sensed that our every move was bein' watched. We barely even talked to each other. At night they put us in a corral sort of place with two guards outside. There was guards on the fort wall, too. I guess that was the first time I can remember ever feelin' slaved. The only time so far I had ever felt really threatened around white folks.

When Mistuh Tolin did get back, I never had seen him more tired. He had been with what they called the center wing of the defense all the way to the Chocachatti place, and they had them a battle on the way.

"We never even made contact with the other two wings," Mistuh Tolin complained while I scrubbed the grime and mud off him. His arms and neck was covered with mosquito bites. There was some dark spots on his legs where he had cut away leeches. "We trekked all that way through that hellish land and saw the enemy maybe six or seven times. Some of the boys got skittish and shot up a passel of cows once." He tried to laugh, but he was weary right to the bone.

"It was awful, Jason. Seems we spent more time fighting the land than we did the Seminole. We were always getting bogged down in the mire and even the mules had difficulty pulling the cannon wagons. There were snakes, and the damn mosquitoes around here are large enough to eat!"

"What happened when you met up with them Seminoles

comin' back?" It had frightened me plenty when I heard about the battle near Fort Alabama. Two militiamen got killed and two was wounded.

"They fired a couple of volleys at the column from a hammock of trees, and our artillery lobbed some cannon balls through the thickets." He got powerful quiet and I could see him strugglin' with thoughts. His fists and eyes was clenched tight closed when he spoke next.

"I killed a man, Jason. We charged the brush and my bayonet went into this man . . ."

My skin felt all crawly. The idea of killin' somebody chilled my blood.

"This cause suddenly doesn't seem too noble anymore. Who am I to say that these people are wrong for wanting to stay on their land? I should have stayed home, like you and Jake told me," he said in a near whisper. "Get married and sit real cozy in the parlor sippin' on that peach brandy Horace makes up so deliciously."

I was quiet—my brain quiet with my thoughts. I wanted to be home in the worst way—to be with Louisa. Before we left for Florida I spent a lot of time with her, takin' her to me in the evenin's, stayin' with her till the pink dawn forced us apart and to our work. She was smooth and gentle, and her kisses set a fire in me that got my knees tremblin' and my brain weak with want. She was my woman. Everybody in the quarters had settled to thinkin' that way. I loved her, and now I missed her somethin' terrible.

End of April the entire command moved out again. They hadn't been gone but a few days when news came in that was unsettlin'. The Creeks was fightin' again back in Alabama. I wouldn't have known about it 'ceptin' I heard these two suppliers talkin' over a newspaper.

"Now's the time we should be up there in Georgia," one man said. I was tightenin' the traces on his wagon. He was talkin' while waitin'. "Says here white folks have been killed, and most of the rest are leaving their plantings and moving to Montgomery or Columbus. They'll be needing supplies."

"It sounds ripe enough except for the fact of those heathen Creeks. I remember the last injun war, and I don't care to be around it."

"True, but you may not have much of a choice. They're fighting in Georgia and in Alabama, and some are trying to get down here to Florida to join those blasted Seminole."

"Old Hickory's got the right idea: ship them out West—into the Territory. The sooner the better."

I had finished my work, and the man led his team and wagon away. I stood lookin' after them and wantin' to take up a paper so bad to read all the facts, but I didn't dare. I just worried over the situation and hoped for Mistuh Tolin's return to the fort.

I saw some Creek Indians durin' that month. They didn't come to fight. They was already whipped. There was more than three hundred of them all around the fort waitin' for a boat to ship them across the Gulf, and then they'd go on to that Indian Territory place.

By the time the militia got back in early May the Washington commanders was in a tizzy about what to do. General Scott took some troops and went up to Columbus, Georgia. The Louisiana militia was gettin' edgy too, 'cause there was a war a-brewin' over their way: somethin' about Texans and Mexicans. Seems a whole group of Texans got wiped out at a place called the Alamo. There was another battle at San Jacinto, too.

The Alabamians stayed until the end of May. Then we started home in straggly groups. Some of the men were reenlistin' with General Jessup to fight at home. He had fifteen hundred Creek soldiers already to fight with. I couldn't understand Creeks fightin' Creeks, but they done it a lot. Mistuh Tolin didn't sign nothin'.

"We'll see what the word is at home," he said to me one night near Tallahassee. "I think I've seen enough of war."

We took a keelboat up the Chattahoochee River to

Eufaula. There was soldiers all over the town, and we saw some Indians in chains: young, old, sick, women and children.

"They're some of Emaltha's horde," a man told Mistuh Tolin. "Been raidin' and burnin' farms. They're huntin' him down, though. Home guard is doin' a good job."

Mistuh Tolin bought a newspaper and it was full of articles about movin' the red man west and some about how the Creeks and Yuchis was bein' thieved of their land by white folks. It all seemed pretty confusin'. Some folks was tellin' of murderous things the Creeks had done, and others was stickin' up for the Indian rights.

The next town out the road was deserted.

"There's been injuns here, right enough," I said as we walked passed burned buildin's. Mistuh Tolin was tight-faced and silent.

After we crossed the Pea River things looked a bit better. We got a ride on a cotton cart with some soldiers who was goin' to Montgomery, then we struck out over the hills when the road headed north. When we got to the valley near the Conecuh I felt suddenly wary. It was four miles more to our fields and another half-mile to the house from there, but nothin' seemed right. Mistuh Tolin sensed it too, 'cause he took off at a trot. I guess we must have run nearly that whole four miles, and when we got to the fence line my heart turned to rock from fear. There was no livestock in the pastures. The fence was ripped down near the corn field and and the earth unplowed. We didn't say nothin', but kept on runnin.'

The canebrake was gone, and the first thing we saw when we splashed across the crick was the orchard. The trees—what was still standin'—was like charcoal drawin's on the sky. The earth was black from soot.

We got to the quarters in about ten minutes. Those brick buildin's was standin' there, but there wasn't a soul nowhere to be seen. Not even a chicken was scratchin' at the earth. My breath was comin' fast and hard when I stopped

47

at Skalley's cabin and went in. There was nothin' there but a few scraps of old cloth, a table, and two straw mattresses. I could almost hear my heart pound, things was so still. I ran quick to Horace's cabin. It was the same way, and I went out the door yellin', "Skalley! Louisa!"

A bunch of crows took off from the trees near the cabin and my voice sounded hollow and far away.

"Ja-*sooon!*" Mistuh Tolin's voice was more like a wail and I dropped the duffle I had been carryin' and ran toward the house.

The house was gone. Pieces of charred lumber pointed at odd angles toward the late-day sky. The smell of burned wood was still about, even though the ashes was cold. Mistuh Tolin stood at the bottom of the stone steps that led up to nothin'. The nothin' that used to be his home—the house my pa had built.

The stone-walled stable was still standin', and the smithy, and the cabin beside it. Jake's chair sat there like it was waitin' for him to set down. A piece of paper fluttered against the door. I took it from the nail it was stuck on and read:

TO WHOM IT MAY CONCERN. Due to the brave and untimely death of Willis Cobb, this estate is being administered by Nathan P. Caulborne, Esq. until the return of the Cobb heir. I may be contacted at my farm in Union Springs.

"Mistuh Tolin." My voice was barely there—cracked by what I had read. "Mistuh Tolin." I took him the paper and held it while he read.

It was like somebody had ripped the soul outta my life. This was the only home I ever knowed. I started rememberin' things on how it used to be—white-painted house with curtains at the windows; sounds of Mattie hummin' as she worked inside; Mistuh Cobb's voice boomin' orders. Even the bad times was good to remember. Now Mistuh Cobb was dead, and the others . . . I looked up the hill to the graveyard behind the house. Mama was buried up there. Kusa and some others. I started climbin' the rise. I heard Mistuh Tolin comin' behind me.

The graveyard was all one: black folks on the left, white folks on the right. I glanced to the right and saw the new stone that marked Mistuh Cobb's grave. There was new graves on my side, too, and I walked to the mounds, already showin' bright shoots of grass on top. The tears started comin' to my eyes as I looked at the names scratched into the wooden markers.

JAKE: 1765–1836
HORACE: 1801–1836
SETH: 1800–1836
BITTY: 1775–1836
CARRIE: 1821–1836

There was little graves with markers and no names, and I wondered which younguns they were. My heart was poundin' as I realized there wasn't a sign for Louisa, but then another marker loomed at me. SKALLEY: 1809–1836. I knelt beside it and saw dark spots where my tears hit the earth. *Skalley.* I touched the mound as though I could feel her breathin' in there. *Skalley.* My tears was hot on my cheeks, and I felt my chest jerkin' with sobs. *Skalley.* My second mama.

"Jason." Mistuh Tolin's hand touched on my shoulder. I don't know how long I'd been sittin' there, but the sky was purple and orange from sunset. "Jason. We've to see Mr. Caulborne." His voice was gentle and controlled. "He's waitin' for the return of the Cobb heirs. That would be us. We're all that's left, you and me." I looked up at him. His eyes was swollen and red, but his face was set stern and tight. "Come on, now."

"Yes, suh." I got up and followed him down the hill. He picked up the old Brown Bess and started up the road to Union Springs.

I went down to the quarters to retrieve the duffle, my steps lingerin' around the buildin's. *Louisa!* I could still

49

hear my voice callin' her, and I stared at Skalley's cabin. Empty. Everythin' was empty. A cold breeze hit me. My stomach got tight. *Louisa!* No marker for her. None for Mattie, or Judith. They was still alive! The hope sprung in me and I ran to catch Mistuh Tolin. They'd be at Caulborne's, for sure, I told myself. Couldn't everything be gone.

8

I was dreamin': It is Sunday and I'm waitin' with the buggy outside the white frame church. Buggies and horses is all lined up and those of us that's drivin' sit around under the trees and listen to the singin' and preachin'. Then the door opens and here come Mistuh Tolin with a pretty miss on his arm. He's gonna drive her home. I go to the horse and get it to stand up straight and good-lookin'. Mistuh Tolin, he waves and smiles . . .

I was dreamin': It's a warm winter evenin'. There's a mouth harp goin' in the quarters and folks is laughin'. Mattie and Horace takes the little ones out of the cabin and we are alone—just Louisa and me reachin' for each other. She laughs, and I chase her around and pull her down with me on the mattress . . .

I was dreamin' . . .

"Jason, wake up. Masta Cobb want you up at the house now. Wake up, Jason!"

I looked up at the round-faced boy who was shakin' me.

"Masta Cobb want you!" he said again.

"Mistuh Cobb?"

"Yas! Masta Tolin! He say come now!"

The walls of the wooden men's quarters at Caulborne's farm was gray and cheerless. I pulled on my brogans and brushed the straw off my back.

"You done slept through breakfast and dinner, too. Masta Cobb done et and dressed hisself." The boy ran out.

Masta Cobb. That was Mistuh Tolin, now. I started rememberin' then. It was like a pressure comin' down on my head, pushin' out all the good dreams of how it used to be, squeezin' away the hopes that everythin' of yesterday was only a nightmare. I felt my chest tightenin' like there was a rope bein' pulled to a hard knot. There was no hope in me. Weren't nobody from Cobb's at this place, and even worse, didn't nobody want to talk about what happened. I swallowed hard, pushed my shirt into my pants, and tied my rope belt as I left the buildin'.

A slow drizzly rain that was good for crops fell down around me. It would sink into the ground right fine and not disturb a row. Seth would have been glad for that rain.

Seth . . .

Mistuh Tolin was standin' with the planter Caulborne on the porch of the big white Caulborne house. There was huge columns holdin' up the porch roof—columns so big even I couldn't get my arms around them. It was the kind of house Mattie said she had lived in in New Orleans.

Mattie . . . Sold off, I knew. That's all any Caulborne folks would say . . . Been sold off.

The rain soaked my shirt as I stood outside the gate and looked across the huge front lawn that was all planted fancy with flowers and bushes. Two horses was tied to the hitch rail and they looked real sad to be out of the barn.

"Jason! Don't stand in the rain." Mistuh Tolin waved me to come up. I opened the gate, ran to the porch, and stood off behind Mistuh Caulborne some five or six paces.

"I know it isn't much, Tolin, but I imagine you could make a go of it," Mistuh Caulborne was sayin'. "You're an enterprising young man."

"Thank you, Mr. Caulborne, but there's still a lot I have to think about. Oh, yes. You said you had a list of the property you sold to pay the debts."

Mistuh Caulborne pulled a piece of paper from his

pocket. "I tried to get the fairest price I could, you understand. Your horses were all taken by the Creeks; the hogs
scattered all over the countryside." He started talkin'
money, and I didn't really listen no more until I heard him
say, "I tried to hold on to your Negroes as long as possible,
but when time delayed . . . well, the creditors insisted. I
think I got a real good price for them, however. Slave
dealers are willing to pay high now that the ships have been
stopped from bringing in Africans. Of course, your bucks
were all killed in the fight, so there was just the females and
some offspring left."

"You have only two women listed here—Mattie and
Judith," Mistuh Tolin said. "There was a young girl, too.
Louisa. Where is she?"

"Oh, yes. Judith said she was a comely wench and . . . she
was, uh, carried off by the Creeks. I doubt if she's still alive,
knowin' the injuns, and your females said something about
her being a few months pregnant."

I had to look up then to see if I was hearin' right. Mistuh
Tolin's eyes was on me, and my mouth dropped open with
shock. Louisa, a few months pregnant!

"I'm sure if they left her alive she would have been found
by now," Mistuh Caulborne was sayin'.

Louisa. Not sold. Not dead (if they left her alive).

My eyes was all blurry as we started down the stairs to
the horses Mistuh Caulborne was loanin' us. Mistuh Tolin
gave me a long thin box to carry, and I held his horse while
he mounted up. Not neither of us said a word while we was
ridin' through the rain to the Cobb land.

"I'm sorry about Louisa, Jason," Mistuh Tolin finally
said when we was in the stable. I unsaddled the horses and
he took a cloth from the rack and helped me rub them
down. "I wish she could have been given a decent burial."

My throat tightened so I couldn't speak, but my mind
was arguin' his thoughts. I just shook my head no. *No!*

He turned away, his face stricken. "Damn! This lousy,
stinking land! It grows grave markers better than anything

else." His voice sounded far away and bitter. "What are we going to do? The two of us can't plant this place back to cotton, and I can't afford to hire in help." He pushed his fingers through his straw-brown hair.

"Where's that box?" he suddenly asked.

"Here, suh." I held it out to him.

"It was found in the ashes. Maybe there's something in it . . . some answers." He sat the box on a bench and fumbled with the lock. "My pa took to gambling with those horses even more after we left. Mr. Caulborne had to sell off most everything to pay what was owed, and there wasn't much here."

"Yes, suh." I thought of Mattie and Judith and the children that had been sold, and wondered where they would end up.

Mistuh Tolin had grabbed a brick and was smashin' at the lock. Then he stopped, near in tears and cussin'. I found a scrap of iron and pried the hinges loose.

"Thank you, Jason," he mumbled at me.

We sat on the bench with the box between us. There was papers inside. Mistuh Tolin looked at them and then passed them over to me. They was old letters dated back in the teens from some people in North Carolina.

"Maybe they was some kind of kin," I said, lookin' at the one signed Raeford Cobb.

"Yeah. They died in the twenties," Mistuh Tolin answered. He was holdin' a long leather pouch. He pulled a paper from it. "To whom it may concern," he read aloud. "I, Willis Cobb, being of sound mind, do hereby will all my earthly belongings to my wife, Nancy Pettigrew Cobb, and my son, Aaron." Mistuh Tolin stopped and looked at me with a half-smile. "This was written before I was born!" He looked back to the yellowed, crinkly paper. "Here's the correction—dated 20 January, 1815. 'My new son, Tolin,' it says." His eyes seemed to dance down the page, then he frowned.

"I'll be damned! Listen to this! 'And on the occasion of

54

my death let it here be known that my manservant, Jake, so faithful to me through the years and who raised me since I was eight, that Jake be made a free man, no longer in bondage to anyone.' "

Mistuh Tolin was on his feet and stridin' around the barn. His face held a scowl. "Isn't that sweet! Poor old Jake. I wonder which of them was shot first? I hope Jake died a free man!"

It sounded mighty hard of Mistuh Tolin to talk that way, and I stared at the stray pieces of straw on the floor.

"Jason! What would you do if you were free?" His words surprised me, and I looked up to see if he expected an answer. "If you were free and had no ties or bonds. You could do anything! What would you do?"

"I couldn't do *anything*, Mistuh Tolin. Even a *free* black man got restrictions."

"Damn it, Jason! I mean just pretend. Pretend you were free, and white, and all alone. What would you do?"

Free, white, and all alone. If I was him, he meant.

I'd look for Louisa, I thought. I'd find her and never let her go.

"Well?" he asked.

I hunched my shoulders, suddenly wishin' I was free to do that very thing. Wishin' I was free, and . . . "There was this man come into Fort Brooke while you was with the column." I started talkin' slow, thinkin' he'd interrupt, but he didn't. "He come in as a courier for one of the generals. Folks said he was a mountain man and an injun-fighter from the West helpin' out with the war. He told about the prairies and mountains, and buffalo." I remembered the excitement I'd felt when that man talked. "He said there was land so big you could ride for days and never see another soul. It's free land, too—no government, no laws —where you worked your way as best you could. I guess if I was free, I'd have to go out there. Someplace where I could stay free and not have to be bound up again."

My heart pounded, fearful from talkin' out to him like

55

that. The rain dripped from the roof eaves. I heard the horses stomp in the stalls, and flies buzzing around the ceiling beam. Seemed like hours passed and I finally looked up to see if Mistuh Tolin was really there or if I was just imaginin' things.

"There was a bundle of food in that oil bag. Let's find ourselves a hearth and see what we can get together." He seemed sort of calm and closed off like he gets when thinkin'. I nodded, wonderin' if I had spoke out too much. We had talked open about a lot of things, but never freedom.

We used the fireplace in Jake and Bitty's cabin. Mistuh Tolin got a small kettle and tin plates from his saddle packs, and I laid the fire. There was some cooked meat and bread and a jar of field peas in the bag, and I realized I hadn't eaten all day. Mistuh Tolin pulled out an apple and a slab of cheese, and I was mighty pleased when he sliced off hunks of the cheese for both of us.

He started talkin', like he did most times, not wantin' comments from me but thinkin' out loud. One thing for sure, he sure didn't want to grow cotton.

"What about Miss Marvena? You still plannin' on marryin' her?" I started servin' the plates and my stomach was growlin'.

"Hardly!" He laughed a hard, tired bark and leaned against the cabin wall. "She's up in Tuscaloosa with her mother hobnobbing with congressmen. What would she want with a poor dirt farmer anyway? I'm not much better off than that trashy overseer her daddy has at their plantation." His eyes suddenly showed a spark of mischief. "Besides, did you ever notice how she twitters when she talks —like a spring bird fresh off the nest. That would drive me crazy after a while."

I thought about Louisa's voice. Soft. A bit of music in the sound. *Louisa.* I swallowed hard on the peas I was downin'. She's alive, my brain declared. And she's gonna have my baby and be strong. Even though I knew I'd never see her again I would keep that thought.

Then I closed it all away. I couldn't think about her no more.

The rest of our eatin' was done with no talk. The rain had stopped by the time we finished. I took the plates and forks and washed them at the pump well.

Mistuh Tolin put out the fire and looked around. "I don't think I could sleep here in Jake and Bitty's place," he said, real sad like. "It just wouldn't be right." He shook his head. "Upstairs? In your room?"

"Yes, suh."

He stared at me a minute and then looked away. "We ought to check everything again, just to see what we can find. Although I suppose the soldiers cleaned up everything when they came through."

The ground was damp and clean-smellin' when we walked out. A puddle off near the hitchin' rail shimmered as the evenin' breeze passed over it. I went to the smokehouse, but there weren't nothin' there. Nor was there in the springhouse. I couldn't even look down the rise to the quarters 'cause of the pain it caused me. I stared into the ashes of the house. So much gone! I tried not to cry. When I went back to the stable Mistuh Tolin was standin' there watchin' me. He was standin' by Jake's chair and there was a bundle on it.

"These are yours," he said. "Looks like somebody hid them behind the trunk over there. Probably Jake, so my pa wouldn't gamble them away." He turned and hoisted a mattress, and started for the stairs.

"I'll take that, Mistuh Tolin."

"You tend to your own things, Jason. I'll manage."

I opened the canvas sack on the chair. There was the hammers, six tongs, chisels, and a good whetstone inside. Down on the bottom was the stake anvil and a set of hand bellows. I lifted out a small iron box that was older than Jake had been. His father had give him that box. Four flints was inside. I looked around the shop and found the bottom tool of the swage in a pile of rags. The pincers and flat bit was still on the wall near the stable door. I added them to the pack and put it all by the forge.

Memories and voices floated to me while I retied that bag. I suddenly heard Jake's big voice singin': *Hammer come down. Hammer come down. Hit that iron* . . . I shivered and looked around again before goin' upstairs.

Mistuh Tolin was stretched out on the mattress on the floor. A lamp was lit, but turned real low.

"What's my name?" he asked as I walked through the doorway.

"Why, Mistuh Tolin, suh."

"*Mister* isn't a name. It's a title. What's my name?"

"Tolin . . . Tolin Cobb." I sat down on the bed, my heart beatin' real fast. He was actin' mighty strange.

"What's your name?

"Me? Jason, suh."

"There was a Jason in my regiment in Florida. Which Jason are you?"

I took a deep breath, scared anythin' I said would be wrong. "Jason. Mistuh Tolin's man, suh."

"Ha! You're wrong! You're not just Mister Tolin's man. You're Mister Tolin's blacksmith man! No! You're Jason, the Cobb blacksmith. Don't you see?" He was sittin' up lookin' at me.

I didn't see at all, but thought he was plumb outta his head from grief and worry.

"Go to sleep, Jason. Tomorrow's going to be a busy day." He turned out the wick on the lamp and lay back.

"Yes, suh."

"And don't ever call me *sir* again."

I opened my mouth, and my brain said *Yes, suh.* I swallowed hard and stared into the darkness. It was then I realized that I was sleepin' on the bed and he was on the floor, and I knew for sure he had gone mad.

Mistuh Caulborne thought he'd gone mad, too, when Mistuh Tolin sold him his land the next evening.

"Tolin! If it's money you want . . ." He paced to the stairs of the porch. I was sittin' by the camellia bush. "Sell Jason! Lord knows, he'd bring a handsome price. I have no need for another smith myself, but there are many, many planters who would welcome the opportunity to get a young, healthy buck like that. Why, he'd bring you nearly nine hundred dollars with his skills."

"Sell Jason?"

I waited. That was somethin' I had worried about since the night before. He had kept talkin' about my bein' a blacksmith, and I figured he was seein' me with dollar signs. A hard, icy knot seemed to grow inside me, and I touched my chest to see if it was cold.

But Mistuh Tolin just repeated his offer. "Twelve hundred dollars for the whole place. It borders your land."

"Well, if this isn't the most confounded thing I ever heard. Your father and I never got along too well, but I respected him as much as any man in the county. I truly dislike the idea of your givin' up the land that your family shed blood to retain!"

"Mr. Caulborne, I've been harnessed to that land since my mother died like a mule to a sorghum mill. Now the traces are cut." Mistuh Tolin sighed loud. "Will you buy the land?"

"I—I'll— Oh, hell, Tolin. Yes! I'll buy the land. And if you change your mind in a year or two I'll return it to you at equal value."

I heard papers rustle. "Here's the deed. I had it drawn up this afternoon at the county office. This titles you to all the land except the quarter-acre above the house."

That quarter-acre—I knew what that was. The graveyard. Mistuh Tolin had me wrought a sign for the gate to the graveyard that morning. COBB, it said, and when Mistuh Tolin returned from town, he erected it hisself on wooden beams over the path that led to the markers.

They went inside and I worried on Mistuh Tolin's sellin' the land. I kept rememberin' what Seth had said: Land is

59

all you can count on. What would we do now, with no land to tend, no place to call home?

I heard the house door open and stood up.

"So what will you do now, Tolin? Join the regulars to fight the Creeks?"

My heart pounded, fearful that he would say yes.

"No, sir. I've seen enough of fighting and death. I . . . I know this person who told me about free land in the Territory. I think I'll investigate that. He said it was a place you could stay free and not be bound up again."

I couldn't believe my ears!

"Umph! The Territory is full of more Indians and wildness! Oh, my . . . But I can see that tryin' to argue you out of it would be useless."

"Yes, sir. It would."

"You take care, Tolin." They shook hands. "And if I can ever be of help to you—in any way—don't hesitate to contact me."

"Thank you, sir."

9

It was June fifteenth when Mistuh Tolin sold his land and started us off to the West. He bought two horses and a pack mule in Union Springs, we put our things together, and just kept goin'. Seems all he wanted to do was make distance between him and his land. My doubts about what he was doin' was still strong, but I was feelin' a relief, too. I didn't want to stay back on that burned-out plantation with all those memories and voices floatin' up at me. They had been there while I worked on the name plate for the graveyard. Skalley had come voiceless and touched my cheek. Jake's hammer song never left my ears. Bitty bustled around the door of the log house, and I heard children cryin'.

There was somethin' about the idea of goin' west that was hopeful, too. Maybe 'cause I'd read so much about it. Maybe, too, 'cause it was what I wanted to do if I could. It was almost like *I* had made the decision to go—had had some say in what we was doin'. But the memories of why we was goin' stayed with me.

In Montgomery the streets was full of folks, red and white, uprooted and shoved around because of the fightin'. I wondered if any of the Indians I saw chained to carts was those that killed my people. Tuscaloosa (Alabama's capital) didn't have so many stray folks, but there was talk on every corner about the war. Mistuh Tolin stopped there long enough to by a passel of books and magazines—must have been nine or ten at least!—and we started on out of town. I had to remind him we was near out of food, so he gave me money to buy supplies. Then I had to remind him about my pass. Colored folks wasn't allowed out at night without a note from their owners.

After I bought the supplies I had to ride an hour in the dark to catch him. I was scared Indians or militiamen was goin' to shoot me, but nothin' happened.

The next six days was spent with Mistuh Tolin readin', and me in worry. He was quiet—too quiet for him—and his eyes looked gray and cold. There was a strong hint of pain in the way he held his mouth, and I knew what that was from. Same as in me—from losin' everythin'. Everythin' that was ever my life—gone. My face must have looked just as empty. Desolate, I think is the word.

When we got to Memphis we both seemed to perk up.

"It means a place of good abode," Mistuh Tolin said as we passed some mansions on our way in from Mississippi. Those estates made Mistuh Caulborne's farm look small.

"The original Memphis was a city in ancient Egypt," Mistuh Tolin continued. His voice sounded good like always when he talked scholarly stuff. "It's only been incorporated ten years, but look how it's grown! They'll be calling it a city before long."

We was soon lost in the traffic. The closer we got to the river, the busier things was, what with surreys and cabs and carriages with fancy red-painted wheel spokes. There was carts and wagons, and freighters with rear wheels tall as a man. A ten-mule team come around a tight corner and backed us up an alleyway. It was haulin' lumber from the docks, and the mule skinner was crackin' his whip plenty to get them gray-noses up the street. Mistuh Tolin's pack horse started fussin'.

"Hold on to the lead, Jason. Lord knows, we don't need to lose anything more," Mistuh Tolin called.

He was right about that, not that we was carryin' much. Jake's blacksmithin' tools made most of the load, and the few clothes Mistuh Tolin had brought back from Florida. I'd scrubbed them as best I could but they still looked mighty worn. I had a bag of clothes, too, but they was in bad sha, . And of course we had blankets and trail gear, like anyone else travelin' two days or twenty.

"It sure smells bad here," I said. We was passin' some long wooden buildings where cloth was bein' made. Across the street was a place for makin' furniture, and I'd heard there was huge cotton storage buildin's where folks stood all day balin' lint.

"That's the smell of industry, Jason." Mistuh Tolin's voice had a bit of a spark, but when I looked at him I could see he wasn't breathin' too good neither.

The river lay flat and calm before us, and I think I expected more than I saw. The mighty Mississippi, people called it, but after gazin' at the Gulf off the coast of Florida I wasn't impressed.

At the walkways near the big boats there was important-lookin' men with cigars, frock coats, and tall beaver hats. They was probably from them mansions we saw earlier. The ladies with them wore wide skirts with long travelin' capes over them. They kept their faces shaded with frilly parasols, and held hankies to their noses like that would keep the stink and roughness of the area from them.

"I wonder how far it is to St. Louey?" Mistuh Tolin said the city name like we'd been told the French people did.

"Six or seven days, at least," I said.

"That far?" He sighed.

"Maybe we could take a paddle boat up—not have to ride the horses all that way." Mistuh Tolin was no horseman and I could tell he was tired of sittin' the saddle.

"Of course! A great idea, Jason!" His eyes sparkled. "We aren't poor folks anymore. I've got forty dollars in my pocket and a draft for ten hundred more. We'll take a fancy steamboat! Stay here while I get the tickets."

He started off through the crowd and I was feelin' a whole lot better. Memphis might have been big and smelly, but it had Mistuh Tolin smilin' for the first time in eleven days. I wasn't goin' to complain about that.

I moved the horses close to a big stack of boxes and looked around. The river stretched off to my left, and the afternoon sunlight glinted off the surface. Folks was sittin' and standin' around on the wooden walkways. Some was colored, some was white; most was poor folks and kids caught up in all the busy comin's and goin's. They seemed to enjoy it all. Me, I was powerful uncomfortable. The noises was screechy—whistles blowin', tootin' from the boats on the river. Men was shoutin' and cussin'. I could hear whips crackin', mules fussin', dogs yappin', and the smell of filth and rottin' food kept flies buzzin' somethin' terrible. Big green-backed flies, and they had the horses and me in torment.

A lot of colored men was workin' down on that river-bank. I don't think I'd ever seen so many colored folks in one place in all my life. Most of them was haulin' bales and boxes, or pullin' on tow ropes to get the barges up to the docks. They was barefoot and their feet would sink clear past the ankles in the muck. I remembered Horace tellin' that a lot of levee work was done by free Negroes, and I wondered how many of those men was free. Freedom had to mean more than that!

"Hey! Get 'im! Stop that nigger!"

That yell scared me near to death, and I saw a middle-sized Negro man come dodgin' and runnin' through the confusion. White men was chasin' him and hollerin'. I figured him to be a runaway, and I wondered where he was from and where he was goin' to. He was comin' right for me and I saw him look real good at the horses. I closed my fist tight on the reins, and he kept comin'. Then somebody tackled his legs and he sprawled out in front of me. Folks was all over him in no time, and I kept talkin' soft to the horses while they snorted and danced around. I could feel my own eyes wide with fright. Soon the noise died down and the man was hauled off—bein' cussed at and beat as he went.

A paper lay in front of me. It was curled to the size of an axe handle where it had been held tight in someone's fist. I picked it up and unrolled it. *Freedom's Journal* was the name.

I'd heard of this paper before, back in '29 or '30, and I knew it was put out by a black man! I never dreamed I'd see a copy.

"Jason! Are you all right?" Mistuh Tolin had been runnin' and was out of breath. "I saw all the commotion down here—" He sighed and clapped his hand on my shoulder. His fingers squeezed tight. "Come on. I don't want to stay down here any longer."

I tucked the newspaper under my blanket roll behind the saddle, and we rode away from the docks.

Mistuh Tolin found a room in a little hostel near the north edge of town. It had its own stable, so I bedded the horses and myself back there. Mistuh Tolin brought me out some supper and stood to talk while I ate.

"We'll be like the Argonauts," he said excitedly. "Jason and the Arg*onaut*. There's just one of me," he laughed. It was the first real laugh since we got off the boat at Eufaula comin' home from Florida. "And I'll be calling on a Captain Drewry at the American Fur Company in St. Louey. He's lookin' for employees to go into the Territory."

Employees was hired folks. Mistuh Tolin said how he was plannin' on gettin' a job, and one for me, too.

"You're hirin' me out, then?" I didn't like that idea, and I worried that the next step might be him sellin' me.

"Well, not exactly . . . I mean . . ." He paced in front of a stall with his hands behind his back. "It's not like it was before, Jason. Alabama is gone. That's out of our life. When I was in Union Springs getting the horses I . . . Well, I figured we could both take jobs and get wages. Maybe we could buy a line of traps and go off to the mountains to hunt beaver." He seemed to relax all of a sudden. "Wouldn't that be great? You always liked those books about the West. That's what I had in mind. We'll spend the whole wonderful winter living in skin houses like the Indians and trapping beaver, then float down the river come spring and back to civilization with a fortune in furs."

I didn't say nothin', although it sounded mighty foolish to me. Neither him or me knew nothin' about settin' a trap line or buildin' a camp in the mountains. We didn't even know what the mountains looked like! But I was achin' to see.

He leaned against the wall and stretched his arms tight on the wood. His eyes was closed and his face looked worried. "It isn't hurting so much now—what happened back there. It's like having a stone in your shoe: the more you walk on it the less you notice the pain, even though the stone is still there. What about you, Jason? You lost more than I did."

"I'm all right, Mistuh Tolin." I could hear the lonely ring of my hammer when I made the sign for the graveyard. I saw Skalley's cabin gapin' its empty door at me. *Louisa!* wailed a deep pain. I pushed it away.

"It's—it's not my fault, is it? Because we went to Florida? I mean—I didn't know—" His hands kept openin' and closin' into fists.

For sure I hadn't wanted to go to Florida, but I'd never thought it a cause to what happened. It was just one more sad thing in my life like my daddy gettin' sold off, my mama dyin'. Just this time it was worse. "I can't see that our bein' there to get killed too would have changed much."

"I didn't hate my pa. Really I didn't," he gasped. "And rejoinin' the militia would have just added more killin' to what's already been."

"You've always done your best, Mistuh Tolin. We all knew that."

He looked at me and tried to smile. "I'm glad you're with

me, Jason. I don't know what I'd do if I didn't have anyone. I just . . ."

I listened to the crickets and peepers in the night. I heard a mouse scurryin' through the hay bin. I wanted to tell Mistuh Tolin how glad I was to be gone from Alabama; how relieved I was that he hadn't sold me off to another planter.

Mistuh Tolin started talkin' about the dreams and agonies he'd been sufferin' for the past ten days. He was tellin' me about one of the books he'd bought, *Manfred,* and somethin' about some Count and the Prince of Darkness. My mind wandered off to thoughts of bein' so far from home; then I remembered that there wasn't no home anymore. The realness of it cut into me and I tried to think of somethin' good to stop the misery.

"Ah, Jason," he was sayin'. "A man of letters is unbound in his ability to deal with life. Knowledge opens the doors to riches and buries superstitions which plague most men's minds."

"You know?" I said when he paused. "There ain't no cotton in the Territory."

"Why, no. There isn't. It's a whole different land."

I felt him starin' at me and I got hot with embarrassment. I cleared my throat and started pickin' up my plate and cup.

"Well, I think I'll do some reading," he said as he took my dinner things. "Good night, Jason."

I nodded to him and watched as he walked away. Then I remembered I had my own readin' matter. Mistuh Tolin had been after me to read those books of his all the whole trip and I pretended at it to keep him happy. But this was goin' to be different. I checked the horses once more, then climbed into the hayloft with *Freedom's Journal.* I got myself situated next to the big open door where the hay was hauled in. The moonshine was comin' through real nice, and I sat back from the openin' just enough so's I couldn't be seen from the outside, but close enough to have light to read by.

There was all kinds of articles in that paper. Most was about how slavery was wrong, and what different groups was doin' about it. None of the groups was farther south than Lexington, Kentucky. There was some writin' about a slave man in Maryland named Henry Blair who had invented a corn harvester. And there was a long article about the Wilberforce colony up in Canada. It was hard to believe: a whole little town of free black folks ownin' land and cattle. They had a sawmill and schools and churches, too . . .

The moon slid up into the sky and left me with barely enough light to find the ladder with. I went down, tucked the newspaper deep in the oilcloth that held the smith tools, and then climbed back up top to sleep.

I took my first steamboat ride the next day, but it wasn't fancy like what Mistuh Tolin had been talkin' about. I'd seen better boats in Montgomery. Once we was out on that big Mississippi River it didn't matter anyway, 'cause it was excitin' and scary, and eye-bulgin' enough as it was.

"Look at it, Jason!" Mistuh Tolin kept sayin' when the river was wide like the Gulf. "Tremendous!" And when the waters narrowed down he was watchin' the land go by like a tiny kid on his first trip to town. He grabbed my arm once, shoutin' "Look!" and pointin' to the shore where a deer was browsin'. It was like he'd never seen a deer before.

Me, I was lookin' at that big paddle wheel turnin' on its iron pipe axle and churnin' up the water behind us. The wheel was taller than I was high, and near as wide as the boat with rows of broad, flat paddles all in lines that rolled and lifted the water. A small house was fixed at the back of the deck and from that was attached long crank rods to the axle. Inside the house was a big boiler-type furnace that was kept stoked with wood. There was water in the top part and the steam from that hot water pushed what was called pistons. It was the pistons that turned the crank-type affair that moved the rods and rolled the paddle wheel. It was excitin' to realize that steam—same as hissed up when I cooled off my iron at the forge—would cause the whole big boat to go.

The rest of the boat wasn't much. It was filled with bales and bags of stuff. There was a lot of wood for the engine, and some livestock bein' trailed on the raft along with Mistuh Tolin's horses. Those horses hadn't been too sure about steppin' off solid ground onto that wooden deck. I finally had to put a bag over their eyes and they come along real peaceable. After three and a half days, they didn't seem to mind at all.

"Jason, look. That must be St. Louey." Mistuh Tolin's eyes was shinin' from the adventure, and I couldn't believe I was really in that city I'd read a lot about. This was the beginnin' of the frontier, I thought. The center of the fur market, and where most folks started for a new life in the West.

Up ahead I could see smokestacks of river boats and barges. There was chimneys along the riverbank and I knew St. Louis had *industry*. The river got crowded with steamers, and folks was polin' keelboats near the banks. I saw two dirty, bearded men in a canoe easin' along. The canoe was piled high with furs, and I stared—barely breathin' 'cause it was all like a dream come true. Our boat slowed and moved up to the dock near some livestock pens. My nose burned from the smell of thick smoke and cow dung, but I was smilin'.

"First off, we'll look up this Captain Drewry about our jobs. We can buy whatever supplies we need, and then bank the money that's left."

"Maybe you should bank it first, Mistuh Tolin. This town don't look too safe." I had spotted a fight on the riverbank and pointed to it. Didn't nobody try to stop it, and Mistuh Tolin and me watched as an old man was beat down and stripped of his derby and boots. His pockets was turned inside out and the three toughs what had jumped him went off laughin'.

Mistuh Tolin seemed to swallow hard and took a deep breath. "The wild frontier, Jason. We're part of that now."

II

Singing
Proud

10

"Buffalo! Buffalo ahead, Cap Drewry," the scout for the wagons huffed out as he rode up.

I looked at Mistuh Tolin, my eyes wide with excitement, and we trotted our horses up toward the lead wagon.

We was three weeks past St. Louis and five days out from Fort Atkinson at Council Bluffs, where we had to give up river travel on the Missouri for movin' on horseback. Mistuh Tolin had us movin' in style, too. We was both dressed in buckskin suits with fringe at the arm and leg seams; and he was wearin' a fur hat complete with weasel head. He had got me a broad-brimmed leather one, and even a new set of long johns and boots like his. We was ridin' new horses, too, 'cause folks at American Fur said eastern horses didn't hold up in the mountains. They was used to eatin' more grain, and different grasses. Mistuh Tolin left the choosin' up to me, and I traded the horses he'd bought in Union Springs for two good mules. I picked real careful on the horses and bought a chestnut for him and a black geldin' for me. They was fine mounts, and I took to callin' mine Dancer, 'cause he was a mite skittish most times.

"This herd better be big enough to bother with," Cap was sayin' to the scout when we got to them. Cap's name was Jebediah, but he was called Cap on account of the boat captain's hat he always wore.

"You betcha. We could stock up enough from this herd to get us from here to Fort John."

Fort John was the old name for Fort Laramie—where we was headin'.

"You goin' with the hunters, Cobb? Bring us back some dinner?" asked Cap.

"Wouldn't miss the chance!" Mistuh Tolin said. "Come on, Jason."

While travelin' up the Missouri we'd been lucky to go out with the huntin' parties, 'cause both of us had shown we was good with dressin' out a kill. Mistuh Tolin had tried his hand at shootin' game, too, and was what these men called a fair shot. What I liked best about that was that we got to see the land. The great rollin' hills had spilled off in front of us like a giant blanket, with cricks and streams tucked in the folds and white-barked trees breakin' up the view. The sky was bluer than I'd ever seen it before.

But from Council Bluffs it had been different. The land was flat and hard, with little grass and nearly always uphill. The Platte River was sluggish in most places, and sometimes faded off into beds of sandy hills and bug-covered water. The wind blew hot and steady day and night, and we got butt-sore from sittin' in the saddle all day. There was times Mistuh Tolin looked so uncomfortable I thought he was goin' to turn us back toward the States. The only good thing I could say about it was that I hadn't seen a single cotton plant.

"Now, this is adventure, Jason. The way it ought to be," Mistuh Tolin whispered to me while he primed the Hall breechloader rifle he had bought in St. Louis. He had got a new pistol there, too: a Colt five-shot.

We topped the rise with the hunters and there they was. Buffalo. Lookin' like great brown rocks on the valley floor. The wind was in our favor and the beasts just stood around croppin' grass or floppin' down on the ground. They didn't bunch all together like the pictures I'd seen, and they looked so heavy I couldn't imagine them runnin' as fast as some folks said they could.

We got closer now, goin' on foot, and inchin' along through the scratchy grass on our bellies so the buffalo wouldn't see us. Mistuh Tolin took up that new rifle and was tense as stretched leather. My heart started poundin' fierce when I was close enough to realize the beasts' true size. The bulls—especially those that was along the outside edge of the herd—was nearly as tall, ground to hump, as a big horse. Their hair was thick and black up by the hump, and it lightened to a splotchy yellow. Huge dirty patches of it was fallin' away from them and trailin' on the ground. There was one bull up the next rise rubbin' his shoulders on the trunk of a tree to get off the loose hair. The tree trunk was worn smooth from where other buffalo had been doin' the same thing over the years.

We was about seventy-five yards away when the hunters readied to shoot. A man knelt with one knee on the ground, his gun set at his shoulder for firin' while a second hunter stood behind or braced the kneelin' man's shoulder with his back and kept his rifle ready. That served a double purpose. There was extra support for the kick of the gun, and also a lookout against Indians who might be huntin', too.

Boom!

I expected to see the animals bolt and start lumberin' away, but they didn't. A bull fell from the edge of the herd, blood gushin' from its nose; its eyes rolled crazy while it died. Another gun fired. A large cow took a few steps toward the herd. The hunters switched places so the man who fired could reload. The other hunter took aim and brought the cow down before she could reach the others. Another cow came over and pawed at the dyin' animal.

"Brace me, Jason," Mistuh Tolin said.

I sat behind him to hold his shoulder while he took the shot. He hadn't used the rifle too much, and he still wasn't used to the kick of that big-bore gun. I felt him quiverin' and saw the sweat rollin' down his neck. His hands was tremblin' and he must have took aim four or five times without pullin' the trigger.

"I've never shot anything so big in all my life!" Mistuh Tolin whispered to me while wipin' his palm on his thigh.

There was a cow movin' even closer to us. I could see the rough nap of its hair. Mistuh Tolin sighted again. Four more buffalo went down, but not from any shots Mistuh Tolin fired. He never fired that gun.

The wind died down, swished around us, and then gusted toward the herd. Snortin' and bawlin' started up and the animals that was restin' lunged to their feet. One of the hunters tried a standin' shot and wounded a young bull, and before he could reload the whole herd was rumblin' across the valley. Mistuh Tolin and me was on our feet with excitement at seein' the thunderin' of the animals as they took off faster than ever to be believed. Soon the dust was thick and it hid most of their shapes, and when the wind shifted again we was covered with a fine powder from the ground they had churned to flour in their leaving.

"Did ya git yourself a buffalo?" Cap Drewry asked Mistuh Tolin when he pulled up with the wagons next to where the butcherin' had started. His face had a half smile like he already knew the answer.

"Aw, he ain't gonna shoot no buffler," one of the hunters, Jim Tolliver, said. "That there boy's a *mangeur du lard.*" Everybody started chucklin'. *Mangeur du lard* was what new folks was called who didn't have no mountain experience. Mountain men figured that new folks would still be tryin' to eat pork and cornbread, and never get the hang of sourdough and buffalo meat. Mistuh Tolin got red in the face.

"He'll be so busy lookin' for settlement comforts out here he'll kill hisself for shore," Tolliver kept on. "Here, boy, have some western food." Tolliver had pulled the entrails from a cow and was holdin' the liver, still steamin', in his bloody hand. He sliced off a piece and handed it out to Mistuh Tolin. Mistuh Tolin's face went pale, and I drew a quick breath. Tolliver laughed and bit into the warm, raw liver. *"Mangeur du lard,"* he said while chewin'.

Mistuh Tolin stomped off half sick and burnin' with anger. I went back to the butcherin' I was doin', my own stomach queasy, and knowin' how Mistuh Tolin was feelin'. He had been joked about ever since we left Council Bluffs, and I could see him gettin' mighty tired of it. Me, folks just ignored. No bad words or good, 'cause I was with him.

When we finished supper that night—a big meal of hump meat fried in marrow with sourdough biscuits (we used the marrow for butter, too) and stewed dried apples—I was certain I was no *mangeur du lard*. Ian Bornston, one of the men on the train who hadn't been teasin' Mistuh Tolin, said as much, too.

"I don't know how anybody could turn away from buffalo meat," I told him. "It's the most tender, best-tastin' stuff I ever ate."

Mistuh Tolin liked it, too, and it was a good thing, 'cause once you got out of the States (that's anywhere west of the Missouri River) everyone ate buffalo—'ceptin' they called it *buffler*. They'd eat all parts of the buffler, too. The liver was especially liked just like Tolliver had ate it. The hump and hump ribs was ate boiled or roasted; belly fat was taken to cook with; bones was saved and the marrow went on everything. The *boudins*—that was the guts—was considered a real treat. They'd be seared over the fire in huge chunks and swallowed almost whole. I didn't get a likin' for that, but the tongue—baked down in the fire coals—was so sweet-tastin' and tender I would never pass that up.

Of course there was times when the buffalo wasn't around. For those times there was plenty of deer or elk, and beaver and panther in the mountains. But mid to late summer, like when we was travelin', was matin' season and the buffalo ran in great bunches on the prairie. Sometimes it took half a day for the whole herd to get through one valley.

We saw Indians a few days after that buffalo kill. It was a group of twelve, all naked and painted. One minute nothin' looked out of the ordinary, the next there they was sittin' on the hills lookin' at us. Mistuh Tolin rode up to me and handed me the Brown Bess muzzleloader.

"I was hopin' this part of the frontier would never come true," he said.

My heart was beatin' fast, but didn't nothin' special happen 'cause Cap Drewry had his men uncover one of the cannons we was carryin' and fire a ball up toward the Indians. They took off before the sound of that cannon had cleared.

"So those were the hostiles?" Mistuh Tolin said with some satisfaction. "I thought they were more dangerous than that."

"Don't be fooled, Cobb. Pawnee are fierce fighters like all these Plains tribes, but they was smart enough to see that their twelve men armed with bows and arrows couldn't go up against the thirteen of us armed with rifles and two cannons."

"Fourteen of us," Mistuh Tolin corrected, and Cap saw me carryin' the gun.

"Can he use that thing?"

"Damn well."

Cap nodded at me and looked thoughtful. "Best he stay armed then."

So we was fourteen armed men. I felt good about it, and it seemed some of the men started treatin' me a bit different.

Mistuh Tolin took up his rifle the next time buffalo was sighted. He didn't even want me to help this time, and though his hands was tremblin' when he first sighted down that barrel, I saw him tighten up real strong before he fired.

The cow he had aimed at crumpled forward and struggled back to its feet. Mistuh Tolin had reloaded in almost the same amount of time. I was crouched in the grass, and I saw that second shot slam into the cow. It went down in a froth of blood.

"You did it! Yes sirree! Clean shots, too. I saw from the hill." Ian Bornston's gruff voice was glad-speakin' when he came to us. "Next thing to do is get Jason here his first kill." He patted us both on the back.

The wagons was rumblin' down to us and Mistuh Tolin's face was one big grin as he walked to the cow he'd killed. One of the other men came over smilin'.

"Didn't think ya had it in ya, Cobb. That was fine shootin'." He flicked his knife and come up with the wisp tail from the cow. "Your sooveeneer."

Mistuh Tolin tucked the tail in the rim of his hat and set to work dressin' the kill.

Cap Drewry wasn't so stiff-lipped after that, and most of the other men stopped makin' jokes about Mistuh Tolin. Only Tolliver kept talkin' wrong.

"Sure, he kin fire a gun. Ain't been doin' nothin' all his life but sittin' and lettin' some niggers take care of him. He learned how to shoot so's to keep them darkies in line. He even had to bring his slave boy out here with 'im for a wet nurse."

Mistuh Tolin flushed and tightened up. I hurt inside. This was the first mention of slave that had come up, and it was like cold winds threatenin' to spoil a summer day.

"Jason's a blacksmith," Mistuh Tolin said strong. Tolliver just laughed.

"Now, that's true, Jim," Cap said. "He's hired on by American Fur—a paid employee."

"Blacksmith. Uh! Wet nurse is what he is!"

Well, sure enough, I hadn't done nothin' to show my trade. There had been this smith at Fort Atkinson, and he made some barrel repairs and the like before the pack train left west. The job wasn't real smooth the way Jake taught me to do it, but the man didn't take too kindly to Mistuh Tolin askin' if I could help, so my tools stayed wrapped in the oilcloth and packed on the mule.

All this talk about me bein' a wet nurse made Mistuh Tolin all the more determined to ride the full distance and work his own load. Sometimes I hardly saw him 'cause he was off ridin' with a huntin' party, or to the side with Cap Drewry learnin' what he could about the fort and the mountains. I spent a lot of time with Bornston, and he took me on the scoutin' trips at times. After two more weeks on the trail our rear ends got callused, and Mistuh Tolin started smilin' again. He even started writin' poetry, and I'd hear him talk it out in flowery words:

> Sweet birds of morning in the sky
> Looking down with nature's eye
> And land whose beauteous sights I spy
> I sing this song with a noble cry.
>
> Great majestic plains stretch out
> Farther than a man can shout
> A voyage through your verdant span
> Is fantastic.

His last lines was always a bit weak.

One thing for sure, Mistuh Tolin looked real good sittin' on the chestnut horse I'd picked for him. He called him Rogue. The sun had blistered his face and hands durin' the first week of travel, but the dead skin had peeled away and left an even tan. There was a smatterin' of freckles across his nose, and his hair was lighter in the five weeks since we left St. Louis. Me, I was ridin' that black geldin' with three white stockin's. The name, Dancer, I'd given him right off was real fittin', but he felt fine under me. He stood nearly sixteen hands high, which was good, 'cause I think I had grown another inch since we left Alabama.

The hills was gettin' steeper and the sky seemed bigger and more vast. The men mostly stayed friendly and we never got asked where we come from or why we was in the Territory. They knew, of course, we was from the South, but it didn't seem to matter to no one 'ceptin' Tolliver, and folks started ignorin' him. The nightmare of Alabama that had sent us out here got tucked in the dark corners of our minds.

11

"Eeeee-haaa!" There was shoutin' and more noise than I had heard since we left St. Louis. Guns was firin' and when I got Dancer settled I saw a group of six men on horses come gallopin' down the hill at us. I was glad that five of them was white men, and I stopped worryin' about the Pawnee, but those men made more noise than the Indians did, and when they come in close I started wonderin' if they wasn't more dangerous.

"Trappers!" Mistuh Tolin announced with a grin. He reined up next to me. "They're ridin' to Fort Atkinson. Look at them! They're more grizzly than I ever imagined!"

He was sure right about that. The men was bearded and dark from the weather and sun. Their clothes appeared to be stuck onto their bodies, and I remembered some of the things Mistuh Tolin and me had read about trappers: they never bathed, and they smelled real bad, and was wilder than the "savages." We had figured it was just some fancy writin' that had been done for the folks back East. Now I knew they was right.

There was an Indian with them. He sat real easy on his horse and was the cleanest of the lot. I shouldn't have been so concerned about dirt, though, 'cause Mistuh Tolin and me hadn't washed off much more than our faces in over two weeks. It was hot summer—hotter than anythin' I ever felt at home—sort of like we was ridin' in an oven. If you didn't keep your skin covered it would dry right up. The only savin' grace was to sweat; then your clothes would stick to you and make you feel a mite cooler. Of course, when that happened everybody couldn't help but smell.

This Indian was all covered up too, and he rode over to where we was and circled around us a bit before callin' out somethin' and pointin' at me. One of the trappers reined up next to the Indian and stared at us. His beard was all smattered gray and stained with tobacco juice, and he had a scar on one cheek that we found out later was give to him by a mountain cat he had tried to den with on a blizzard night. He was wearin' a fur hat and his leather coat showed some beadwork under the dust.

"Wal, I'll be damned!" He spat tobacco juice into the dry grass. "First preachers, then wimmen, and now coloreds." He shook his head and spit again. "Time's a-changin'. This ol' child be glad to git out."

"Wonder what he meant by that?" Mistuh Tolin looked puzzled.

Ian Bornston rode up next to us. "That trapper's been in the mountains nearly as long as I been out in these parts." Bornston had told me he come fifteen years ago. "Come out when he was about your ages, I guess. He says the beaver ain't shinin' no more—that is, they jest about trapped all the beaver out of the mountains—and times is gettin' hard. Why, the pack train that went to the rendezvous last month was carryin' womenfolks."

A rendezvous was where the trappers would meet with a pack train once a year to cash in their fur takin's and buy supplies they needed for the next trappin' season. The tellin' was that it was a wild affair with liquor flowin' all around, and gamblin', and Indians with their skin houses that they called lodges. I ached to see it.

"Wiggins and his group." Bornston nodded toward the mountain men. "They're movin' their lines. Some is goin' up to the Dakotas. Wiggins, he'll probably head south to the Sangre de Cristos near Santa Fe."

"You say there were women with the pack train?" Mistuh Tolin said with surprise. "I can't imagine bringing a woman through this wildness."

"They have to be the hardy type. Not a trip for society folks, no sirree."

"Jason, can you imagine Marvena Caulborne out here in all her hoop skirts and fancy dressings?" We both laughed and Bornston rode off.

Wiggins and the other mountain men who had rode in camped with us that night. They told some fine tales about beaver, bad winters, and grizzly bears. They also talked about Indian women and what it was like bein' with one of them—in such detail that I had trouble sittin' still.

"I jest hope them wimmen in the Sangre de Cristos treats me as well as the Crow wimmen do. If not, it's gonna be a cold winter." Wiggins hadn't seen a white lady in six years—'cept the two missionary wives that had been at the rendezvous.

Mistuh Tolin seemed to delight in the raw language, and when we rolled into our bedrolls he muttered somethin' to me about some girl in Montgomery that I shouldn't have heard. I almost felt guilty for knowin' that kind of thing about a white lady.

One thing I will admit: it was mighty strange to be gone so long without the sight of a cotton skirt or hearin' even one soft, gentle voice.

Come mornin' the trappers headed east, and we kept on west. There was nothin' before us or behind us that showed signs of people, and the sun was so bright it hurt my eyes when I looked anyplace but right on Dancer's black neck. I figured there had to be somethin' that could cool off this heat, and I started thinkin' about the quarters back home durin' the lay-back at summer's end. Nothin' to do but sleep late and fish, and rest in them brick cabins. Skalley always had honey water to drink. The thoughts of it almost made me dizzy from want; but wantin' didn't do no good, 'cause I was still burnin', and when I looked into the distance the heat seemed to wiggle right up from the ground.

Camp was made early one evenin'. Cap Drewry kept watchin' the sky and the wagon men was tyin' their mules in a large stand of trees that was near. Cap had bunched the wagons close into the trees and then he set about checkin' all the ties on the wagon canvases. Mistuh Tolin and me went to help.

"Are we going to have some rain? Sky's sort of cloudy," Mistuh Tolin said as he looked up.

"I can smell it," Cap answered. "Gonna blow real good. I felt it this mornin'."

Some of the men was takin' dry wood and puttin' it under wagon tops. They stuffed some of their belongin's there, too.

"Tie your things to a wagon axle so's they'll be off the ground," Bornston told us when we was tyin' the horses. "Then take a spot under the wagon and you boys'll see yourself a real plains storm, yes sirree."

The sky was gettin' dark as night and birds raced like darts to get into the trees. We no sooner got the horses settled than the rain started. The drops was big and heavy, and they stung when they hit 'cause there was ice in the center. Folks started callin' "Hail!" The wind got real cold and it was so strong it was all Mistuh Tolin and me could do to get under a wagon bed. We stuffed our bundles and packs on the axle and lay flat against the ground.

It was like the sky had opened and poured a river onto us. The water was filled with hail the size of goose eggs that clattered on the wagon sides and pounded the canvases. Pieces rolled under the wagon and made cold spots on our legs where we couldn't push them away. The black sky grew bright, and jagged lines of white streaked down. The thunder sounded like trees bein' split and felled all around us; then it rumbled and boomed until I didn't think I could stand the noise a moment longer. The earth shook and the wind lashed at the wagon like it was a toy to be flipped over, while the heavens fell down on us with a giant water whip wantin' to beat us into the ground.

I tried to peer at the horses, but the only thing I could see was solid water. Once when there was a lull in the wind I thought I heard the shrill brayin' of some mules, but the water kept everythin' hidden. Water was fallin' through the air, it was rollin' in muddy rivers through the wagon tracks, it was streamin' from the wagon sides and flowin' across the ground like waves blown on a beach. The sound was a hundred drums bein' beat in my ears. I was soaked from layin' on the ground, and the wind lashed water in my face and down my neck.

Then, just as sudden as it started, it was over. In the distance was a sometime rumble, and the evenin' sky brightened to a hazy pink, then fell back to darkness. The clouds hung low and churned over us like hundreds of silent gray sheep. The water still flowed under me, and there was little dryness to anything.

I felt Mistuh Tolin's hand on my arm gripped real tight. "Jason?" His voice was nearly a whisper.

"Uh-huh." My heart was poundin' and I could still feel the shakin' earth when the thunder sounded far off. Mistuh Tolin didn't say nothin' else, but I heard him almost shudder when he sighed.

The ground was slick with mud. Walkin' in it was like tryin' to get through one of the spring bogs back in Alabama. The wet stuff clung up around the ankles of my boots as we made our way to the trees where the horses and mules was. Hail was piled against the tree trunks, and branches lay all over where they had been snapped off by the storm. The air was rid of dust and still smelled cold, and the clouds started to break and show the sky again.

Mistuh Tolin's horses was scared aplenty, but fine. I talked to them and stroked their noses to calm them. There was a wagon mule that had pulled loose from the picket and been struck on the head lots of times with hail. It was down in the mud and not even strugglin' to get up. One of the mule skinners put a pistol to its head and killed it with a single shot.

"We got some hail damage, Cap," Jim Tolliver called.

I looked to where he was. The wagons was sunk four spokes deep in the mud, but that wasn't the problem. I followed Mistuh Tolin over to the wagon.

"Two lids smashed," Cap grumbled.

"What's the cargo?" Mistuh Tolin asked.

"Flour. Let's see if we can't scoop the mess out before it ruins the whole barrel." He set to work gettin' the pasty mixture out before it soaked through to the bottom.

"We'll have to sleep cold tonight, too," Cap continued talkin' as he worked. "All the wood is wet through to the centers."

"Does that mean eatin' cold?" a wagon driver asked.

"Nope. Cooks got buffalo chips. They'll do us."

Buffalo chips was the dried droppin's from the buffalo. They didn't smell none, and they made a hotter fire than wood. I had noticed the cook pickin' them up on occasion and wondered about it. That night I was glad for it.

Bornston was tendin' a man hurt from bein' struck in the jaw with a branch. I set to work with some others clearin' parts of the trees and ripped canvas out of the campground. I could tell it would take nearly a day of strong sun to dry up the mud enough that we could pull out of there. Nobody seemed to do much complainin', and I figured storms like that was commonplace.

Mistuh Tolin had finished helpin' Cap with the flour. Bornston gave me a lantern and I found us a place on top of the wagon we had stayed under durin' the storm. We untied the canvas and dumped off the water. Mistuh Tolin checked the cargo—kegs full of DuPont gunpowder—and it was fine. We turned the canvas dry side up and I got our packs from where they had been on the wagon axle. Other folks was gettin' on top of the wagons, too.

"What about your tools?" Mistuh Tolin asked after he

had checked his books. He started unwrappin' the oilcloth. "You don't want them to stay soaked."

I spread out a blanket, then pulled off that wet leather shirt. I put on a dry cotton one. It sure felt good.

"Where did you get this?" Mistuh Tolin's voice was quiet and full of surprise. I looked up and saw he was holdin' my copy of *Freedom's Journal.*

I could feel my heartbeat gettin' faster. I hadn't hid that paper from him intentional, but I hadn't been too sure whether it was somethin' he should know about. It was certain that Mistuh Tolin's thinkin' was different than a lot of folks' or I'd have never learned half of the things I did, but my readin' *Freedom's Journal* was a lot different than readin' that *Manfred* book of his.

"I—I found it in Memphis, Mistuh Tolin; after that fight at the docks." I tried to keep my voice steady, and I wasn't too sure what I was afraid of. He was sittin' with his legs over the edge of the wagon and readin' the paper.

"Have you read it?"

I nodded yes.

"Mighty fine, isn't it? A whole colony of Negro people living in Canada." He looked over at me. The light flickered across his face and I couldn't see real good. I could tell he wasn't smilin'. "Is—is that where you want to be, Jason? Up there—livin' with them?"

"Me, suh?" I got sweaty. That was the first time I'd said *sir* since that last night in my room back home. I tried to smile. "Goodness knows, I wouldn't want to be up there in the North where they gets snow and all. I wouldn't know what to do in snow. Besides, they's free Negroes, Mistuh Tolin." My voice sounded high and I knew I was talkin' dumb like Mattie had taught me to do with the white folks.

"Yes, but they didn't all start that way," he said quickly. "There's a lot of runaways up North. All over the North! Why, there's whole communities in Pennsylvania and Ohio, and up in the New England states. You've got a skill,

Jason. You'd be welcome there, I'm sure." His voice sorta trailed off.

"You think I'd run away, Mistuh Tolin?" I remembered the man at the docks in Memphis, and I thought about Kusa.

"I wouldn't blame you if you did, Jason. I—I couldn't blame you at all." His voice sounded tight and whispery. He put the paper back on the oilcloth and I heard his feet squish down in the mud. They made odd sucking sounds as he walked away.

My breathin' was hard and jerky, and I took up an old shirt to wipe the tools. Part of my brain was thinkin' on how my pa had worked to buy his freedom—what a prize freedom was thought to be. But another part was thinkin' of those men at the docks sweatin' in the filthy mud. I also knew that I couldn't have stood havin' everythin' ripped apart back home and then run off to live with strangers— black or white. Mistuh Tolin and me could talk about nearly the same things in our lives. Good times. Pain. And we did, too. And now I was in the Territory . . .

Maybe I was wrong not to want to run away, but I had nothin' I wanted to run to.

I pressed that shirt soft onto the tools, and a singin' started in my head: *Hammer come down. Hammer come down. Hit that iron make a mighty good soun'.* I looked across the darkness and saw Mistuh Tolin standin' by the chuck wagon. Him and me was the only folks here who'd know that song. We was the only ones who'd get a whole picture in our minds when we heard it. That was important.

89

12

Fort Laramie was on the broad meadow near the blendin' of the North Platte River and the Laramie crick. The walls of the fort was nearly fifteen feet high and made of sod bricks. It was topped with strong wooden stakes that Mistuh Tolin called palisades, and there was clay blockhouses on each end of the wall.

"Part of what we'll build is another gate—make us double safe against hostiles," Cap told as we rode into the fort on a cloudy mid-August day.

Steps led up to a walkway by the gun loopholes, and some men was loungin' up there. The walkway was also the roof of the lodgin' rooms where Mistuh Tolin and the others would be livin'. I wasn't too sure where I'd be. Across the middle part of the grounds was a big log tradin' house where Mistuh Tolin was gonna work as a store clerk. A plump Indian woman, wrapped in a bright-colored shawl, was stirrin' a boilin' pot of wash. There was the start of other buildin's, too, and way to the back I spied a small shed and a clay-walled corral where the animals was kept.

"It ain't safe to leave the horses out in the grassland unattended at night," Bornston told me. "Horse-stealin's a great pastime for most injuns hereabouts."

Most everyone in Cap Drewry's train had been to the fort before, so the greetin's was cheerful. Mistuh Tolin was took up on the walkway and I followed along. From that high you could see all the way to the crick, and clear to the woods and northern hills in the other direction. It was impressive.

Mistuh Tolin was given a room in the barracks-type place along the wall and somebody moved my gear in there, too, while we was lookin' around. Mistuh Tolin didn't complain. It was already late, and so we just turned in as soon as the stars come out. I never moved out of that room for our whole stay, and hardly nobody thought nothin' of it.

Next mornin' Mistuh Tolin started the inventory and puttin' up of the goods that had come with the pack train. I set to buildin' a forge in the shed near the corral. Mistuh Tolin didn't supervise my work none, so I just went on like I knew it was to be done. I used Mistuh Tolin's mules to haul rock, and 'cause the mortar that had been shipped out wasn't too good, I searched the crick banks and found a good yellow clay to brace it with.

I helped with the buildin', too. There was men at the fort who knew how to use a broadaxe so good it was a pleasure to see, and then we'd hitch the new-felled trees to the wagon mules and pull them into the fort. Mistuh Tolin got good at mule drivin', and I learned a whole lot of things. I built the toolhouse almost by myself with an easy, sharp-notch cut that could be done with only two strokes of the axe.

"You gotta watch yourself there," a man named Ned Saunders cautioned when I first started on the toolhouse. "You're used to swinging a smithy hammer. Can't wield an axe that way." He showed me the best way to do it, then left me on my own. When I was finished, Saunders was real admirin' of my work. I told him about my pa, Marcus, and how he had been one of the best carpenters in Alabama. I couldn't help grinnin' my pride about him.

"He'd sure be proud, Jason. You done a good job."

"Thank you, Mistuh Saunders."

91

"Ned. The name's Ned. Don't hold with all that *mister* business."

I watched him walk off, thinkin' on how nobody out here seemed very formal. It was hard to get used to, but I liked it. Most folks just had me call them whatever Mistuh Tolin settled on. Bornston, Cap—and now Ned Saunders.

Ned was a slight man with dark hair, maybe thirty years old, who was born along the Illinois River. His folks was both drowned in a flood when he was six, and he got raised by a tribe of Omahas. They passed him on to missionaries when he was seventeen, but he didn't stay with them long, bein' growed already. He'd lived out of the States all his life, and for two years he'd been a scout for American Fur. He knew a lot about everythin' that had to do with livin' on the frontier, and he took to teachin' me. I listened real good.

Other folks at the fort was generally friendly, and they got more so when they saw me workin' at the smithy. Talents was important things in that western territory, like Ned's talent for scoutin'. Some said he could read the sign of a panther on the rocks four days after it had passed.

"I saw him track an eagle in the air once two hours after sunset," Ian Bornston laughed. He was a mighty good tracker, too, but noted most for his doctorin'. "Ol' Ned's got a gift. An' Cap here's got a gift, too. He can smell weather. Ain't that so, Adam?"

Adam Vogel's talent was for drinkin' liquor. He'd start off in the mornin' with a shot of whiskey, and he'd drink right on through the day. The crazy thing was that it never affected him none. He was the same at sunset as he was at sunrise.

"That's true," Adam said. "Cap can get up in the morning, take a few deep breaths, and tell if the day's going to be fair or cloudy; light rain or storm. I was with him two years back when he predicted the first snowfall almost to the minute, and later he knew when we'd see the first false spring."

Adam was drinkin' a wild berry wine while he talked. He had even took wild grains and started makin' beer. There was a vat of the stuff behind the storage house that was dark and strange-smellin'. I tasted it once and it was kinda sweet—and potent. Half a glass made my head swim.

"Winstead here has a real knack for cookin'. That's why we let him fix the grub all the time," Cap put in.

" 'Course there was a time when he couldn't cook worth a damn," Bornston said. "Didn't that happen till he met this widow lady in Virginia. She was packin' her stuff for to move to the Ozarks, wasn't that it, Winstead?" The man just chuckled. "An' lo, if Winstead didn't set to help her fix a bent axle and the whole dang wagon came crashin' over on him. There he was buried up to his eyeballs in all of her frillies and unmentionables, and when she come to him he was out colder than a trade axe in a snow bank. Land's sake, she say, what cause you to pass out like that? And when they looked around they come to see that he had been struck on the head with this big leather-bound cookbook what had been in her family for nigh on to a century. Ever since that time, yes sirree, Winstead's been cookin' up a storm."

Folks all laughed at the tale, and Mistuh Tolin and me got another touch of what was everybody's talent: yarnin'. Most of what was said had beginnin's in fact, and then it'd get spun out into what might have been true; and if somebody was real good at yarnin', the story would seem so fantastic that you had to laugh at yourself for listenin', and even then you'd think maybe it was true. Yarnin' wasn't hard for Mistuh Tolin and me to understand, 'cause we'd grown up with it.

"Jake used to spin tales out until I'd think they were true," Mistuh Tolin told them all one night. "And then he'd throw in just enough lies to make you know he was teasin'. Like that one about the snowstorm in the Smokies when he was a youngster. Tell them that one, Jason."

"Me?"

"Go on! You can do it much better than I."

So I told about the snowflakes that was the size of dinner plates, and how they stuck to his hair and coat like glue. The snow piled up to his waist, he'd said, and I put in all the details just like Jake did. I relaxed into it real soon and was talkin' good about how he was nearly buried in only ten minutes' time and wouldn't have been alive to tell the story if a huge black bear hadn't come along and got so mad not bein' able to find his den that he roared and melted the snow away with his rage.

Folks laughed and hollered at that talk, and at first I wasn't sure if they was laughin' at the story or at me, 'cause I had acted it out real good and put in a lot of detail. But as I listened to more yarnin' from others I realized that it was the story they liked.

"You're a real mountain crittur, Jason," Ned said when we left the dinin' hall. "You can really spin a yarn."

Brian Honicutt was at the fort, too. I'm not sure what his talent was. He handled an axe all right, but nothin' fancy. He didn't know trackin', and he wasn't a very good shot with the old flintlock he carried. He was out from Ohio and lookin' for a partner to free-trap with in the Siskadee. (Free-trappin' was when you didn't work for American Fur, or Rocky Mountain, or no other company.) He took up with Tolliver—the man what had come with us from Council Bluffs. They was a fittin' pair, too, 'cause they both seemed to like makin' trouble. Maybe that was their talent.

I could see the problem with Brian Honicutt before Mistuh Tolin even suspected it, in the way Honicutt watched Mistuh Tolin's every move. He admired the fine buckskin clothes (Honicutt dressed in homespuns), and when Mistuh Tolin would go out with his Hall breechloader and ridin' on that well-formed chestnut horse, Brian Honicutt seemed to glow with hate and envy. He was the only person at the fort to make me call him *mister*, too. That rankled Mistuh Tolin some, and Brian started doin' everythin' he could to get Mistuh Tolin into a fight. Mistuh Tolin ignored him.

One night when Mistuh Tolin and me was sittin' with Adam Vogel, Ned, and Bornston, havin' our supper, Honicutt and Tolliver come into the hall for some drinks. "You know," Brian said, "I really don't understand what a rich plantation boy would come way out here for. Don't you miss seein' those cotton fields, and hearin' your darkies sing to you at night?"

Mistuh Tolin didn't even look up, and Adam poured hisself another bit of wine. He started a conversation with Mistuh Tolin, and we all figured Honicutt would go away.

"Bet your daddy is some real rich planter, huh? Bet you went to one of those fancy schools back East so you could learn how to act better than everyone else. That why you talk up poetry and stuff all the time, huh?"

"Mr. Honicutt, my father was not rich, and I didn't go to any school at all. What I know is by my own will and teaching. Perhaps if you spent more time reading a book rather than looking for trouble you'd be a more pleasant individual."

By then everybody was watchin' and listenin'—probably hopin' for a fight. There was some trappers in from the mountains, and I could tell they wanted to see some action.

Honicutt smiled real easy. "Well, don't that beat all. He talks all fancy, but he keeps company with a bastard nigger boy. Sleeps in the same room with him!"

My stomach hollowed out when he spoke, and I felt my hands start to sweat. Mistuh Tolin's eyes got dark and sparked with anger. Honicutt saw it and kept on talkin'.

"Now, when I was back in Ohio there was folks that kept tryin' to say that niggers was men like the rest of us." He snickered. He had an audience, and started puttin' on a show. "But we all know they're pig-iron dumb and bastards every one." He turned to Tolliver. "Why, I saw this little burhead boy one day runnin' down the street, and I asked him, 'Boy, where's your daddy?' 'My daddy, suh? I ain't got no daddy,' he said. 'Why, everybody's got a daddy. How'd you get born if you didn't have no daddy?' 'My mama had me in a cotton field,' he said." Brian laughed real mean and leaned across the table to Mistuh Tolin. "Is that how that boy of yours come? His mama out makin' it with cotton balls?"

My head was in a rage and I tried to keep it from showin'. Saunders stood up fast and stopped Mistuh Tolin from flyin' into Brian. I was on my feet and tremblin' like a leaf in a hailstorm. Brian's hand moved to his side.

"Don't nobody need to be drawin' knives, Brian," Adam said as he plucked the knife from Brian's sheath. Most everybody else stood back. "You've had a bit too much to drink. Go sleep it off."

"No," Ned said. "They got to fight it out. Brian's been bad-mouthin' these two since they got to the fort."

"I'm ready!" Mistuh Tolin growled.

"It ain't your fight, Tolin. It's Jason who was laid on the coals tonight. Let's take it outside and get it settled once and for all."

My heart beat so fast it felt like a stone in my chest. I couldn't fight that man. He was white. If I raised up my hand to him, anyone there could kill me dead and nobody would even blink.

Ned tapped on my shoulder. "Come on, Jason." Everybody was startin' outside. I looked over at Mistuh Tolin.

"Go beat his guts out!" he said. My mouth dropped open. I was sure he didn't know what he was sayin'.

Ned grabbed my arm and pulled me to the door. He seemed to understand how I was thinkin'. "This ain't the States, Jason. There ain't no laws out here exceptin' survival. You can't survive when folks is like Brian Honicutt. Give 'im hell—for Marcus."

The men had formed a huge circle and I could see the wall guards watchin' from their posts. Even the two Indian women of Adam was standin' on the steps to see. Brian stepped into the circle with a strange look on his face. He was squat and chunky, and big-boned from farm work. He probably would have beat Mistuh Tolin easy, but when I looked at his face I got the slight feelin' he was scared. It shocked me.

"Go to it, Jason," Ned said.

Nobody else said nothin', not wantin' to side with either of us. My arms felt as weak as ducks' down, and I walked a couple of steps into the circle.

"Come on, let's see you fight." Brian put his fists up like I'd seen pictures of prize fighters doin'. He plodded around with his jaw set hard and threw fake punches at me. Time slipped by. He didn't jump me, and I was just standin' there too scared to do anythin'. I could see Brian's confidence buildin'.

"Come on, Jason. Smash him one!" Mistuh Tolin said strong.

"See there, boy? Your master done told you what to do. Smash me. Come on, boy." Brian rolled his fists in the air and leaned back like a barnyard cock.

I tightened my fingernails down on my palms and raised my hands a bit. I licked my lips and tried to keep from shiverin'. Folks started chucklin'. It was like I could hear them thinkin' 'Bastard nigger boy *is* made out of cotton balls.' I sweated from the laughs and grins I saw on the faces. I couldn't see Ned and Mistuh Tolin, but I imagined that they was laughin', too.

Then Brian started laughin'. "Look at 'im! Damn! Funniest thing. His eyes all bugged out. He's scared silly." Brian wiped his eyes with the back of his hand, still laughin'. "But, but—" He got control to talk. "He's a good ol' nigger. Free or slaved they all know better than to hit a white man. Bur-head, black-assed, cotton-balled ni—"

I hit him. My fist smashed into his half-opened mouth and his head jerked back. He went down hard on the ground, and I stood there with my knuckles achin' where

I'd knocked out some of his teeth. I was so scared I thought I'd faint away, and I kept waitin' for a rope to settle down around my neck.

"Get 'im, Brian!" Tolliver was urgin.'

Brian was up and his face was hard and mean-lookin'. There was blood all over his lips and down into the stubble of his beard. He came at me with a fury—his fists caught me hard in the stomach and I tasted part of my dinner in my throat. I fell to the ground and he charged in on me. There was yellin' and shoutin' from everybody and Brian's fist crashed on the side of my face. I thought my jaw was goin' to give way, and I fought back. I forgot everythin' but tryin' to get him off of me. I pounded my knuckles into him and slammed my knees up on his chest. I pushed hard, got on my feet again, and backed away.

Brian was rollin' his eyes and lookin' like a mad bull. Strange sounds came from his throat and he came at me again. I jumped aside and let him throw hisself against the men behind me. They righted him and pushed him back. I felt blows in my stomach again, but I grabbed his shoulders and flung him away. He started back. I clenched my hands together and waited till he was almost on me, then I swung my knotted fist like a club and caught him square on the side of the head. He went flyin' sideways. I heard him groan and turned to meet him again, but he didn't come. He had crashed into the porch beam of the hall and was layin' in a heap on the log step.

Wasn't nobody movin', and all I could hear was the raspy breathin' of Brian Honicutt and the poundin' of my own blood in my ears. My gasps was like air suckin' through a bellows.

"Well, I think that does it," Adam said in an easy way. He stepped over Brian and walked back inside.

"Is there anyone else here that doesn't think Jason's a man?" Mistuh Tolin said as he walked to me. Nobody said nothin'.

Folks started back to their business. A few of them was

---

smilin', and Cap Drewry slapped me on the back when he passed. Only Tolliver went over to Brian Honicutt to see how he was.

It was over. I had beat a white man and I was standin' —alive!—bein' congratulated by folks. Mistuh Tolin and Ned was grinnin' like two possums in a henhouse. I let my shoulders go slack and they walked with me to the water barrel, where I cleaned the blood off my hands and face. This ain't the States, Ned had said. I looked back to Tolliver and Honicutt as they started off for their camp. My jaw and ribs was throbbin'.

No. This sure wasn't the States.

13

I carried bruises from that fight for more than a week, but
it was worth it. Jim Tolliver and Brian Honicutt left the
fort the next mornin', and everyone seemed to treat me a
bit different after that. More like I was part of the crew.
They joked with me friendly and I took to sippin' whiskey
and water with them in the evenin's even at times when
Mistuh Tolin wasn't there. I surprised a lot of the men
when I took up an old issue of *The Saturday Evening Post* and
read a few things.

Mistuh Tolin stayed busy a lot at the store, and I worked
at the smithy. We both helped with the buildin' and huntin'. Ways between us got easier and we even talked some
about Alabama—how we was glad to be gone, and how we
missed everybody.

"Some mornin's I wake up and I think I just know I'm
gonna hear Judith callin' the pigs, or Seth cussin' at some
mules," I said one night.

"Seth." Mistuh Tolin's voice sounded so sad it brought
me from my mournin'. I had never really considered them
to be that close.

"You know, he was the same age as Aaron would have
been," he went on, his voice sorrowful. "We wanted to do
so much with that place, Seth and me; but we never had the
money for seeds or tools. He kept me going and doing

anyway. 'You got to love the land,' he'd say. 'Like it was your kin.' " I heard Mistuh Tolin sniff loud.

"Mistuh Tolin, how come you stayed back there? How come you didn't just leave since it wasn't what you wanted?"

"And leave you all behind?" He tried to laugh, but there was pain in his eyes when he looked at me. He got real solemn and studied his hands while talkin'. "My pa . . . my pa and me, we argued, but . . . I loved him, Jason. I kept thinking that maybe . . . that someday he'd know that. I thought if I stayed and worked like he wanted me to, he'd see me for me and . . ." He sighed heavy. "There was so much left unsaid, Jason. So much!"

I understood his pain better than ever then, and I was glad I didn't have no burden of unsaid emotions. That's why all of us at Cobb's was so close, and I know I spoke clear to each my need for them—my carin'. I was that way with everybody . . .

I turned out the lamp and lay back hearin' nothin but quietness from Mistuh Tolin's bed.

Most of our times was easy goin', but there was once Mistuh Tolin got real mad. He came into the room while I was shinin' up his ridin' boots.

"Damn it, Jason! Don't you have anything better to do than fiddle around with my things?" His face turned hot red and he kicked the boots away from me. "Oh, hell!" He slumped onto one of the rope beds and covered his face with his hands.

"You gettin' cabin fever bein' out here at this fort, Mistuh Tolin?"

"No. no. It's just that you—you don't have to do things like that out here. I don't want you to. Just forget all that kind of stuff."

"What? Are you going to wear muddy boots then?"

"No!" He jumped up in a rage. "I can clean my own boots! I can curry my own goddamn horse, and wash my own stinking clothes. I don't want you to do any of it! Now get out of here and do something *you* want to do!"

I knew to leave him alone when he was feelin' hot like that. I headed out toward the river and found Ned. We spent the rest of the day ridin' around the prairie. He taught me more about the land; how to track; tricks of survival. We didn't get back till near dark, and by then Mistuh Tolin seemed to be feelin' better.

Before the geese started south, and when the work was near finished at the fort, Ned took me out with him for some scoutin'. We'd be gone for four or five days, he said, and I didn't even think to ask Mistuh Tolin if it was all right. I just packed a bedroll and some supplies on Dancer and rode off.

It almost scared the life out of me when we went ridin', bold as you please, into this Indian camp the second afternoon out. It didn't bother Ned; seems he had known they was there for a long while, and he spoke their language, too. The people was Cheyenne, and they had nearly thirty-five lodges set up near a sweet-water stream.

"Ain't that somethin'," I mumbled while starin' at them big tepees.

"They're real comfortable, too, especially with a big ol' buffalo rug on the floor, weaved sleepin' mats and all," Ned told me.

He started talkin' with two men that appeared to be leaders of this group. He untied a pack from his horse and let it slide to the ground. It was filled with mirrors and beads, ribbons and other trinkets that the trappers called googaw or fooferaw. There was also two trade axes, three traps, tobacco plugs and a sack of coffee. These gifts was to show how friendly we was, and to encourage the Cheyenne to come down to the fort and trade. My mind didn't stay too long on this bargainin' and talk I couldn't understand, 'cause I was too busy takin' in all that was around me.

The lodges wasn't set all close together like drawin's I'd

seen. The whole camp was spread over about eighty yards square, and there was dogs and horses tied to lodge poles. Little brown children laughed and played games between the tepees, and the smell of the cookin' fires blended with the dry smells of the season. An old woman started beatin' a dog that had stole some meat from a dryin' rack. Her voice was shrill and she chased the dog away. Broad-chested, tight-muscled men with long hair sat cleanin' rifles and shapin' arrow shafts. Dogs was barkin'. Hides was bein' tanned. And there was women!

These wasn't the first women I'd seen since leavin' Council Bluffs, 'cause Adam had two that worked for him around the fort all the time. What I was seein' now was different. They was tan-skinned, wide-cheeked, slender-hipped creatures with dark hair braided or wrapped with leather ties. Their leather skirts was all bordered with fringe, and they wore short leather dresses at top—some with beads and painted colors around the neck. A group of four was workin' over a green hide, and wore only their skirts! I started rememberin' the things Wiggins had said about women, and it got me feelin' flushed.

My mind was switched from those soft thoughts when Ned said somethin' I could understand. "They want us to see their horses. They're right proud of their mounts, and we might do some business with them before the winter sets in. Fort's low on horses."

The two men rode with us through the half circle of lodges. They was older leaders of the tribe, but when we started toward the hills we was joined by three young men. One of them rode up close to me till our horses bumped shoulders. I kept control of Dancer, who didn't like bein' crowded, and looked over at the Indian. His skin was smooth and the color of polished cedarwood. He was wearin' leather leggins and breech clout, and a fringed leather shirt like I had on. His ear was pierced with copper wire and there was two teeth of some animal hangin' there. He reached over and patted Dancer's strong neck. Then he

103

grinned real broad, showin' a set of strong teeth. I smiled back, not knowin' if I should, but he seemed friendly enough.

We went over a hill and there was a huge meadow dotted with grazin' horses. I don't know who was more excited, me or Dancer. He started whinnyin' and jumpin' around. I wondered if he had once been part of a big wild herd that roamed the prairies and thundered through valleys. I held him tight-reined and stared. There was nearly two hundred animals out there!

"These are their horses?" I couldn't keep my surprise from showin'.

"Yep. A fine lot it seems to be, too," Ned answered as we got closer to the herd.

Young boys was all around the meadow watchin' the herd, and the warrior I'd smiled at called to one of them. The boy hazed a fine-lookin' dun geldin' out of the herd. Its black mane and tail was shiny and the stripes on its legs went into black hooves that looked to be polished. The Indian tossed a rope around the horse's neck and pulled him up close. He slipped from the horse he was ridin' to the back of that buckskin so smooth the horse hardly tossed its head. He rode right up to me and said somethin', still smilin'.

"He says it's a good horse," Ned relayed. "Says you have a good horse, too. He wants to see which one is best."

"He wants to race?" I watched the Indian fix a hackamore around the dun's head.

"He does, but you ain't gonna do it. I don't want to ride double back to the fort if you lose." Ned said somethin' to the man, and his smile faded a bit. The Indian said somethin' to the camp leaders and they started talkin' with Ned. Pretty soon we was all headed back for the camp with the young men ridin' hard into the village trailin' the dun horse with them.

"So what's happenin'?"

"I said the race wouldn't be fair with his horse just fresh

from the pasture and yours two days on the trail, so the race'll be ten sleeps from sunset. They're gonna bring the whole camp down to the fort. That injun's name is Stone Finger."

My heart was pumpin' hard and I felt kind of sickish over what Mistuh Tolin was goin' to say when I told him I got involved in a horse race, and from the way Ned was talkin' it wasn't just for sport—it was for stakes. High stakes: Dancer.

"I'll be damned!" Mistuh Tolin roared. "A horse race! As if that kind of thing hasn't brought me enough trouble in my life." He scowled at me.

"I looked that buckskin over real good, Tolin," Ned said. "I think Dancer can beat him."

"Dancer's a strong six-year-old, Mistuh Tolin."

"That's right, and Jason and that brave are near the same size. Weight will be in our favor 'cause the buckskin ain't as deep-chested as Jason's horse. We'll talk them into a long-distance race and—"

"All right, all right!" Mistuh Tolin laughed and shook his head. "I don't know why I'm so concerned. It's you who'll be on foot if you lose your mount," he said to me.

Afternoon of the seventh day the Cheyenne showed up at the fort. They seemed real restrained after the way I'd seen them the week before. The children and women stood wide-eyed and quiet. The warriors was all painted up for ceremony and was ridin' proud. I tried to make out Stone Finger, but didn't see him. Some women was ridin' old mares and ponies, and the tepees was all rolled up and tied on the backs of ponies. The dogs barked, and that was the only sound.

"There'll be a day to bargain, a day to trade, and then the race," Ned told me after he'd talked with the tribe leaders.

A bunch of us from the fort walked up to the palisades to watch the tepees go up.

"You and Dancer goin' to be ready?" Adam asked after a sip of whiskey.

"Yep. I've been takin' him out twice a day and runnin' him good. We're ready."

"Ya nervous?" Bornston asked with a grin. "The bettin' sheets is showin' a lot of fortunes ridin' with ya."

I sucked in a deep breath and tried to smile.

"You need to help with the horse work. You got a good eye for livestock, I hear," Cap said. "Maybe that'll keep your mind off the race. And you, Cobb."

Mistuh Tolin was starin' into the meadow through Adam's spyglass and watchin' the Cheyenne women work. He seemed fascinated by the whole scene and hadn't heard Cap talkin'.

"Tolin Cobb!" Cap said loud and thumped his shoulder. He wagged a warnin' finger and grinned. "You watch yourself. Cheyenne ain't as free with their women as some of the other tribes."

Mistuh Tolin flushed. I laughed at him. "I stared, too," I confessed.

So we bargained a day and looked over the horses that was in the new corral we'd built. Each horse was figured to be worth a handful of fooferaw and an axe or blanket; or one trap and a string of beads. There was lots of combinations set, and the Cheyenne strolled around the fort store studyin' the materials, testin' the axe blades and such. I kept lookin' for Stone Finger. He wasn't there.

Next day Ned and me selected twenty-two good horses to keep at the fort. The Cheyenne collected their payment, and then the Indians who wanted more from the store came forward with what they had to trade. Fur pelts and buffalo robes suddenly appeared from under lodge covers; and beaded shirts with fringed yokes, and knife sheaths and gun covers. There was some impressive things presented, and the noise of the tradin' mounted to a high pitch. Ned and the two other men at the fort who could speak Cheyenne was busy talkin' back and forth with everybody. I watched it all from near the stable, and I was still lookin' for Stone Finger.

"Maybe Stone Finger decided not to race," I said to Ned when I went in the store after all the tradin' had ended. "I haven't seen him nor his horse."

"He's probably makin' medicine up in the hills for a good race," Cap said.

"No self-respectin' Cheyenne would back out on any agreement," Ned answered. "He's around."

I just nodded, not knowin' if I wanted him to be, or not.

The Cheyenne set out a feast that night and invited the whole fort crew. Not all went, though, 'cause there was those who was certain it was a trick to get us all in the open so they could steal what they wanted. Mistuh Tolin and me went, and it was a fine meal with fresh venison and smoked, dried buffalo meat. The whiskey barrels was brought out. The whiskey had been cut five parts to one with water, and some black pepper was added to give it some bite. The Cheyenne didn't seem to notice, or if they did they didn't care.

After the feastin', pipes was passed around among the few fort people that was there and leaders of the tribe. An old woman tossed more wood on the fire and a crowd of warriors come over, glowin' from the fun and whiskey. All sudden like, this tall Indian stepped into the firelight. He held out his arms like he was goin' to grab hold of the sky, and yelled such as to set my hair on end. Everyone got quiet, and he started talkin'.

Ned squeezed between Mistuh Tolin and me. "He's tellin' about his braveries. Countin' *coup* it's called." And Ned told us what the man was sayin'.

Another warrior leaped into the light and started talkin' his tales when the first was done. Saunders kept translatin'. It went on for over an hour, till it seemed all the warriors must have spoken, but they hadn't. A powerful-built figure

107

pushed through the crowd and circled the fire with steps so strong it seemed to make the earth shake. He stopped in front of me. It was Stone Finger.

Saunders said his words to us: "I am Stone Finger. I wear the feather of the eagle. I have killed two of my enemy, the Crow. I have killed three of my enemy, the Snake. I have stolen twelve horses from the Blackfeet." Everyone made cheerin' noises to that—the Blackfeet was considered to be some of the hardest fighters on the plains. "When my bow failed me I killed a mountain ram by driving the arrow into its heart with my fingers. I wear his teeth for strength." He touched his earring. "I have some of the finest buffalo ponies of my tribe. Tomorrow I shall race against the man of victory skin and *I* shall win. I talk to the winds, and I shall ride with the winds. I have spoken." He looked at me with glittery eyes.

"You're next. I think he's challenged you," Ned said as he slapped my back. "If you don't give an answer he'll figure his medicine worked."

"What do you mean?"

"Go out there and count *coup*. Tell him who's really gonna win that race tomorrow."

Mistuh Tolin's mouth gaped a bit, and my hands went limp. Ned prodded me again, and I stood up and looked square at Stone Finger. "I am Jason," I said, soft. And then it was like I'd been taken over by a strange power. I remembered all the tales I'd read about the West, and the way Jake would tell his stories and make everyone hunch up and listen. I knew I could do it, too. I stepped past Stone Finger and into the light.

"I am Jason. My strength comes from Jason of old," and I thought of the book I read and reread in the nights in Alabama. Ned was translatin' my words into Cheyenne. "I have the strength to lift the wrath of undergods. I have walked through flames and been touched by lightnin'!" I pulled off my shirt and let the firelight show my burn scars. "The power of lightnin' has taught me how to bend iron and mold hot metal. If Stone Finger talks to the wind, he talks to my horse, Dancer. *He* is the wind. I have spoken."

Stone Finger and me faced each other. His eyes was still glittery with excitement and what looked to be anger, but there was a little smile on his face.

Then the feastin' was over. Countin' *coup* was over. My heart raced as I heard the sound of drums and chanted music. Stone Finger seemed to melt away into the blur of people around me. Ned took my arm and we all started back to the fort.

"Damn, if you ain't somethin' else!" Ned said. "That was mighty fine for a settlement man. You convinced them, all right."

"I wasn't sure. I didn't have no killin' to tell about, or horse-thievin'."

"Oh, the killin' ain't much. That ain't considered a big *coup* out here. The big *coup* is to come close to death and not get killed. Stone Finger had taken lives, but they think you've walked through death and back again a couple of times. The biggest thing he did was take horses from the Blackfeet, and he probably did that when they was down with smallpox this past winter. You really got him, though, talkin' about Dancer bein' the wind. He's got to beat you now, or he'll lose face for a while with his tribe."

"What did he mean when he said 'man of victory skin'?" Mistuh Tolin asked.

"Oh, the Cheyenne black their faces for a victory scalp dance after a war. Lots of tribes do it. The Sioux black up when they dance before a war."

I looked at Ned with surprise, but he was busy tellin' the people back at the fort what I'd done. Mistuh Tolin joined in the tellin'. I thought again about the man of victory skin. That was the first time I'd heard of black faces as bein' good. It made me feel special.

14

I got to run a race and I got to win it proud, I said to myself while I worked with Dancer the next mornin'. It was like it was the most important thing I'd ever done. I brushed Dancer out and put the stirrup band I'd fashioned over the blanket. No saddle that day. I wanted to feel every muscle when that big horse ran. I smiled that I was about to race a horse around a fur-tradin' fort against a Cheyenne Indian. It was somethin' I'd read in a book, but now *I* was in it. *I* was goin' to be the hero! Man of victory skin.

I barely heard the talkin' when I walked Dancer out of the fort gates. The autumn air was bracin', and cold, but I pulled off my shirt like Ned had suggested, to remind the Cheyenne of my *coup*.

"Good luck, Jason," Mistuh Tolin said. "I don't know when I've been more excited."

I just nodded, stayin' tight; concentratin' on what I had to do.

Two miles, the race was to be. Out from the fort to the trail that ran beside the crick, back up and across the plains to a stand of cottonwood, and then a half-mile sprint back. Men from the fort and the Indian camp rode out along the course to see that we held to the plan. I mounted Dancer with one easy bound and held him tight-reined till he fought me and bucked a bit. Stone Finger was showin' off his horse, too. Then we sat side by side. The horses was tense and blowin'. Ned fired the gun and we was off.

Dancer took out like a shot and then settled into an easy lope that stretched us into a good lead. I had to look back to see where Stone Finger was. It was too easy. I started worryin'. Down to the crick; along the trail: Stone Finger was closin' the distance. Dancer held to his pace. Up the hill to the plains: Stone Finger pulled up beside me, and an arm's length ahead. I urged Dancer toward the cottonwoods, but he held to the same even pace. The dust spurted up in my eyes from the dun passin' us. I heard Dancer blow hard against it. I started sweatin'.

At the cottonwoods we had lost almost three strides. I could see the black tail of the dun as we turned toward the fort. I hunched over Dancer's neck and smacked his chest with the end of the reins.

"Come on, Dancer," I pleaded. "This is a race, not a mornin' ride."

His ears twitched and I felt his muscles tighten. I teased him again with the reins, breathin' hard into his mane, keepin' my body low over his. It seemed his long strides was suddenly doubled. The ground streaked beneath me until I had to look away from it. When I did, I saw the rump of the dun only a length in front, but the finish line was only thirty feet beyond that.

"Come on, Dancer." I tightened my knees on his sides.

We passed Stone Finger like he was trottin'. We seemed to soar across the ground. The passin' wind took my breath away and Dancer's body was like a welded, powerful machine. We'd done it! The knot of people from the fort was cheerin' wild in front of me. For me! I had won! I rode Dancer around to calm him and held my hands high. My face hurt from smilin,' and then they all closed in on me.

"*Weeeeoooo!* You did it!" Mistuh Tolin grabbed me off the horse and danced me around. "I wasn't sure you were going to make it for a minute."

"Dancer didn't know what we was out there for till

111

almost the last. When he caught on—"

The men was poundin' me on my back and screamin' in my ears so I couldn't hear to talk. I held Dancer's reins close under his jaw while he snorted and pranced. It got quiet, and folks stepped back. Stone Finger walked up with his dun horse on a lead rope. The tan coat was nearly black from sweat and Stone Finger held the rope out to me while he studied Dancer's sleek form. Dancer had thin, white froth at his mouth, and that was all the race had strained him.

I took the rope. Stone Finger started talkin' in a slow, even voice.

"He says your words of last night have been proved," Ned told me. "Your horse is a black wind with clouds at his feet. He says he is not shamed to losing to such as this."

Stone Finger walked away straight-backed and strong-legged. I admired his whole manner, and I held tight on that rope, bein' glad those words was spoke to me. It was *me* Stone Finger was honorin', and I held my head up proud.

"They're calling Dancer the Black Wind," Mistuh Tolin told me that night. I'd come late to the room after spendin' extra time at the stable.

"Yep. Ned says to keep a close watch on him. It would be a good *coup* for whoever could steal him." I pulled off my boots and words got spoke I hadn't planned. "It feels sorta nice bein' looked up to like folks did me today."

"And you've every right to it," Mistuh Tolin said easy. "What do you plan to call your new horse?"

I squinted at him, tryin' to figure the way he said that. "You—you got a name picked out?" I was suddenly scared that he was goin' to end all my proud feelin'.

"*Me* have a name? I don't care."

I swallowed hard and said what I knew was true. "But it's—it's your horse."

"The hell it is!" He stared at me funny. "Next you'll be

telling me that the clothes you're wearing are *my* clothes."
He laughed.

"Then you—you're givin' me the horse?"

"No! I'm not *giving* you the horse. It's been yours since Stone Finger handed you the lead." I stood there like a statue. His blue eyes got dark. "Jason, you won that horse with your own hard work and enterprise. I claim no right to that—or to anything! Not anything! Do you understand?"

I studied Mistuh Tolin's tense face. I nodded yes. I understood that there had been a lot of changes in my life in the past three months. What these changes meant I wasn't sure, but it was givin' me a freedom . . . *Freedom.* That was a dangerous word to think, but it seemed true. Maybe it wasn't written down and set by law, but I was livin' the way I wanted to. I didn't do no work for Mistuh Tolin at all no more, and what I worked for was mine.

No. Not quite. Mistuh Tolin held my pay from American Fur.

So I was livin' a dream, and one that wouldn't last forever. Yet while I had it, I figured to enjoy it. I'd worry on the dark side later.

The Cheyenne stayed at the fort for two more days. There was more tradin' and gamblin' and horse racin'. Mistuh Tolin tried his luck at a stick game that was a lot like throwin' dice. He lost his fur hat, but won it back later along with a leather gun case with fringe on the muzzle end as long as my hand. When the tribe left there was good feelin's on both sides, and the Cheyenne said they'd trade in the spring if the beaver take was good. I kept Dancer tied outside our room door for three weeks after that. I wasn't takin' any chances.

"Snow's started up in the mountains," Ned said a few days after the Cheyenne left. He had come down to the smithy where I was. "Cap says it's probably two to four inches."

"That's more snow than I've seen in my whole life," I laughed while takin' an iron piece out of the coolin' bucket.

"That's just the start of it! Are you nearly finished here? It's eatin' time."

"I'm at a good quittin' place. Fixin' up a special bakin' rack for Winstead. It's nearly finished." I wiped off my tools and put them neatly on the racks I'd made. My leather apron—one I'd made from a thick buffalo hide—I hung near the forge so it wouldn't get stiff from the cold. I looked around to see that things was in order, and smiled—real proud with how well I was doin'.

Ned and me walked silent to the dinin hall'. I looked to the hills and could see the last bits of gold from the aspen leaves still showin' among the dark green of the pine. The sun was like a glowin' coal over the hills, and the land was glitterin' with evenin' frost. I could hear the wind bringin' in the cold, and I knew it was nearly time to start wearin' the big, heavy capote Mistuh Tolin had bought me. He was wearin' his already.

"Well, I thought you was gonna work through your supper," Cap said when we got to the hall.

"I forget the time when I'm down there. The huntin' party's not back yet?" I scrubbed my hands at the corner water barrel and got my meal.

"Nope. But I saw them cuttin' over the east meadow about an hour ago. I expect them any time," Adam said.

"You think Cobb will have bagged himself another elk?" Cap asked. "He's a good hunter."

"If he don't get lost in the woods," Ned said with a laugh.

I had to smile, 'cause Mistuh Tolin had no talent for much more than sightin' the gun. He always thought it amazin' that anyone could tell when and what type of animal had passed just by lookin' at its tracks.

We was just started on our second helpin's when the door banged open. Mistuh Tolin was all bundled in his capote with the hood pulled up around his ears. Bornston and the others just had on wool jackets over their leather shirts.

"Jason! I saw Ol' Lucifer! Finally!" He sat down beside me. "Biggest damn bear ever existed!"

"Grizzly?" Cap asked Bornston with surprise. "Where was it?"

" 'Bout a day's ride west on the slopes," Bornston said.

"Tearin' away at this tree. He was nearly ten feet tall!" Mistuh Tolin was sayin'. "We shied way around him."

"A late winter," Cap mused. "But hard, if he's prowlin' down that low."

"And there was moose in the lakes. Fantastic animal! Ugly as sin, but big!" Mistuh Tolin went on.

"So what did ya bring back?" Ned asked.

"Two young buffalo, three deer, and an elk. Tolin did it again," Bornston said as him and the others was gettin' their meals. Mistuh Tolin was still sittin' with his coat on.

"Looks like you better salt this one down, Cobb, so's you'll have it when you and Jason take off with your trap lines." Cap winked at Ned when Mistuh Tolin wasn't lookin'. Me, I slowed my chewin' and waited for Mistuh Tolin's response. This was the first been said of our bein' trappers in a long time.

"Yes. I suppose it is that time," he said with a slight smile.

"You should've been gone if you was goin' down South Pass way. Late winter or not, I'll bet they've got plenty snow already," Bornston said. "Why, I've seen snow in the Siskadees so high it'd take nine men on each other's shoulders to see over the top."

"That's over fifty feet!"

"Snows so much up there the trees grow sideways," one of the others put in. "Jest layin' out flat across the ground where they couldn' bear the weight."

Mistuh Tolin hunched deeper in his coat. Adam changed

the subject and spoke to Ned. "I hear tell there's Arapaho south of the peaks."

"Yep. I'm headin' down that way in a couple of days. See if we can't get them to trade with American Fur. Don't think Rocky Mountain got to them yet," Ned said. "Say, Jason, why don't you come along—if you ain't gone trappin' yet. You, too, Tolin. Beautiful country. Different than around here."

It sounded real good to me. Mistuh Tolin just nodded and finally took off his coat and went for his meal.

"So what about the trapping, Jason?" Mistuh Tolin asked when we was back in the room. "I hope we haven't waited too late to go. Where do you think we should head?"

"Me?" I stirred up the coals in the fireplace and tossed on another log.

"I know how you've always wanted to see the mountains. I had thought the fort would be closer to them than it is."

"Mistuh Tolin, I . . . well, I really got no urge to trap."

He looked at me surprised. "But all the reading you've done about it, and the scouting you've learned from Ned. Why, I'd feel quite safe with you planning the trail."

"That kind of thing is useful anywhere. I like the land a lot, but not to hole up on a bluff in the snow waitin' for the beaver to show in the spring."

"You're just saying this because you don't think I'm up to it!"

"No! I'd—I'd miss my forge; and I sorta like havin' lots of people around."

"Really?"

I nodded. "I thought you was the one who really wanted to go."

"Oh, it would have been fun—I guess." We both seemed to relax, and it was agreed: we wouldn't go trappin'.

When we told Cap and the others they seemed to know it would get decided that way.

"I couldn't see you off from your work that long," Adam said to me. "You're an iron man."

"Iron and horses," Bornston put in.

I smiled, feelin' good.

"So there's no reason you can't go south with me," Ned said. "Be gone maybe two weeks. Can you spare him that long, Adam?"

"He'd a-been gone longer had he trapped," Adam said as he poured a bit of wine in his glass.

"We'll just tell the horses to keep their shoes on till Jason gets back."

I laughed, but when I glanced at Mistuh Tolin his face was sorta pale. I realized they hadn't said nothin' about needin' him around.

It was strange havin' more friendly concern over me than him. It was like our roles got reversed. I was movin' strong in a way of life I'd always wanted. Mistuh Tolin was tryin' hard, yet nobody seemed to take him serious at all. Some other folks might have felt sassy about that, but I couldn't. I wanted him to feel good about hisself like I did. I wanted us both to shine. Right now Mistuh Tolin wasn't livin' much different than he had in Alabama—always tryin' to prove hisself. It gave me a cold feelin' that there wasn't no fairness in the world at all.

15

Ned, Mistuh Tolin, and me set out for the mountains the next day. Bornston went along, too. We passed played-out beaver dams and rode up the pine-covered slopes. We saw all kinds of game, some wolf tracks, and some of those flattened-out trees all silver along the ground. Snow was already on them. Then there was no trees at all, just blue-gray rock bumpin' and pushin' up through the snow.

The trail got narrow and rough. I was ridin' my dun horse I called Cheyenne, and it minced through the pass with careful steps. My breath came hard in my chest up by the peaks, and even with the sun shinin' at midday we was cold. But I loved every minute of it. Once I walked Cheyenne out on a short ledge. The mountains was curvin' off to my right, and I could see all the way to the plains and where the sky met the earth to the east. I wanted to yell out *Hello! I'm here!* but at the same time I didn't want to spoil the perfect stillness.

Arapaho surrounded us on the trail the fifth day from the fort. Ned palavered with them in sign talk, and they took us another day on the trail to their camp. Those Indians was quiet folks when we rode in. They looked us over real well—children and women linin' the pathway we was led through to a big lodge that must've been for some chief. We was took inside and fed some meat and potato-like things, then we sat while the chief filled a big pipe with loose tobacco.

"You two do just what Ian and me do," Ned cautioned. "These folks is high on doin' things just so. We don't want to offend them none."

When we left the lodge I could tell that some agreement had been made, and all them Arapaho suddenly seemed friendlier. Mistuh Tolin had been real nervous durin' all this goin's-on, seein' that this was the first time he'd met up with any Indians outside of the protection of the fort.

"You flash some fooferaw and you two'll get yourselves a bed-warmer for the night," Bornston muttered.

"What?" Mistuh Tolin didn't seem to understand, but I had an inklin' of what he meant.

"A woman! Ned and me already have ourselves arranged."

"You shouldn't have no trouble, Jason. They seem to know about Black Wind, and we told them you was the one who owns him. Probably all you got to do is smile nice at one of 'em."

"That certainly couldn't be true!" Mistuh Tolin seemed shocked, but I started castin' my eye around the camp. "No. Definitely not! Come on, Jason." He pulled on my coat sleeve just as I made eye contact with a roundish, pleasant-faced girl. "It's totally unthinkable to take advantage of these people this way."

I nodded and looked back over my shoulder.

It was around the time of my twentieth birthday when we got back to the fort with promises of trade from the Arapaho tribe. Mistuh Tolin was mighty relieved to be back and he plunked down tight in the room like he was never gonna move again. When Ned came in a few days later to see if we wanted to go visitin' with him to a Crow tribe, Mistuh Tolin said *definitely not!* But I went, and I took plenty of fooferaw. Like Ned had said, ownin' Black Wind gave me some extra respect and I made my own arrangements this time. I was real glad for it, too, and even got me a handsome pair of moccasins. That same tribe came to the fort and stayed nearly ten days. Spring Star (that was the Crow girl's name) was just as friendly as when we first met. I never told Mistuh Tolin what I was up to, I'd just take off like I was goin' huntin'. I'd picket my horse behind her daddy's lodge. We had some good nights.

Four other tribes came to the fort to trade before the winter set in. Crow and another Cheyenne challenged Black Wind. They both lost. I won a fine Green River knife, a Hudson Bay blanket, a leather shirt all trimmed with beads, and another horse. This bay mare wasn't as fine an animal as the dun, but the good thing was, everything I'd won was mine and nobody ever questioned it at all.

Winter came on hard at Fort Laramie. The wind blew across that flat land and the crick froze. A lot of men had took off to the hills with trap lines, or to snuggle into an Indian lodge for the winter. Those of us at the fort settled down for the long winter lay-back. The evenin's was filled with yarnin' and drinkin' a fair share of Adam's brews.

Mistuh Tolin holed into the fort like a bear to his den. He rearranged the store, read a lot, and took to whittlin' fish hooks and such. He didn't even want to go huntin'!

Me, I enjoyed ridin' out on days when the air was so cold it would freeze my nose hairs and make my breath look like puffs of steam. It was good to feel Dancer's heat when I'd lean over his neck. I became a regular member on the huntin' parties, and Ned taught me more about trackin' and readin' the land. That's how we spent the winter.

"Look at that day!" Mistuh Tolin exclaimed as we stared over the palisades to the meadow. The snow was white and glossy, and thigh high right outside the fort door. The wind gusted and came warmish on us. Even so, Mistuh Tolin pulled his capote closer around him and scrunched his fur hat on his head. "I think spring is finally on its way," he said happily. We crunched down the steps.

"I don't know. Cap says this mildness won't last."

"Oh, it has to! In early March back home the ground would be ready to start harrowing. A good time for early crops." He had been talkin' more and more about home.

"You know how Cap is with the weather. He seems to know."

Mistuh Tolin just grunted. "What time are you and the others going hunting?"

"Be leavin' in about an hour. You want to come along?"

"Oh, no. Ned says you're one of the best hunters at the fort."

I had to grin at that, 'cause it was a fact that I brought in a lot of game. "It's that rifle of yours," I said. "Can't help but be good with that. I like the way it feels."

"That Hall is a nice piece, all right."

We ate hearty and I saddled up Dancer. Ned and Bornston was ready to go. Cap watched us with a scowl. "Keep an eye on the clouds," he warned.

Thing was, there weren't no clouds in the sky. Nary a one.

We rode out and scouted for game sign. Ned let me take the lead, but after two hours things didn't look too promisin'. I spotted dips in the snow that had been made several days before.

"What animal?" Ned asked as I examined the tracks.

"Elk, looks like. Probably a bull."

Ned nodded. "When?"

"Maybe two, three days?" I tested the depth of the icy crust and fingered the powdery snow that had blown on top. "Three days," I said, confident. When I looked up Ned and Bornston was smilin', and I knew they agreed with me.

"Wal, you taught him some," Bornston said to Ned. "I'd ride the river with this child any day. Yes sirree."

On the way back to the fort we crossed buffalo sign, but

the tracks was near a week old. The sky started cloudin' to a dull gray, and the sound of the horses' feet crunched loud in the still air.

"Let's check that section over there, and then head in," Ned suggested.

We spread out and I took the tree line on the far side. The snow got deep from driftin' in the gullies of the meadow, and Dancer had to lunge through in some places. It was then I saw the fresh track of a heavy animal in the snow. I headed Dancer for the sign. A short-legged animal with broad girth. Buffalo! Probably a hangback from that small group that had been through before. The sign led around the trees and then up a draw. Dancer and me followed. I looked to signal Ned and Bornston before I was out of their sight, but they was lookin' off another way, so I went on. The snow seemed deeper, and Dancer's weight pushed him through the crust up to his gaskins. I got off and went on foot after findin' a shallow place for him to stand. Followin' those tracks was gettin' easier, so I knew I was close.

I spotted a mangy cow buffalo in a clearin' that was blown shallow of snow. She looked old, and sure wouldn't make good eatin' for none but a panther or a bobcat, but it was buffalo. The hide could be used, I figured, and I'd come this far . . .

I thought I heard a shout from far off. Ned? I listened, but was so anxious to shoot that buffalo I didn't go back. The cow was standin' and gruntin', and when she saw me she charged, half fallin', down the hill. I tried to sight the rifle, but she was too close, too fast. One of her horns caught me when I jumped aside. It ripped right under my capote and jagged a hole in my thigh. The snow was spotted with blood and I fell back with pain and the shock of it. The buffalo kept crashin' through the trees.

I didn't feel the pain after a while. The sound of the cow faded. Then I heard Dancer whicker for me, but when I went to walk, my leg gave way. I had to prop myself with the rifle as a crutch. It was then I heard the wild howlin' sound like devils out of hell. Snow started comin' down in thick, frosty globs. The wind blew hard like it had in the summer storm on the plains, but now it was so cold I could barely move. Above the howl of the wind I could hear the clicks of the ice-covered branches slappin' together. I had watched these storms from the safety of the fort twice before durin' the winter: blowin' and blowin'. Cold. It was so cold!

I turned to go back to Dancer, but there wasn't nothin' before me but thick flakes of white snow.

"Damn snow!" I didn't remember ever cussin' before, but I cussed that snow, and my not bein' on Dancer, and the numbness in my leg that made it hard to walk. My hands started feelin' heavy with cold—freezin' even through my gloves, and I kept droppin' that big-bore gun and flounderin' for it in the snow. I wanted to cry. My feet had no feelin' at all, and I bumped into somethin'.

"Dancer?" I saw the dark shape like a shadow in the white air. I pulled myself onto his back and felt him start to move . . .

16

Fire! Seems that so much of my life was decided by fire. Fire in the canebrake; fire in the forge; fire at the Cobb plantation that burned away everythin' but my life. Now there was another fire—the same kind that took my mama. It was in me and I was burnin' with it. I lay in the blankets and saw all them other fires whirlin' in my mind. I heard myself cry out, but I couldn't stop from doin' it. Once I hollered and a hand touched my forehead. I looked up and saw Mistuh Tolin all wavy through my eyes. That was a comfort.

Cold would come on me sometimes. It was like I had spikes of ice for bones, and I'd start shakin' till my teeth rattled. I was so cold I couldn't even open my eyes to look around, but I felt certain I was at the fort in the room Mistuh Tolin and me shared.

"Jason. Can you hear me? Come on, man. Sit up. Here, take some of this." Mistuh Tolin's arms had to pull me upright 'cause I had no strength. A liquid burned down my throat. It was my throat that was hot, not the liquid. I was sure I was breathin' flames, and there was a deep heavy pain in my chest when I coughed.

The whirlin' in my brain was the worst of it. I couldn't keep a thought long enough to get it said. I found out later that was from the medicine Bornston was givin' me. I'd start tryin' to call for somebody, then forget who it was. Sounds were frightenin'. Sometimes when the door would close the noise slammed right through my head, and Mistuh Tolin movin' a chair was like a file raspin' in my ears. I remember one time seein' Skalley's face. I called out for her, and she changed to Louisa, eyes dancin' and happy.

"Louisa?" I was half sittin'.

"Shhhh." It was Mistuh Tolin's heavy whisper, and I sank back into a crazy-dreamed sleep.

Pretty soon I started puttin' the pieces together. Mistuh Tolin would come and feed me warm broth. I started sittin' up on my own, but my head still spun if I moved too fast.

"Wal, you lost a lot of blood, boy," Bornston told me one day when I complained about bein' dizzy. "I filled you full of laudanum and quinine, and hoped for the best. I didn't know if this ol' niggur was gonna see you pull through."

Bornston was talkin' mountain-man talk, and *niggur* was how folks spoke about themselves or others they was with. He didn't mean it like I used to know it. He could have said *beaver* or *child* or *crittur*. It would all have been the same.

"Jason. By God, you had me worried," Mistuh Tolin said the afternoon I finally seemed well enough to get out and around. His face was tired and pale.

"I just felt like gettin' cared for, that's all," I joked. I looked in the mirror by the wash basin. I was thin, and had an inch of whiskers.

"It's not funny! If something had happened to you, I—" He slumped on the bed. "You look awful."

We both laughed, and I set to shavin' and gettin' clean again.

"You surely didn't miss much the last two weeks," Mistuh Tolin told me when I finally hobbled over to the hall. My right leg was stiff, and tender to the touch up near my hip. Mistuh Tolin had fashioned me a cane to use. "I've heard more wild stories about the mountains. If we had gone out there, I don't know if I could have stood it." He opened the door for me and smiled as he spoke. "I'm glad you're better, Jason. I truly missed your company."

"Well, hello! Look who's about!" The men in the hall was real friendly to me and I got pats on the back all around, some so hard it was all I could do to keep balanced with that one leg bad.

"Winstead's got a fine stew bubblin'. He must've known you'd be up today," Ned said cheerful, and he went off to get me a bowl of it.

"Here you are, Jason. This'll perk you up. Bornston wouldn't let me bring you any before now." Adam set a big glass of whiskey and water before me as I sat down.

Mistuh Tolin sat down with me and the others and they told me again how the blizzard had hit in real sudden; and how Ned and Bornston had looked for me before it started snowin'.

"I thought I heard someone callin'," I confessed.

"We figured you to have holed up already," Ned said. "We cut up the ridge and barely got a shelter together before that storm came in on us. Had all those pine boughs twisted into a wickiup and the snow piled up on top fine. So much snow I thought we'd be buried alive."

"I never have figured how you could breathe in there," Mistuh Tolin commented.

"Fire from the inside melts a hole in the top, ain't that so, Ned?" I said. He nodded.

"Yes sirree, it was sure a shocker when I peeked out at the sky nigh to evenin' and saw that bulk of Dancer standin' there," Bornston went on. "He must've smelled our smoke, though I don't know how in that howlin' wind. Mountain horse, he is; had to be, to get you to us that way."

We had been trapped in the hills for three days—me losin' a lot of blood, and then takin' sick from bein' so long unconscious in the weather. I lost the tip of my left little finger to frostbite. That had Bornston worried a heap. I remembered none of it. Not a speck.

"It was a miracle you came through it, Jason. A miracle for you, and a blessing for me," Mistuh Tolin stated.

I felt real quiet inside—even frightened at what I'd gone through. I thought maybe I should go burn offerin's to the sky like the Indians did for thanks to the great powers of life. What I did do was take an extra measure of corn to Dancer that evenin'. He whickered and nuzzled me, and I stayed with him until I felt the cold through my coat, and Mistuh Tolin came to get me back inside. Dancer got special care for a long time after that.

The spring weather came not long after that, and brought in free trappers and Indians with pelts to trade. Activities was like in the fall, but in a grander style with more people, more horse racin', and plenty of whiskey. Stone Finger's tribe returned, and while nobody challenged Black Wind, they did invite us to feast and count *coup* with them one evenin'. I had a lot to add to my boasts now, with survivin' the blizzard and bein' gored by a buffalo. Stone Finger gave me a necklace of gold nuggets and ermine tails.

"That's gold, sure enough," Cap said with awe as he examined the necklace. "Wonder where they dig that stuff. Wouldn't I like to find that place!"

"I don't know as I should keep it," I said.

"You can give it to me," Adam stated. "I'll have no trouble with keeping it."

"The Cheyenne don't value gold like we do," Ned explained. "But you'd shame Stone Finger mightily by not accepting his gift, Jason. He give you that as a bond of friendship. You ought to give him something in return at a time when he can't refuse it or bring it back to you."

So the night before the tribe was to leave I put the Hudson Bay blanket I'd won outside of Stone Finger's lodge. I tucked a piece of iron in the blanket that had formed in a loop at the top and hardened to a round knob. I knew he would make a good necklace from that.

I lost the bay horse that spring to a Crow brave who had said he wanted to race. I worked it all out in sign talk I'd been learnin', but I didn't quite understand right, 'cause it turned out to be a *foot* race. I got a lot of teasin' about that.

A trapper came in with a Brown Bess muzzleloader just like Mistuh Tolin's and challenged me to a shootin' contest.

"Five shot, for speed and accuracy," he said. That meant we was to see who could load and fire five shots in the quickest time and there was penalties for bein' too far off the target with the shots.

I had my five shots finished just about the same time as him, but every one of mine was right on the yellow-painted circle that was on my target tree. I won a badger-skin knife sheath and a necklace of wood beads and grizzly claws. That necklace was a handsome thing, and I took to wearin' it most of the time. The gift from Stone Finger I saved for special times, and kept it carefully packed in a rabbit-fur pouch.

Spring Star's tribe came in with a load of furs and she was glad enough to see me. She was thin from the winter, but our times together was warm and full. Mistuh Tolin took to eyein' a gentle-lookin' gal of that tribe, and I think he was about to make his arrangements when he found out she was married.

"Married, huh," he said to Adam when he told him. "That means the same as in the States. Hands off."

"Very true. Crow men don't hold to their wives fooling around. You've just saved yourself a flogging."

"That woman probably don't want to risk losin' her nose, anyway," Cap said. "That's what happens with unfaithful wives." And he made a slicin' motion with his hand against his nose. "Right off!" It gave me chills to think about it.

The pack train that came through on the way to the

rendezvous was bein' led by a Captain Stewart. He was glad to have a good blacksmith when he arrived. I shoed some mules and repaired iron tires on the wagons. Seems part of the train was crossin' over the Rockies and goin' to the Whitman mission near Walla Walla. I started wonderin' about that land west of us. I wanted to see the Rockies, and the green valleys on the other side.

Stewart had four women with him, and the fort nearly turned inside out to please them. Men who hadn't shaved all winter suddenly took up a razor. The cussin' slacked off a bit, and so did the wild, bawdy stories. Stewart also brought along a man by the name of Alfred J. Miller. He was one of them folks that painted pictures of things. Seems Stewart had a brother who was sick away back in Scotland—across the ocean—and Stewart wanted his brother to know what the land looked like in the wilds of America, so he brought this artist to paint pictures to send back to him. I watched the man work and marveled at how he could make little dabs of color look like trees and hills.

The train didn't stay too long 'cause Captain Stewart was plannin' to surprise the trapper mountain-man Jim Bridger with a whole suit of metal armor like I'd seen in pictures of old-time wars. The time they did stay at the fort was long enough to make Mistuh Tolin miss a whole lot of ways and things he had always hankered for: gentle talk with women, starched shirts, loose tobacco, smooth cotton pants and pigskin gloves. He started gettin' restless.

"Jason, I know you don't want to go back, but we won't stay long. I want to get the funds from the bank and invest in something. Wouldn't it be nice not to work for American Fur, or anyone? Be our own boss."

"Are you sayin' we'd come back?"

"I can't see why not, or we could go into Michigan Territory . . . buy some land."

"Michigan Territory?" That was North. That was freedom land.

"Or some place." His face drained of color.

I started gettin' that skittish feelin' again and old thoughts settled on me. I was a slave . . . I had no say. I should fight it! Tell him, *No, I'm stayin' here!* What would he say?

I looked to where he was sittin' on the bed, fiddlin' with his pocket knife, and I suddenly knew what he'd say. He'd say, *All right, Jason.* And he'd leave.

I drew in a deep breath and couldn't seem to think in that room at all. I walked out and up to the walkway, all the time picturin' Mistuh Tolin ridin' off all alone, and me standin' all alone watchin' him. I hurt inside, and I stared at that free land I loved so much. I knew I was goin' to leave it.

17

There was six people in our party when we left Fort Laramie the end of June. We was all well armed, too, 'cause the word was out that the Sioux nation was blackin' their faces toward white folks. Bornston was with us on that trip, and Pike Walters. He had free-trapped north of South Pass that winter, but didn't fare too well. He was headed to Council Bluffs to join a party that was goin' north into the Dakotas. That's where Bornston and a man named Coe Price was goin' too. An old-timer named Taggart come along to see us through.

"I give up trappin'," Taggart told Bornston. "Figure to start guidin' wagon trains. Folks is gonna be movin' out this way, ya know." He scratched at his red beard. "The good years is comin' to an end."

In the evenin's we would sit at the fire and swap stories we'd heard from other mountain men. By now I had realized that I could spin a yarn about as good as any crittur, and I got to layin' it on real fine one night about my fight with the buffalo and gettin' caught in the blizzard.

"Listen to him!" Bornston exclaimed with a laugh. "Sounds like one of those whoppers told by Black Harris!"

Black Harris was a mountain man known for his lies. I never found out if he was really black, or if it was just a name they give him.

"I shore wish ol' Dancer could talk," Pike drawled real slow. He was from Tennessee a few years back, and about Mistuh Tolin's age. "Would be good to know just how true it all is."

Mistuh Tolin picked it up and told a real good tale about the big horse race with the Cheyenne. "They call the horse Black Wind, and Jason is the man— How did they put it, Jason?"

"Man of victory skin," I said with a smile.

I took first watch that night with Taggart. The moon was hangin' low and half full. There was a mistiness around it and I figured there'd be rain in another day or so. A coyote yapped in the hills, then yowled at the sky.

"Listen to that sad critter. Ever hear such a lonely sound?" Taggart asked me as he sat down on a rock. We had our backs to each other and talked real soft.

"I don't care for it," I admitted. "But I like the call of the wolf. It's strong and deep—sorta like he's countin' *coup.*" Ned and me had listened to those howls of the wolves lots of nights when we was out from the fort. Each one sounded different and the voice that started the singin' always ended it after every wolf in the pack had said its piece and the little ones tried their voices. I smiled as I remembered that, and thought about church singin' at the revivals and knew how the wolves must feel when they was done.

"The wolf sings proud, not scared," I said after a while.

"Ain't many folks that hear it that way, Jason. Me, I been out here a long time, and I know the wolf. He's proud, all right, and free. Ain't like that there coyote always runnin' and lookin' over his shoulder."

I listened again to the coyote and got chilled. I saw me sittin' on a hill and hollerin' out. How was I callin'? I had counted *coup,* that was a fact. Had me a good life this past year, but now I was changin'. I was goin' from wolf— proud and free—to coyote—scared and lookin' over my shoulder.

I shook my head against the thought. It wouldn't be that

way. I'd learned too much. I might play the part of a slave, but I would always be different. I'd always sing proud.

That coyote hollered again and I thought of Mistuh Tolin tryin' his voice all these years and never yet said his piece. I had no call to think about him like that, but I did, and it saddened me.

We met up with a war party of Sioux near the Loup River. They came down on us whoopin' for blood and we turned tail and run. We rode into a draw that was backed with boulders and thickets, and Coe Price and me kneeled all the animals over onto their sides so's the Indians wouldn't stick them with arrows and leave us afoot. Pike had hisself a bullthrower (that's what we called a Hawken gun) and he caused two of them Indians to go under right off. They kept their distance after that, so we picked and shot, and sweated, and watched till the sun threw long shadows on the grass.

"Think they're gone?" Pike asked Taggart.

"Nope. Jest waitin' us out, I suspect."

The animals was tired from layin' so long in the draw. We cut the ropes that cross-hitched their back leg to a foreleg, and let them up since it was nearly dark. Mistuh Tolin and Price squirmed their way back through the thickets to see what was there. They were gone about five minutes when we heard shots. I charged back to see what happened.

"Mistuh Tolin?" A shove on my shoulder sent me rollin' to the side, Mistuh Tolin atop me. A shot kicked at the ground where I had been.

"Don't say anything," he whispered. "They're close."

I saw Price's legs all crazy in the weeds and I knew he'd gone under. I tensed up and stared into the darkness. Mistuh Tolin laid down his rifle, took out his knife, and held it in his teeth; then he pulled out that Colt pistol from where it was tucked in the back band of his pants. I unhitched my knife. Taggart come up so quiet I didn't know

133

he was there till I saw him from the corner of my eye. I signaled him where the trouble might be comin' from, then we just laid out and waited.

A big volley of shots and arrows zinged in right near us, but we didn't fire back. Flies buzzed and a cricket started chirrin' next to my elbow. I flicked some sweat off my eyelid with my finger. Then there was a big loud yell and four Sioux came through the brush at us with their faces painted in stripes. They must not have suspected we was there, thinkin' we got killed in the earlier shootin', so they just charged. Mistuh Tolin snapped off three shots with his revolver and two of them went down. I fired that muzzleloader, but it didn't seem to do no good and this Sioux was near on top of me with a hatchet. I caught him in the stomach with my knife and shoved hard. Taggart used his rifle butt and clubbed the fourth Indian so strong it made a loud whack.

Everythin' was silent. I held my breath lest another Sioux be layin' in the brush waitin' to hear me. That man I stabbed was layin' all over my arm and still breathin'. I could feel the weight of his body, and smell his sweat. My hand was sticky with his blood. He moaned a bit, then the breathin' stopped. My stomach started turnin', and I felt like I was bein' held under a pillow.

"Taggart! Cobb!"

"Yo!" Taggart answered Bornston.

"Five of 'em done rode off. They quit. Any of you hurt?"

"We lost Coe Price," Mistuh Tolin reported.

I got sick. Seemed like my insides couldn't heave enough as I rolled away from that dead man. I lay off in the bushes pantin' for breath and Mistuh Tolin came over to me. His face was drawn and solemn.

"I did the same thing down in Florida when I killed that man on my bayonet." He sat with me till I got over the sick feelin', and we went back to the draw.

We buried Price in a shallow grave and piled it high with rocks. Taggart got my stomach churnin' again when he scalped that Indian he killed and tucked the hairpiece in his belt. We went down to the Loup and made camp, and chilly as the night air was, me and Mistuh Tolin went in the icy water and soaked for nearly ten minutes as if to clear away the ugly scene. Bornston patched up a wound on Taggart's shoulder, and then the two of them stood first watch. They didn't even seem thankful that they still had their hair.

Bornston and Taggart made no comment about the fight all the way to Fort Atkinson, but when we got there they was full of the tale. Taggart showed off the scalp he had took, and started braggin' on the three young critturs what saved the party from the Sioux. He made it sound real heroic, even my killin' a man.

"Then Jason run his blade to the Green River in this warrior what was steamin' down on him with a tammyhawk, while I laid open the skull of another with the butt of my rifle. It was a good fight. *Waugh!*"

To take somethin' to the Green River (that was the hallmark on the hilt of a knife) meant to put it as far as it can go. That's what Bornston did with his part of the tale, too.

"Wal, we had lit out from the river, all right, and laid them mules and horses down in the draw. Pike here takes up his Hawken and makes two of them red devils come right off. Cobb nailed the coffin on two, and then Pike got one more in the showdown. Yes sirree! Them beaver shine!"

We was suddenly the talk of the fort, and we got sorta swell-headed about it. Didn't nobody tell about me gettin' sick from killin' a man. Of course lots of folks didn't really consider Indians men—sorta like the planter don't really think of Negroes as more than plow horses.

I started wonderin' if that man I killed had a family. Maybe a ma, or a woman who was gonna cry for him. I thought about Stone Finger and if he was at war somewheres dyin' on somebody's knife. That Sioux brave was part of my *coup* now. Well, I convinced myself, it don't make no difference. It was him or me. But I started worryin' 'cause I didn't have no woman to sing a mournin' chant for me if I'd gone under. I thought about my mama, and Skalley—and Louisa.

"Jason, I'm going over to the store," Mistuh Tolin said late that afternoon. "Is there anything you want?"

"I don't think so." There was nothin' I seemed to need. I had two pair of britches, four shirts, not includin' my fancy leather one, and good coverin' for my feet and head.

When I next saw Mistuh Tolin he was dressed in broadcloth pants and a white shirt; he had on new boots and a fine felt hat. There was more packages under his arm.

"Look at this," he called, and he showed Pike and me a little gun that was smaller than his hand. "A derringer. Only holds two shots. Just look at that design work!"

I shook my head while he showed off the gun, then he started off toward the mission schoolhouse.

"What's he gonna do over there?" Pike asked.

"Oh, he just likes schools. Never got to go back home, and he always wanted to be a teacher."

"Think he'll do that when he gets back to the States? He sounds like he's got the knowledge for it."

"I don't know."

"What about you? What are you gonna do, Jason?"

"Me?" I had no answer for that, but Pike saw a young gal that caught his eye and changed his thoughts.

"Think I'll get me down to the barbershop for a shave," he decided. "Hear tell there's gonna be a dance here tonight."

Not long after dark, lanterns started showin' up in a huge circle right outside the fort gate. Somebody had a fiddle and there was a couple of accordions. Music got goin' fine and they brought a whiskey barrel out of the saloon. Women there was right few, but them that wanted didn't have no trouble gettin' dance partners. I itched to swing me a lady, but there wasn't none there for me. Pike couldn't find that girl he had noticed earlier, so him and me settled down to see the fun. Bornston and Mistuh Tolin joined us.

"That's good, toe-tappin' music," Bornston said after lightin' his pipe. We all agreed. "Go git yourself a gal, Cobb —you and your fancy duds. Let's see ya kick the dust around."

"That there boy can't dance nothin' but fancy East Coast stuff." The voice that was talkin' was rough with liquor. We looked up and saw Jim Tolliver. "Now, if you want to see some dancin', get the nigger to dance. Never seen a nigger that couldn't dance."

I knew right off he was meanin' me. He was talkin States talk now, not mountain talk. I looked around for Brian Honicutt. He wasn't there. I hoped this wouldn't end up in a fight. With settlement folks around, the outcome might not be as nice if I won.

"Get on, Tolliver. Ya got too much whiskey in ya," Bornston said. "Let the boys alone." He put an arm around Tolliver's wobbly shoulders and tried to march him off.

"Come on, Cobb. Don't tell me that slave boy of yours don't dance!" Tolliver laughed. Bornston pushed him off in the direction of the corral. I sighed heavy.

Pike pulled out his big skinnin' knife and started pickin' at his fingernails with the tip of it. "That boy's got a way about him that just rankles a man to the core," he drawled real slow. "Can't see that a person should put up with that. Not nobody at all!" He looked at me when he said that, then stared real hard at Mistuh Tolin. "Was that right what he said about Jason bein' your slave?" Pike's voice had a bit of an edge on it. Mistuh Tolin didn't say nothin'. "That why Jason goes around callin' you *mister* all the time? Hell if I'd do it, Jason. You're too good a man to have to kowtow to anybody!"

Mistuh Tolin had already got up and walked away. I listened to his footsteps crunch on the dry, sparse grass.

"He's a good man, Mistuh Tolin is," I said to Pike.

137

"If he's so good, why don't he let you make your own way?" Pike tossed the knife and it landed deep in the ground; the handle quivered a bit.

"I do, Pike. I'm doin' fine."

"Why don't you take off, Jason? Come with Bornston and me. We're goin' up to good country in the Dakotas. We could use another strong arm, what with Coe bein' killed and all."

I didn't say nothin'.

"You been a free man out here. Are you gonna give that up?" Pike stared at me. I started pullin' at some blades of grass that was between my feet, not knowin' how to tell him how it was.

"Seventy miles down that river and you're back in the States. Missouri's a slave state, too. Hell, I saw the Georgia militia ride onto my pa's place in Tennessee and hang a freed man who worked for us. Claimed he was a runaway who'd stole some money. Didn't matter how much my pa talked, and that man even had freedom papers. They didn't listen. Cobb might be a good man, but he's takin' you right back into that."

I put my hands over my face, my elbows restin' on my knees. I couldn't think. The music seemed too loud, the fiddles scrapin' into my brain. Finally I dropped my hands and looked at Pike.

"I can't explain it, Pike. I know what you're sayin' is true, but Mistuh Tolin and me . . . It's different . . . We grew up together. He taught me how to read, and lots of other things. The Creeks wiped out everythin' he had—burned it to the ground. They stole my woman and killed the only folks either of us ever loved. We got memories, him and me, and if there wasn't that to share we'd have nothin'. Not neither of us."

"It's a high price you're payin' for memories, Jason. A mighty high price. And you still call him *mister*. That ain't right."

The music was still goin'. Folks was havin' a good time.

Pike went off to get some more whiskey, and I left before he got back.

Mistuh Tolin and Pike didn't speak none the next day. In fact, Mistuh Tolin didn't speak to no one. Pike and Bornston had hitched up with five other men and they was gettin' ready to leave the followin' mornin'.

Pike come around after dark to where Mistuh Tolin and me was sittin' by our fire.

"Jason? We'll be pullin' out in the mornin'," Pike said as he squatted down next to me. "You comin'?"

I looked over to where Mistuh Tolin was readin' some book he had pulled up close to the lantern. I wished he would say, *Sure, Jason, that's a fine idea. Let's both go,* but I knew it wouldn't happen. I shook my head no.

"Well," Pike sighed. "We'll be gone afore sunup." His hand rested on my shoulder.

"I wish you shinin' times, Pike," I said.

"Thank you, my friend. I hope your way be clear."

III

Vanishing
Dreams

18

A steamboat came down the Missouri two days after Pike left. It had been up to Fort Pierre in the Dakotas and was brimmin' with furs from the trappers up there. The boat was a big side-wheeler with double stacks and two decks. A real beauty, but neither Mistuh Tolin or me got too excited.

"Beaver's shinin'!" a fur-company man said.

"'Tain't no matter," grumbled a trapper. "St. Louey don't pay 'nough to git another season started with. Laid out a whole plew for a plug o' baccy." *Plew* was trapper talk for a beaver pelt.

"Get better prices for buffalo than for beaver," a well-dressed man commented.

I suddenly longed to see some buffalo with their shaggy, thick coats all matted and caked with mud from the wallows, but I helped load up our stuff and walked the horses onto the lower livestock level. Cheyenne cut up somethin' awful, and I suspected he was goin' to miss the wild land as much as me.

It seems I noticed all the bad things goin' down the river, like bloated animal corpses in the water with a cloud of flies hoverin' over them, or half-eaten antelope rottin' in the sun with buzzards pickin' at the smelly carcasses and ants crawlin' through the empty eye sockets. Mistuh Tolin was quiet, too—powerful quiet. He stared at the muddy waters of the Missouri for what seemed to be hours. Then he read newspapers that other folks left layin' around. That seemed to make him feel worse.

The steamboat was nearin' the landin' where the Missouri and Kansas rivers flow together, when Mistuh Tolin started stirrin' to get his things together.

"I thought we was goin' to St. Louey, Mistuh Tolin," I said.

"No. I don't think so." His words was clipped and he went to the captain to get back part of the money for our passage. He looked sick, and I commenced worryin'.

Signs of settlements was showin' along the east banks—houses and dogs, and straight rows of corn wavin' green in the wind. We passed a string of cotton fields and there was some Negroes hoein' the rows. I remembered again where we was: the States.

"Here, Mistuh Tolin. Best you carry these." I unfastened my knife and handed out the muzzleloader. He frowned at me. "I don't know what the Missouri laws are, but places back home I'd be in trouble bein' armed."

He took the things and turned away real quick.

Independence Landin' was where we was. The town of Independence was off the river a few miles, but the Landin' was so filled with people and wagons you'd never have known there was no town. With the territories openin' up, there was big wagon trains of settlers startin' off on the Sante Fe Trail. Folks was movin' across the river into Indian Territory, too, and some was headed out to California. That was over three months away. Others was goin' down the river to the Ozarks and then on to Texas.

While the boat was bein' tied up I watched a gang of workers strugglin' with a wagon to get it off the cliffs and to the docks. Most everythin' had to be lowered with ropes and pulleys 'cause the hills was too steep for the oxen teams to get a wagon up or down.

"Haul! *Heave!* Haul! *Heave!*" I could hear the leader callin' the rhythm. The wagon inched down. The sweat beaded shiny on the workers' backs. The team I was watchin' was all Negro—probably free, if you could call it that.

When we went down for the animals I had some trouble convincin' Dancer that he should step onto land and through all the people that was bustlin' around. He started buckin' and jumpin' like he had a bur under his tail. The dun started cuttin' up, too. Mistuh Tolin took his horse, Rogue, and the two pack mules, and I had to do a lot of strong-armin' to get Dancer and the dun settled. Finally, a big white man in a tan suit helped get the crowd moved enough so I could take the horses through. I touched the brim of my leather hat in thanks, and started toward where Mistuh Tolin was waitin'.

"Wait a minute, boy!" the man called. I looked back. "Those are fine horses you've got there." His manner of speech was slow and easy—like back in 'Bama. He was a rich man. I could tell that by the way he walked. I stood a few inches taller than him, but he had a way about him that made me feel like he was sittin' on a mountain. His smile was fixed and stiff, and his brown eyes reminded me of a hawk spyin' a rabbit's nest. Mistuh Tolin come back to me.

"Is this your boy?" the man asked Mistuh Tolin.

"We're together."

The man's smile brightened and he tucked his thumbs in his vest pockets. "You've just come from the Territory, I see. Any luck with the trapping?"

"We worked at the fort for the season," Mistuh Tolin replied after a moment. "I've no furs to trade."

"Hmm. I hear a strong touch of Alabama in your voice. Is that so?" Mistuh Tolin nodded. "I used to be an overseer up near Montgomery. Perhaps you knew the people. The name of—"

"I'm sure they were no friends of mine," Mistuh Tolin said real fast.

My heart beat double time as I realized what this man

was drivin' at. He was lookin' me up and down like I would inspect a new bovine before purchase.

"I take it you're not a landed man."

Mistuh Tolin didn't answer.

"Send the boy ahead with the horses. Let's talk business, son."

Mistuh Tolin backed away from the hand that was reachin' to rest on his shoulder. "There's no reason you can't speak to both of us."

"All right. We're in a time of woes. Economic setbacks. I'm sure you know—"

"What do you want?" Mistuh Tolin demanded.

The man seemed a bit annoyed with Mistuh Tolin's manner, but he kept on. "My name's Fannin. Percy Fannin, and this boy looks to be good with horses. I know an estate owner in Texas who could use a boy like—"

"Are you offering a job?" Mistuh Tolin's voice was harsh, and I wished I had taken the horses on, not wantin' to hear myself bein' bartered over—not wantin' this awful reminder of where we was.

"Why, no, son. I want to buy this here boy from you. What's your price?"

Mistuh Tolin's blue eyes got cold and he turned away real quick. "Come on, Jason." His face was gettin' red-splotched on the cheeks. My heart was poundin' hard with pain and fear as we started up the bluffs. That Fannin called to him, but Mistuh Tolin didn't even look back. In fact, he was quiet and solemn all evenin', hardly sayin' a thing as we set up camp in a lonely spot near a crick.

Sleepin' was hard for me that night. I dozed once and dreamed of white-topped mountains and herds of buffalo, but when my eyes snapped open to some small sound, I thought of Percy Fannin. I had no fear of Mistuh Tolin sellin' me off. He had chances to do that before, and there was also the way he was—the changes in him since we'd been at Fort Laramie. Still, havin' to deal with people like

146

Fannin was unnervin', and I remembered what Pike had said: It's a high price you're payin' for memories. But it was more than memories.

Mattie and others always warned me not to think of Mistuh Tolin any different than other white men, yet I'd also been taught to read people's feelin's—know their thinkin'. I was pretty good at that, and I knew my own feelin's, too. It wasn't Mistuh Tolin I wanted to be rid of, just slavery.

Mistuh Tolin stirred several times, and I wondered if I was trappin' myself with silly notions. Well, I figured, we're on the border, so if I have to, I can leave. I'll *be* a runaway—go back to the Territory.

Mistuh Tolin was up before me, and he had the coffee boilin' already when I pulled on my shirt and rolled my pack. I could tell he wanted to talk, so I leaned back against the saddle and waited. He poured coffee for us and sat on his saddle, his elbows restin' on his knees.

"We've got problems, Jason," he finally said. "No. *I've* got a problem." He drew a long breath. "There's no money. All those plans I had about investing, getting our own place . . . The banks closed down—a panic, they call it. I heard about it first when the Stewart train came into the fort. Anyway, all that money is gone."

"You mean the eight hundred dollars you banked in St. Louey?"

"Yes. There was too much land speculation, and they changed some laws back in Washington. The bank had put out more money than they held in securities and— Well, that bank in St. Louey folded three weeks ago. Completely out of business . . . and our money with it."

I don't know what he wanted me to say, but as I sipped my coffee I marveled at how we was again in the same circumstances: me losin' rights to all my property I had in the Territory, and him losin' all he had too.

"Damn! I've made a mess out of everything!" He threw his cup and it clattered against a tree. The coffee made a dark stain on the ground. "What can I do, Jason?"

"Well. How much money do you have?"

"Sixty dollars."

"Is that all!" I know my voice was loud with surprise. I couldn't believe that all the wages from both of us workin' at Fort Laramie could be gone 'ceptin' for that. Mistuh Tolin didn't look at me, and I started wonderin' how desperate for money he was goin' to be. Percy Fannin's sharp, hungry eyes came to mind. I buried the thought. I knew that wouldn't happen, and I felt bad for even thinkin' it.

"Sixty dollars will last over a month with us knowin' how to live off the land. You can probably find a job. And —and you could . . . hire me out down at the docks." Those words came mighty hard.

"Don't be ridiculous!" He sighed like he hadn't slept for weeks. "I *should* be able to get a job—perhaps clerking at a store. Of course, I'd prefer to teach—I think. Maybe we could hire on with a missionary, like the one that runs the school at Fort Atkinson." He started soundin' hopeful as he dreamed up the plan. "I'd help out with the school, and they'd be in need of a blacksmith. It would serve us both!" He looked at me eagerly.

"Maybe we could hire on with American Fur again," I suggested.

"*You* probably could." He looked sick again and his mouth opened to talk, but he didn't say nothin' for a few minutes. "Nothing's going to change with us. Just like it was at Fort Laramie. Partners. Okay?"

"Mistuh Tolin—"

"Let's go see what we can find."

All the while we was breakin' camp he kept talkin' about how we'd get on with a wagon train and go west into "unchartered territory . . . pioneers in a new land!" It sounded fine with me, but deep down I knew he wasn't really a pioneer man. He would manage if he had to, but he was better suited to mild climates and sleepin' under a roof.

———

148

Not far from where we was camped there was a barren meadow grazed out and dry from all the earlier travelers. A group of fourteen wagons was pulled up there, and the people was plain-dressed and quiet.

"Maybe missionaries," Mistuh Tolin whispered. But their eyes was suspicious and scowlin' as we rode up.

"Who be you?" a bearded man asked. He walked out from his wagon with his rifle layin' in his arms. He didn't look friendly at all.

"We're looking for a group to move west with. Are you missionaries?"

"The only true emissaries of the Lord, and our flock is solid. We are Mormon. Move on with you, and tell whoever sent you that we'll not be infiltrated!"

We moved on, all right, and was glad to do it.

Farther east we found another wagon camp set near a wide stream. There was good grass for the stock, and the folks was movin' at an early-mornin' slow. Friendly and smilin', Mistuh Tolin tipped his new felt hat a lot and said hello. He helped a girl with a balky milk cow, and talked with her brothers for a while. Most of the folks was from Kentucky and other parts of Missouri. They took real well to Mistuh Tolin's Alabama speakin'. There was Negro folks among them 'cause even though these folks was poor, some had bondsmen.

"Hey, you." I heard a whisper at me while Mistuh Tolin was talkin' to a family. I looked back and saw about five young Negro kids starin' at me.

"You see! He *is* colored," one of them said.

"We thought you was injun. How come you to dress like that?"

I grinned and fingered my bear-claw necklace. I almost made up a tale about bein' the adopted son of some Ute chief, but instead I told them about Fort Laramie and travelin' west.

"You a freedman?" one of them asked.

"I—I make my own way," I said slow.

149

They kept starin' at me like I was somethin' special, and they followed us around for a while till they got called for some chores. It made me feel real good.

"They're movin' out of the States in three more days," Mistuh Tolin said excited as we moved toward the outer edge of the camp. "They're just waitin' for a wagon conductor—and, Jason, they've got no teacher among them!"

"Looks like they got no smith neither," I said as I spotted a wagon with axle trouble.

Right soon I was heatin' up a fire and unrollin' my tools. Folks took notice and we was ringed by a crowd. I fixed the axle, some bent plow blades, and split chain links. There was yoke bindin's to be tightened, scythe blades to be straightened. Mistuh Tolin helped out by workin' the hand bellows. It was hard work without a good forge like the one in Fort Laramie, but I managed. The work also helped me take my mind off my worries. We was goin' on like partners, Mistuh Tolin and me, just like he had wanted, and bein' back in the States hadn't changed him at all.

"A sack of beans, a handful of shot, two dollars in gold coin, three eggs and a free lunch—not bad, but you did all the work," Mistuh Tolin said as we started over to the crick to set up camp.

"Mr. Cobb?" a soft voice called to us as we crossed a rough road. "That is your name, isn't it?"

Mistuh Tolin and me looked up at the young miss who had called to him from the seat of an old surrey. There was a round-faced Negro woman sittin' beside her. She nodded to me.

"My father and I would be honored to have you to our house for supper." She flushed. "My name is Samantha Johnston, and my father is Angus Johnston of Maple Lane. He admired the way you helped the travelers today, and wishes to know you better."

Mistuh Tolin tipped his hat and I got tense—wonderin' if her daddy was lookin' to buy slaves like that Fannin man. Mistuh Tolin seemed to be thinkin' the same thing.

"Miss Johnston. I hope you aren't a friend of Percy Fannin's." His voice was cool.

"Percy Fannin! Oh, gracious. I should say not!" Her face got cherry-colored. The Negro woman looked real mad and stared at Mistuh Tolin.

"In that case, we'd be pleased to accept your kind invitation. First, we would like the opportunity to freshen ourselves for the occasion." His voice was soft as fresh corn silk, and he flashed a big smile.

"Certainly. Our house is a short ride out the road toward town, and up the lane lined with maples. There's a meadow and pond in front. You shouldn't miss it. Please come whenever it is convenient for you."

Now, that little miss seemed to get real flustered when she talked, and her face reddened some more. Pieces of dark hair waved from under her bonnet, and I knew Mistuh Tolin was well enjoyin' what he was lookin' on. She no sooner turned that surrey around than Mistuh Tolin lit out for the crick. He was washin' and shavin' before I could blink good.

"I'd say you found that miss right pleasin' to see," I teased while I washed.

"I'd say you were quite right, Jason. I don't know how *you* managed out in the wilds without a soft voice to hear on occasion, but *I* thought it was quite unpleasant."

I smiled and wiggled my toes in my fancy Crow moccasins. "There was some moments," I said. I pulled on my beaded leather shirt and topped it off with my ermine-tail necklace. Since this Johnston man didn't appear to be a threat, I was lookin' forward to bein' entertained by the Negroes of Maple Lane while Mistuh Tolin ate. It would be good to brag on that life I had so enjoyed . . . to talk out those good memories.

151

19

The lane to the Johnston house was nearly a quarter-mile long and big, wide-leafed maples grew up tall on one side even after the path curved toward the house. I couldn't see the end of them trees. The spaces between the trunks was all closed in with trailin' vines and berry brambles so it was almost like a wall. The other side of the lane was open to a broad meadow with a small pond near the center. Anyone at the house could see whoever was on the lane soon as they turned off the main road, so it wasn't at all surprisin' that a man was standin' on the porch when we got there.

"Hello! I'm Angus Johnston." He took long strides off the porch and held our horses while we dismounted. He was a short man, and bald except for a fringe of grayin' hair around the sides and back of his head. "I'm so glad you could make it." He shook Mistuh Tolin's hand and then turned to me, his hand outstretched. "And you are the smith. Your name?"

"Jason." I took his hand timidly and wondered at his openness. His handshake was firm and his palms rough from work.

He smiled, but seemed puzzled. "Welcome to Maple Lane, sirs." His brown eyes was friendly.

No bondsman showed up to lead me off. The man kept

talkin' while Mistuh Tolin and me loosened the cinches of our saddles.

"Yes, with the money decline back East and the idea of free land in the West, the country is crowded with those who think only to further their own station with little regard to the needs or wants of others. It's rewarding to find two people who will be generous with their time and knowledge."

He motioned toward the house. I hung back and looked again for a brown face. I'd no desire to sit out the evenin' with just the horses for company, but Mistuh Tolin grabbed my arm and pulled me along with him.

It was strange to walk into a white man's house through the front door. The livin' room was wide with a huge brick fireplace coverin' one wall. A bookcase was on the other wall, and Mistuh Tolin looked at those books with envy—until Miss Samantha came in.

"Please, have a seat, gentlemen. Is there tea, Samantha?"

"Certainly, Father." Miss Samantha seemed to float from the room with a soft rustle from her plain cotton dress. I expected her to call a servant—probably that woman she was with earlier—but she disappeared around a corner.

Mistuh Tolin sat on a high-backed chair and he frowned at me. I edged onto a padded divan with curved arms.

"Tell me about yourselves. You've just come from the Territory, that's evident. Probably why your generosity hasn't yet been tainted."

"Yes. We've spent the past year in the employ of the American Fur Company at Fort Laramie. Beautiful country there."

"You were trapping?"

"No. I was a store clerk, and Jason was the fort blacksmith. It was quite enjoyable except for the cold and the illness to Jason."

"Oh, really? How did it happen?"

Mistuh Tolin smiled to me to tell it, and my mind thought of the glory way of mountain yarnin'. I held myself back. "I was caught in a blizzard while huntin'," I said quiet.

"Yes, and he had been gored by a buffalo cow. He lost a lot of blood, and part of his finger to frostbite. It was a miracle he got back at all," Mistuh Tolin put in.

"Gracious! That sounds quite harrowing." Miss Samantha was carryin' a tray with cups and a china teapot.

"And how did you happen to come west?" Mistuh Johnston asked.

"Well." Mistuh Tolin took on a bit of color. "Our—our families were killed by Indians and so we just started traveling together. Partners, actually. It was Jason's idea to come west."

"We'd be most interested to know of your travels in the western land. It has always seemed so intriguing to me," Miss Samantha said as she poured the tea.

I must say I was a mite nervous about sittin' and bein' served by a white lady, but Mistuh Tolin didn't seem to even notice. He commenced tellin' all the nice things about the Territory and what the land looked like. I sat there and stared at the little china cup and saucer I was holdin'. The white was like fresh snow, and there was small pink flowers painted on them. I took a sip of tea and when I put the cup back on the saucer it made a ringin' sound like a little bell. I couldn't help but smile, and when I looked up Mr. Johnston was lookin' right at me.

Dinner was a frustratin' affair. I never in my life had sat at a fancy table with white cloth all draped down. Mistuh Johnston sliced off slabs of crisp-roasted pork and served our plates with quartered potatoes. Green beans steamed in a bowl with butter meltin' all over them, and the cornbread must have been made with a lot of milk and eggs. It tasted like cake. It was all quite a bounty after frontier food, and a thick, brown-topped custard was on the sideboard for dessert. I struggled to remember which hand to put the fork in, and how to cut the meat like refined folks. I was sort of relieved when the meal was over.

"Samantha tells me you mentioned the name of Percy Fannin," Mistuh Johnston said after he lit the pipe when we was back in the front room.

"Only to ascertain that you were not friends of his," Mistuh Tolin said quickly.

"That pleases me to hear you say that. Mr. Fannin and I cross paths occasionally, but we certainly are not friends. How is it that you know of him?"

"Well—ah—"

I started talkin', then wished I hadn't when I saw Mistuh Tolin's face. "I was havin' trouble with Mistuh Tolin's horses at the boat dock, and that Fannin stepped in—"

"Actually he wanted to—to hire us for a friend of his," Mistuh Tolin cut in.

Mistuh Johnston's eyebrows shot up. "Hire you?"

"Yes, sir. But he didn't impress me as a very savory character," Mistuh Tolin added quick.

"No. No. He's not."

Mistuh Johnston puffed on his pipe and stared at the floor. Miss Samantha fiddled with a little hanky. I suddenly knew it was time to leave. Mistuh Tolin and me got up at the same time. He said all the proper things and we all went out the door. Mistuh Johnston took up a long spyglass from the shelf on the porch and peered into the darkness toward the main road.

"There are horsemen sitting on the road out there. I just made out their shadows, so ride with care." We pulled into our saddles and I looked out the lane.

"Highwaymen are all over the area," Miss Samantha said.

"Yes. They'll take every piece of property you own." Mistuh Johnston was lookin' right at Mistuh Tolin, but I got his meanin'.

"We haven't much, but what we have is well protected," Mistuh Tolin said strong. He unsheathed his rifle and handed it to me, then took his pistol from his travel bag and tucked it in his pants band. "Thank you for the warning."

We went quiet down the lane, then sat for a moment and studied the road. "What do you make of it?" I asked. Any horsemen that had been there was gone.

"I don't know. Everything's quiet enough."

We started back to the camp area and I couldn't help thinkin' on bein' in that house. I had heard there was white folks that didn't hold to regular ways—Quakers and all—but actually bein' there was strange. "That was such a fine meal," I finally said. "I've never had anything like that before, but—somethin' went wrong near the end. I guess I'm too used to speakin' out."

"No. It was I. I was the one who made the mistake. A very bad mistake."

I looked over at his tense figure and my heart was poundin' fierce. Things was goin' in riddles, and I wanted to know the answers real bad.

At the wagon camp we found a quiet spot for the night. Mistuh Tolin started a small fire, and turned to me. "Jason, there are things we have to talk about," he started.

The answers to the riddles, I thought. His face was drawn and pained, and I think I was holdin' my breath. The sound of horses made us turn, and we looked up on a stocky gray mare and that Percy Fannin. There was two rough-lookin' men ridin' with him. One was tall and thin, and had a mean curl to his lip. They was both carryin' heavy guns and ugly looks.

"Well, Mr. Cobb. Seems you've had yourself quite a day. I didn't realize that your finances were such that you had to hire out your boy for breakfast eggs."

"What we do with our time and money is none of your business at all. Now, would you please leave this camp."

Fannin just chuckled. "Goodness, son. If I didn't know better I'd say that your visit with Angus Johnston was rather damagin' to your Southern character." He frowned suddenly. "You *do* know who that man is, don't you?"

"I take him to be a person of high intellect, excellent moral fiber, and with integrity to the finest degree."

"He's an abolitionist!" Percy Fannin spit into the dirt as though the word had poisoned his tongue. "One of the worst kinds. He not only spouts his unsanctioned beliefs whenever and wherever he goes, but he aids and abets runaways!"

My eyes widened. I had figured that the Johnstons weren't slave-holdin' people, seein' as how Miss Samantha cooked the dinner and served it herself. But an actual abolitionist!

"Now, about this boy of yours. I can make you a fine deal. Since I now know he's a blacksmith, and seemingly quite good for such a young buck, I'm willing to offer you —seven hundred dollars."

"I have asked you to leave this camp!" I could hear the rage startin' in Mistuh Tolin's voice.

"Yes. Well, I can always declare him a runaway and take him from you. Wouldn't you rather get somethin' for him?"

Mistuh Tolin's pistol was out in a second. He had the hammer pulled back and the trigger slid real smooth out to his finger. My stomach muscles tensed and I looked to where the muzzleloader was, 'cause if they was goin' to take me I wasn't goin' to go without a fight.

"Fannin, get out of this camp!"

"How about seven hundred and fifty dollars? That sounds fair. It's a lot of money for a young man who has no land."

"I will not—cannot—sell Jason, and you cannot declare him a runaway because—because he's a free man!"

It was like I'd been struck with a mountain of snow and I tried to keep my mouth from droppin' open.

"Free! That's a slick trick, but I'm sure an Alabama man wouldn't—"

"If slavery is what Alabama stands for, then perhaps you'd better list me on the side with Angus Johnston. Jason Cobb is a free man, and a better friend to me than I deserve! Now get the hell out of this camp!"

Jason Cobb?

157

I heard the horses trampin' in the dirt and Fannin mumblin' somethin' as him and his men rode off. I fiddled with my saddle packs, then looked at Mistuh Tolin. His face was covered with his hands.

"It's true!" I was amazed, yet calm. He turned away. "Mistuh Tolin. I *am* free, ain't I?"

He sniffed loud and marched to his horse. "Yes! You're free, goddamnit. So go on and leave. I don't blame you a bit." He pulled a leather pouch from his possibles bag. "Here!"

"How long?" I took the pouch, still feelin' quiet inside. "Did your pa do it—in his will?"

"No. No. *I* did it. Lord help me. I did it and then I was too much a coward to tell you. Pike Walters was right. You're too good a man to kowtow to anyone—especially Tolin Cobb. I've used you, Jason. I'm sick with the thought of it! I would have never been hired on with American Fur if they hadn't needed a smith. And today— that was the proof of it—no one needed an unskilled, romantic dreamer. They needed a blacksmith. I benefited from your skills, your knowledge, your very existence! Damn!" He held out his hands helplessly and shook his head. "I've bound you to me by deception when you were legally free."

"I *am* free." I looked at the leather pouch and started openin' it. "I have been manumitted." I opened the folded paper.

This hereby certifies on this Wednesday, 15 June 1836, that Jason, personal man of Tolin Cobb, is now a free man of color and that his name to wit be called Jason Cobb. He is granted a certificate of registration and is of the following description: age—19 years; color—black; stature—six feet, ½ inch; he has a burn scar on his left shoulder and upper back. He was born in Bullock County, Alabama, of a slave mother and was manumitted by his master, Tolin Cobb, for the rest of his natural life. He is a blacksmith by trade.

There was a registration number and fancy signatures, and I looked back to the top of the paper. Wednesday, 15 June 1836. That was the day we left Caulborne's. I had been free for over a year.

"Jason Cobb." I said the name aloud. "Why didn't you tell me? You shoulda told me." I wondered if I would have felt any freer if I'd known it was legal.

"I—I started to. Lots of times, but—I was afraid. Then when I found that newspaper, *Freedom's Journal* . . . Oh, Jason, I was sure you'd go North and I—I didn't want to be alone."

I folded the paper and put it back in the pouch. There was a thong on the pouch, and I tied it in a loop and hung the bag around my neck with that ermine-tail necklace I prized. "Jason Cobb." This was what I had hoped for, but I still couldn't believe it. "You've given me your family name."

"What else? I thought of Carpenter, since your father was a carpenter, but Cobb was the only thing that fit. We're all that's left, Jason. You and me—and a graveyard full of markers."

COBB. I had hammered that out at the forge before I left. I curved that iron, formed it with my tools—Jake's tools!— at the forge Jake built, and Jake had been with the Cobbs since before the Revolution. COBB. I had tempered that iron so it would never rust. *Miz Cobb, she want to manumit you,* Mattie had said.

Pictures of back home rolled through my mind. There was Mattie stirrin' up bread in the kitchen, and Horace and Seth cussin' out a team of mules. Skalley tendin' a garden with a baby close to her breast . . .

Louisa! I wanted her to know. *I'm free!*

I saw Jake sittin' in the quarters tellin' stories . . .

"Jake sure would have liked that mountain yarnin'," Mistuh Tolin said, almost like he knew my thoughts.

"And fights with injuns. He had hisself some battles."

I closed my eyes, and there was Judith sewin' clothes for

159

her little ones . . . *Louisa* (carried off by the Creeks . . . a few months pregnant, Mistuh Caulborne had said). And mixed with all the memories was a boy with two shinin' blue eyes, a grin, a friendly laugh.

"There's another thing." Mistuh Tolin's voice was clear and forceful. "You've no reason to call me mister. You never have. Don't say that anymore. Please."

Don't call him mister no more? It truly made him like everybody else—like Ned Saunders and Pike Walters. I had been friends with them, but with not near so much between us as with me and this man I'd known all my life. It was like that name—no, that title, *mister*—had been a chain around my mind. Now it was gone. I sat down next to him wantin' to say how I felt but lackin' the right words. The fire was gettin' low and throwin' flickery shadows all around.

"Remember that time we went out in the orchard and was makin' snares for birds?" I started sayin'.

"Yeah. You were supposed to be mending a fence, and I should have been at the settlement putting in a new seed order, but neither of us did anything until late afternoon —just lying in the orchard talking and weaving grass snares."

"Then you helped me mend the fence real quick so Jake wouldn't whup me, and *you* got whupped 'cause you was late home for supper." We both laughed a bit. I had been twelve then.

I felt no hatred or anger. It was Tolin I'd grown up with, hunted with, cried with. He took care of me when I was sick at the fort; the only person who understood how I felt after I killed a man. We had more than memories. Much more.

I got up and went to my bedroll.

"Are you leaving, Jason?"

"No." I felt so quiet inside it was amazing. I spread out my sleepin' pack. "I don't want to be alone neither."

20

I woke up early the next mornin' with the sound of creakin' wagons and a lot of noise in my head. It was barely dawn, but kids was runnin' around and dogs barkin'. The twenty wagons at the camp was movin' out. Tolin pulled on his boots real quick and grabbed his new hat. When I caught up with him he was already at the lead wagon that was roundin' the bend.

"Where are you going? Do you have a wagon conductor?" he called.

"I be him," a gravelly voice said. It was the thick, round-stomached man who had ridden into our camp with Percy Fannin the night before. He was carryin' a coiled whip.

"The train wasn't to leave until Friday."

"We're leavin' today—down the Texas Road. Settlin' some folks in along the Arkansas."

"That's Indian Territory."

"They'll make room if they hafta," the man snorted. "Mr. Fannin said to move today and not to take you in. Says your boy there is a runaway."

"He's not my *boy!*"

"Don't want ya if'n he's a runaway."

"He's a freedman, and a blacksmith. These folks need a blacksmith."

"Free, huh?" Tobacco juice hit the dust by Tolin's feet.

"Got no room for ya." The man rode away.

Tolin raised his fist. "And we've no need for you!" he shouted. "That stinkin' cracker. They were more than happy to give us pay for your work yesterday when they thought you were a bondsman. Damn! Jason, this is ridiculous!"

I watched him fume and knew he didn't realize what a special day this was for me. The first real day of freedom. The sun was peachin' up the sky and there was meadowlarks and mockingbirds singin' sweet and clear. The smell of cookin' fires still hung in the air, and it was mornin' cool that fooled you on how blisterin' hot the day was goin' to be. What a mornin'!

"We can see if there's another train due to form up."

"It's pretty late in the season for people to start long treks west." We walked to our camp. "That Percy Fannin surely does get around. What right does he have to keep us off a train?"

"Why should he even care what we do?"

"I don't know. I don't want to know." I felt Tolin lookin' at me while we walked. "You don't have to stay with me, Jason."

"I know."

He looked worried. "You aren't going to change, are you? From the way you were at Fort Laramie? I mean, hell! —it was good out there with us. Like partners, you know?"

"That's what you told Mr. Johnston, that we were partners. Say! Why don't we ride out to Johnstons'? I'll bet he'd know of places that would need a teacher and a smith."

"The Johnstons! I couldn't face them. It's enough I have to look you in the eye after what I've done. I've probably fouled up your whole life."

I wondered what I would have done last June if I'd known I was free. Started North? Ended up workin' on some river crew and gettin' kicked around like those men I'd seen in Memphis? "This last year has been fine for me," I said as I set the coffee to boil.

162

"You could have gone with Pike and Bornston. I could *feel* you wanting to go."

"I didn't need freedom papers to go with them." I watched him pull the cups out of the pack. "There ain't no slaves in the Territory. No slave laws, neither. If I'd really wanted to go I could have left and there was nothin' you could have done about it."

He looked over at me and I could see his eyes change from worry to calm as he understood what I meant.

"You know," I went on. "Jake told me once that I had to know you like I knew myself. I guess I do and . . . well, that's why I came back to the States. I couldn't ride off and—"

"And leave things unsaid?"

I nodded, feelin' near to tears.

"We *are* friends, aren't we, Jason?"

"We're friends—Tolin."

He looked grim and gripped the cups tightly. "God *damn* this stupid world that we had to go through all this hell to know it!"

Everything was settled between us. We both knew it, and it was easy to accept once it was said out. We fixed ourselves a breakfast of those eggs we had got the day before, and some dried meat left over from our time in the Territory. There was plenty of coffee and we was feelin' full.

"I still think we should go to the Johnstons'," I stated strong. "I'd like to take another look at a real live abolitionist, and—well, I saw the way you was eyein' Miss Samantha. Why should you give it up?"

"You're crazy! That girl wouldn't want me to rest her feet on. They think I'm a slaveholding man, Jason, and that goes against everything they believe in."

"But you ain't no slaveholder! We'll ride out and talk. I won't call you *mistuh* no more. I'll remember my last name. Freed folks always got two names."

"And another thing. Don't keep referring to stuff as my things. Half of everything in the camp is yours, including

163

that crazy black horse, Dancer, and the muzzleloader."

I looked up in surprise. I had expected rights to things I'd got in the Territory, but nothing more.

"I decided this from the very beginning." He reached around to his blanket and tossed me my belt. I caught it and thumb-shined the handle of my Green River knife. "So, here, carry your own money, too."

"Money?"

"Of course! Your pay from American Fur. It's all in company notes and coin, so it's sound. After expenses there's one hundred and thirty dollars there."

"You said there was only sixty dollars left!"

"I said *I* had sixty dollars. You didn't spend all your money on fancy clothes every chance you got."

"I didn't know I had any to spend."

He looked at me sharp—fearful. I grinned at him and we both laughed.

"I feel funny with all this money and you havin' so little," I admitted.

"I wanted it to be more—some of the bank money was yours and, hell, the company was paying you more than me to begin with. Like I said, they wouldn't have put me on at all had I been by myself." He flopped on the dusty grass.

I wondered how it would have been had *I* been alone. Would they have hired a free black man? Would I have gotten fair treatment at the fort without Tolin settin' the standards?

I held the purse and felt the paper crinkle as I squeezed it. "One hundred and thirty dollars. *Whew!* What do I do with it? I mean—well, I could get robbed!"

Tolin started laughin' at me and I got mad at myself for actin' so dumb. I turned away from him and thought of places I could carry the purse. I finally settled on my pants. I hardly ever took them off. Mountain-man pants didn't come with no pockets, so I took my old, too small, homespun britches out of my duffle and cut a hunk out of the leg with my knife.

"What are you doing?" Tolin finally asked when I was gettin' a needle and sinew thread out of my bag.

"Makin' a place for this money. You don't expect me to carry all that out in the breeze for folks to get a whiff of, do you?"

"Just put it in your possibles bag. That's where I've been carrying it."

"Nope. I'm takin' no chances, thank you!" I sat myself off near a thicket so I couldn't be seen from the road, and sewed the pocket in my pants. I didn't put it on the outside, neither. I sewed it inside so I could feel that rough material against my leg. Then I took the purse, pulled out the two half-eagle coins, and stuck the notes in the pocket.

"There!" I tied up my pants. "Now I feel better." I put the half-eagles in the pouch around my neck with my freedom paper.

"Goodness, Jason. You've got me wondering if I might be too careless with my money."

"I'll not carry my money anyplace but right with me. It's too easy to lose a possibles sack, or have it stole. But there ain't too many folks that want leather pants that been wore a whole year."

Tolin started laughin'. "Now you're going to have to take your britches off when you bathe."

"Sure enough, but since that doesn't happen too often I'll worry about that later." I grinned and put my hand out to help him stand.

"All right, my friend. Where are we off to? I'm not going back to the Johnstons'!" Tolin said as he started breakin' camp.

"Then it's Independence! That name has a good sound to it."

Independence was laid out all neat with fences around the buildings. Main Street was a real wide, beat-down track and there was covered wagons with folks comin' through to pick up supplies. There was carriages, and a big coach that took passengers from that town to St. Louis. Two dogs snapped at the wheels as it rolled along. The courthouse was a big affair on that street with grassy slopes rollin' up to the front of it and trees standin' tall and shady. On the other side of the broad street was buildings and stores and offices for important folks. We saw a sign by one door: "P. Fannin, Slave Trader. Negroes Bought and Sold." I got a real creepy feelin', and me and Tolin rode way over on the other side of the street.

One thing Independence didn't need was another black-smith. They had one shop that didn't sell nothin' but signs and fence gates that had all kinds of loops and fancy doin's on them. The man wrought out people's names in frilly script writin'. It was fine work, and I walked through his things and studied them real close.

There was a farrier at the livery stable, and there was this other man—a huge, black-haired man with a thick neck and shoulders like an ox. He didn't wear no shirt, and had on a big leather apron to protect his hairy chest. I knew right off there was no way I could work as a smith in Independence while this man was around.

The minute I stepped off Dancer he grumbled somethin' that was full of cussin'. What it amounted to was *No Gawkers*! There was a sign up by the forge, too: "All work to be paid for in cash." That was probably why my services had been needed by the wagon train.

Tolin had gone in some of the stores, and when he rode up to me, he had a real sour look on his face. We went off down a little street, and he told me what had happened.

"Everything around here is *very* established," he said. "I even talked to a preacher in the dry goods store and asked about teaching at a school or church. First thing he said is, 'You aren't from Missouri.' Then he asked what denomination I was, and didn't seem too happy when I said Episcopal. And *then* he asked me where I went to school—"

A youngster came flyin' into the street right in front of our horses. We whoaed up quick.

"Don't make no difference whether they send the kids in here, you tell your folks that!" the shopkeeper was yellin'. "I'm not sellin' supplies to no Mormons—big or small!"

Tolin had jumped down from Rogue and was helpin' the boy to his feet. "We nearly trampled him! Why did you push him like that?"

"You friends of his? Well, he don't need to be around here. Mormons aren't supposed to be comin' through Independence anyway!"

"He can go anyplace he wishes!" Tolin declared. "And how can they leave the area if you aren't going to sell them supplies for travel? Do you expect them to eat grass?"

"Governor Boggs set up a whole damn county for them to the north. They can just get on up there to Far West with their own kind!" The man huffed back into the store.

"Are you all right?" Tolin asked the boy. He stared at Tolin with suspicious eyes and then ran off. "That's a hell of a thing! Throwing people out of stores; can't find a job unless you're Missouri-born; slave traders can even hang out their shingles! I think this town is misnamed!"

"You very well may be right," a voice said.

Tolin swung around, and I twisted in the saddle to look over my shoulder. It was Mr. Johnston.

"I see Independence hasn't been treating you kindly," he said.

Tolin seemed dumbstruck, and he reddened a bit as he looked at the man.

I'm a free man, I thought with a smile. "It don't seem that we fit in too well here," I said quickly. "The blacksmithin' is hammered up tight, sure enough, and, uh, Tolin, he couldn't find no job neither." I suddenly figured this might be the time to get everything cleared up, so I talked on. "We even had trouble at the camp last night."

"I'm sure Mr. Johnston doesn't want to hear our problems," Tolin mumbled.

"Of course he would. He said himself he didn't like that Fannin man. I think he'd be real interested to know how

Percy Fannin came out and tried to buy me off you last night. Why, I don't even think he believed it when, uh, Tolin told him I was a freedman. He said somethin' about you, Mr. Johnston, messin' up Tolin's Southern thinkin', but Tolin here has been set in his ways long before we ever got to Missouri." I stopped and let my words sink in.

Mr. Johnston's eyebrows bounced up and down a few times and he got a slight smile.

It seemed the power of words was full in me and I didn't know how to stop. "I suspect you weren't too sure about my status either," I started again.

"Jason!" Tolin was gettin' alarmed.

"You see, we don't always know how to play it: master and slave, or just good friends. It depends on who we're with—and just comin' back from the Territory the idea of bein' in a slave state had us a mite confused."

There was silence where we was. I could hear the sounds of horses from the other street, and even some murmured voices from the store we was in front of. Mr. Johnston mounted his horse and sat there lookin' at us with a half smile on his face. Tolin got up on Rogue. His face was pale even under his tan.

Mr. Johnston started chucklin'. "Have you two young men seen quite enough of Independence?"

I nodded.

"The concept will always be strong with us," Tolin blurted out.

Mr. Johnston laughed in a good way and pulled a watch from his vest pocket. "It is nearly noon. I would be pleased if you would accompany me home for dinner."

"Sir?" Tolin was surprised.∙

"Dinner, lad. I certainly hope that the bad experiences of the past day haven't deadened your appetite. Come along. We can talk more about the concept of independence, and perhaps arrange some employment for your young bodies." He turned his horse back toward Main

---

Street, and it was evident he expected us to be comin' with him.

I grinned at Tolin and turned Dancer to follow. I was eager to know more about this man and his "business." The thought was fascinatin'.

"Jason!" Tolin said with an anxious whisper.

"Don't say nothin'," I said quickly. "Just you start thinkin' on how glad Miss Samantha will be to see you again. Come on."

I took the lead and rode off after Mr. Johnston, trailin' *my* mule and *my* dun horse. Mistuh Tolin—that is, Tolin—he came along, too.

21

Conversation on the way to Maple Lane was constant. Mr. Johnston rode between Tolin and me and talked while we was ridin'. Actually, he asked questions.

"So, Jason, the freedman," he began. "Your last name wouldn't be Smith, by some chance, since that's your trade?"

"No, sir. Seems Tolin and me share a common last name. Makes the friendship closer."

"Cobb. Yes," he mused. "I'm a blunt man, Messrs. Cobb, and that is one reason I appreciated your declarations back there, Jason. I'll continue the trend with another question. Have you always been friends, or were you at one time master and slave?"

I was a bit startled, but Tolin didn't hesitate at all. "Mr. Johnston, we have always been friends even though we were at one time master and slave. I have no better friend in the world than Jason. He saved my life when we were young, and his companionship has been a continued blessing to me through the years."

I felt a sight embarrassed havin' Tolin talk like that, but he was right. We had always been friends. I was glad I could finally think that without feelin' guilty.

"Another question," Mr. Johnston went on. "Did Mr. Fannin appear distressed at not being able to buy Jason?"

"He certainly did! He expected that my apparent poverty would make me eager for his tainted money, and he was so angry he even left word that the wagon train wasn't to take us in."

"He's a dangerous man. He counts on the travelers through here needing extra cash, and so to be willing to sell their 'property' as he puts it. He has a group of thugs who have even stolen oxen teams from persons who had young bondsmen. Of course, they could buy new teams only after selling their slaves to Fannin. The livery man is in his employ, and I think the blacksmith in town has his sympathies with Fannin."

I could believe that!

"Mr. Johnston, that Fannin said you're an abolitionist," I said easy.

He looked amused. "Oh, ho! I *am* an abolitionist. That doesn't seem to bother you, Tolin."

"Certainly not, Mr. Johnston. As my mother used to say, 'Every man has property to his own person; this nobody has a right to but himself.' "

That sounded like Miz Nancy's talkin'.

"It's a quote of John Locke, but it was one of her favorites," Tolin continued. "That's why I freed Jason as soon —as soon as I was out from under my father's rules."

"Hmm. You appear to have a good education," Mr. Johnston observed. "And you, Jason, are quite eloquent."

"The Cobbs have a history of excellent speakers, and Jason has been reading for a number of years." Tolin smiled at me proudly.

"Reading! Excellent! Yes, excellent!"

Maple Lane looked a bit different in the day than it did in the late afternoon shadows. I saw things that wasn't visible before. Behind the house a ways was three small cabins, and then there was fields of corn and beans. A frame house sat in a little valley near some cottonwoods, and there was lots of garden space and chicken coops. On the far side of the main house was a large barn with a stable attached. I heard a donkey bray, but I didn't see one.

When we got to the house there was a Negro man standin' on the porch. He was stocky, and he carried himself real straight. I could tell just by lookin' at him he was free, but then it wouldn't be no different at Maple Lane.

"It's you, Angus," he said to Mr. Johnston. "I wasn't sure when I saw these young men with you. There's no trouble?"

"No, Lucien. Everything's fine. I found my young friends in Independence feeling very perplexed, so I brought them home," he said as we dismounted. "Lucien. These are Messrs. Tolin and Jason Cobb. Gentlemen, Mr. Evans."

Mister Jason Cobb!

"Mr. Evans." Tolin offered his hand.

Then I shook Mr. Evans's hand, too. I could see right off that we wasn't to treat him no different than we did Mr. Johnston.

"Is Samantha about?" Mr. Johnston asked.

"She's gone visiting, I believe."

"Ah, yes. Well, I'll leave her a note and then show you two around Maple Lane. Lucien, can you come with us? Miss Rose and Cleveland can watch things here."

Mr. Evans did join us, and him and Mr. Johnston told us about a lot of things. Mr. Johnston had lived in Missouri since 1806, and the land had been his father's. His father had been one of the folks against makin' Missouri a slave state in what was called the Missouri Compromise way back when the territory first came into bein'. Mr. Johnston had continued his father's fight against slavery. He even backed the Mormons' right to stay in Independence when the rest of the citizens was runnin' them out back in '33.

"I just believe in the Constitution," he explained. "When it says 'liberty and justice for all,' it should mean just that!"

"And where do you live, Mr. Evans?" Tolin asked.

"We live at Maple Lane. My wife, Henrietta, keeps us real well in the house by the cottonwood grove."

"And a beautiful family he has, too. Dorothy is sixteen now, just three years younger than my Samantha, and off in Illinois at a Quaker school," Mr. Johnston said. "And then there are his boys, Ben and Charles. How old are they now, Lucien? Seems they do the work of men; I have trouble remembering."

"Ben is nine, and Charles is fourteen."

My curiosity wouldn't rest. "How come you to settle here?" I was wonderin' if maybe Mr. Johnston and Mr. Evans was one time master and slave.

"I was slaved in Louisiana. I worked for my freedom and came up here. Angus gave me a job, him and his missus, and later I bought Henrietta free from the town magistrate where we used to live. That was the year Mrs. Johnston passed on, bless her soul, and Angus asked us to stay on here and take part in the farming."

"Lucien makes it sound so simple, but I would have been lost without him. He is well versed in farming techniques, and for the first time this land began clearing a profit. And then with my dear Clair gone, and little Samantha to raise . . ."

"Now, Miss Rose and her boys got here just two years ago." Mr. Evans changed the subject quick. "You haven't met Titus and Cleveland yet. They are much about your ages, I suspect. The last of fourteen children old Lula had."

"Yes. Miss Rose, bless her, is such a pure soul. We don't call her Lula—you two remember that—it's always Miss Rose. That was the name of her old Kentucky mistress who freed them in her will. The Lord's will, Miss Rose says."

Mr. Evans started chucklin'. "There are times when she gets the feeling that she can talk on like a preacher. I think she could recite the entire Bible from memory, but mostly she does work that doesn't require much of being up and about. It was her who made that donkey sound when you rode up. Do you remember?"

Tolin said yes, and I remembered, too. "That was a signal, wasn't it?" Mr. Evans looked at me with a slight smile.

"Mr. Fannin told us you helped runaways here."

"Fannin!"

"Yes. It seems he had his eye on Jason," Mr. Johnston said.

"Are you part of the underground railroad?" Tolin asked.

The two men was quiet for a long spell—probably tryin' to figure if we was to be trusted or not.

"Yes, lads," Mr. Evans finally said. "Maple Lane is a known station for fugitives. We give them food and clothing. Help out as much as possible."

"If we can guarantee passage to the freedom lands of Illinois for the twenty or thirty people a year who come this way we feel very content," Mr. Johnston said.

"Why do you send them up to Illinois?" I asked. "Why not right across the river into the Territory?"

"Well, Jason, the Territory isn't all that stable, and most of the people who come through here haven't enough skills to carve out a living on their own. They need a place where there will be jobs, and adequate shelter. And there are people right now in Washington who are attempting to have the entire Missouri Territory designated as slave land."

"Not only that," Mr. Evans added. "Most of the land in the Territory has been settled by slaveholding people except for way north across the Rockies. The Arkansas valley is filled with slave-labor plantations and farms, and of course Texas, and the new state Arkansas, are already slaved. Even Indian Territory."

"Yes, many of the tribes in Indian Territory are slaveholders. Particularly the Choctaw and Cherokee."

I noticed that Tolin didn't say much durin' all this talk and information, but he'd look at me sometimes and I'd see the same fire in his eyes that he had that mornin' after we admitted we was friends.

We walked a good mile around the farm part of Maple Lane. Mr. Johnston showed us the grain storage, the smokehouse, and the gristmill as well as pointin' out the corn and oats, and the pasture of sheep. The way the crick and tree line ran, it was nearly impossible to come up onto the main livin' area of the farm without bein' seen, or without makin' a lot of racket. I knew there must have been hidin' places aplenty in the orchards or in the different maple groves that was along the field lines. Mr. Johnston didn't point out nothin' like that, and I didn't blame him none. That was valuable information, and he really didn't know us that well.

When we got back to the barn I saw that our horses had been cared for and our packs put on the porch of one of the cabins. Mr. Evans left us and went toward his house just as Miss Samantha stepped out on the back steps of the big house. I must say she looked powerful pretty standin' there in a pale print dress and her dark hair braided and twisted in two rolls at the sides of her head. Now it wasn't for me to be seein' her in that way—with her bein'a white woman and all—but I couldn't help knowin' what Tolin was feelin' then. I wished I could see a dark face smilin' at me like that.

"I have some dinner prepared," Miss Samantha said. "You must be famished from walking so."

She was right about that, and we washed at the pump and went inside. Again, I was sittin' at a table and the cloth rumpled all down on my legs when I pulled my chair in. The big bowl in the center was filled with steamin' chicken and soft dumplin's, with gravy that was pure pleasure to taste. This kind of meal didn't bother me none at all, 'cause it was all served in big bowls. I didn't have to worry about which hand to put the knife in or none of that stuff.

Miss Samantha didn't seem surprised that her daddy had brought us home, and she talked open and friendly just like he did. She did have trouble lookin' at Tolin without a flushed cheek.

"What part of the South are you from, Tolin?" Mr. Johnston asked as we ate.

"Alabama, sir."

"Oh! Then you'd know a lot about the Choctaws we were speaking of outside."

"Actually more about the Creeks," Tolin said. "We lived in the eastern part of the state."

"That entire removal situation is quite unfortunate," Miss Samantha said. "Those people—slaveholders or not—were forced to give up everything and move out to desolate land. They tried so hard to keep what they had."

"They shed a lot of innocent blood doing it, too," I said bitterly.

"Yes. The Seminoles and their sympathizers," Mr. Johnston said. "I read where the Chickasaws are finally being removed to the Territory, and the Cherokees have nearly exhausted their legal fight in the courts. The rest of that tribe will soon be moved, too. I suppose they realized they had to relinquish their rights to the land."

"Either that or be slaughtered by the unprincipled soldiers of the area. I'll never forget what happened at that one plantation." Miss Samanatha shook her head sadly.

"Yes. We had a woman come through here this spring. She had been on an Alabama plantation when the Creeks, I think it was, raided in '36. The way she explained it, the Creeks were running from the soldiers and had come to their place for horses—I guess they had a lot of them there—and the planter fired on them. She said all of the Negroes there took up pitchforks and whatever they could, to defend against the Creeks, and it was then the soldiers came."

"Just horrible! They assumed the Negroes were rebelling to join the Indians. They fired on them, and killed nearly all of them, and even set fire to the house and canebrake because they believed more had taken refuge there."

"It would have been a total slaughter if the commanding officer hadn't ridden in and stopped them. This woman—what was her name?—she escaped by hiding with her children in a graveyard. She and another woman."

"Judith. That was the name."

By then Tolin and me had stopped eatin'. We was starin'

at each other as they talked—hurtin' from the words.

"She was separated from her children when they were sold to a slave trader a few weeks—" Mr. Johnston's voice stopped sharp. "Good Lord! Don't tell me you knew the people!"

Seemed like hours passed before I got voice enough to say somethin'. "It was the Cobb place. It was our home you're tellin' about." Tolin got up from his chair and walked into the front room. "We had been in Florida—the Seminole War. When we got back we figured the Creeks had done it all. Mr. Caulborne must not have had the heart to tell us." Miss Samantha got up and followed Tolin. "Judith got away, and Mattie . . ."

"Jason, if I had known!" Mr. Johnston slumped back in his chair. "I assumed you two had been west longer than a year. I—"

"Mr. Johnston, did Judith make mention of a girl—a girl who was carried off by the Creeks? Louisa?" *Louisa!*

"Your sister?"

"No, sir. She was my wife—not with a preacher and all, but my woman just the same. She was carryin' my child."

Mr. Johnston sighed heavy and shook his head. "No. I don't recall the name, but you might talk with Lucien and Henrietta. Judith stayed with them for the six days she was here."

"Thank you, sir." I excused myself and went to the door of the livin' room. Miss Samantha and Tolin was sittin' on the divan and talkin' quiet. I saw his hands knot into fists. She patted them. I took up my hat and went out through the back door.

Mr. Evans was sittin' with his family at dinner when I knocked at the side door. "Jason! Come in." He opened the door for me. "This here's my wife, Henrietta." It was the woman who had been with Miss Samantha in the surrey. I took off my hat and stood for a minute. I felt Mr. Evans puzzlin' over my quietness.

"I've—I've come for some knowledge, Mr. Evans. Mr.

Johnston tells me a woman named Judith stayed with you this spring."

"That's right. Was she kin of yours?"

"In a way. He said she told about a plantation gettin' burned by soldiers in Alabama, do you recall that?"

"Oh, yes. It was a terrible thing!" Mrs. Evans grieved. "Sit down. Did you know those people?"

"It was our home, ma'am. Tolin's and mine. We come back from Florida and it was all burned. Everyone gone." I drew in a deep breath and tried to keep my voice strong.

"Bless you, child. Dear Lord! Judith said you all was close folks. Dear Lord."

"In the tellin' did she say anythin' about a girl—she'd only be sixteen now. Louisa?"

"She did say that name. I recall it," Mr. Evans said as he set to thinkin' on it. His two boys was starin' at me, not eatin'.

"There was markers for near everyone in the graveyard. Judith and Mattie, and some of their younguns got sold off, we know, but Louisa . . ." I was trembly inside from wantin' them to know somethin' definite.

"She was carried off by the Indians. Yes, that was it. A young girl, Judith said, who was running up to the graveyard to hide. She was running, and the Indians were riding to get away in the trees, and the soldiers were coming behind and firing."

"Yes. I remember, too," Mrs. Evans said. "This Indian grabbed her up and carried her off on horseback. Judith said the girl would have been killed for sure if it wasn't for that. They never saw her again. Mercy, what a terrible thing."

I blinked away the comin' tears. I had to know I was hearin' right. "She was saved by the Indians?"

"That's the way of it. A miracle, it seems."

She was saved by the Indians! It sounded strange, when I had been hatin' them all this time for what had happened. But Louisa was alive! Louisa! Saved by the Creeks.

22

Tolin looked pretty bad when I saw him later on, and I figured I must have been a sight, too. We walked together to the cabin where our things had been put, and stood on the little porch lookin' off at nothin' for a while before we hoisted our gear and went inside.

The cabin was real nice. Nothin' at all like slave quarters. There was two rooms: one in front with a hearth and table and three chairs; and another behind that with two beds, a dresser, and a chair. There was curtains at the windows and a rug on the floor in each room.

"Mr. Johnston told me you asked about . . . about Louisa," Tolin said as he put his duffle on a bed. I nodded. "You really loved that girl, didn't you?"

"She was my woman," I said quietly.

"Louisa was so young—all sparkles. I knew about the baby, but it's hard to think of her as a woman."

"Well, she was, and . . ." I sat on the other bed and stared at my hands. Louisa was like a dream—a private part of me I'd never talked about with Tolin. "And when you settle with a woman, you stay with her. Jake taught me that. Like him and Bitty. It was that way at the Cobb place."

"I remember. Mattie and Horace. Seth—he loved Margaret so much. Your mama and the carpenter. She didn't take up with another man after he was sold away from the area."

"Skalley and Kusa, too. It was just that way," I added.

"Did the Evanses know anything? Had Judith told them more?"

"Louisa was carried off by the Creeks, just like Mr. Caulborne said, but it was to save her from gettin' killed by the soldiers."

Tolin's fists slammed onto the bed. "It's all so God-awful horrible! Soldiers! And no one even told us the truth! I was hating the wrong people!"

"Would you have wanted to know the truth? Could you have stood hearin' the way it really was? I couldn't. I *know* I couldn't. I would have been hatin', but it would have been —it would have been different." I didn't say what I was thinkin', that I would have started hatin' white folks— maybe even Tolin; that I would have run off and hated, and never been like I turned out to be. Right then I liked myself pretty well, and I couldn't have dreamed of bein' different.

"I'll not go back, Jason. Not ever! No matter how nice Mr. Caulborne was to give me the option to rebuy. I thought that when I sold the land, but now I can't. I've already talked to Mr. Johnston about it. I'm joining him in his fight against slavery. It's got to end, Jason!"

I was listenin' to him, but I was thinkin', too. "She's still alive somewheres," I said quietly.

"Louisa?"

"Yes. I had always hoped it, but now it seems for sure. She wasn't found dead; there was no word of her bein' captured."

"That's not certain, Jason. The Creeks would have sold her off. Soldiers could have taken her." He must have seen the fear on my face. "Jason, that's part of the life we lost. Don't think on it. You'll drive yourself crazy!"

I nodded and sighed. I knew he was right. A notion of goin' back to Alabama and searchin' for her started in my mind, but was drowned in fear of travelin' deep into slave country. My chest got tight, and I closed my eyes against the stingin' tears. *Stop thinkin' on it!*

180

"Did Mr. Johnston say what kind of work he might have?" I asked as I started unpackin' my things.

"Well, there's always plenty of farm work. A real farm, finally. And I'll be helping with the smuggling of Negroes. He can't pay much, but I'd work at it for free if I had to." He took a deep breath. "I'm hoping you'll stay, too, Jason. It's not like we talked about with a blacksmith shop and my teaching, but . . ."

It was strange thinkin' that I didn't have to stay just 'cause he did. I was a free man. Legally. I could make my own choices, go my own way . . .

I chose to stay. I think that was mostly 'cause it was the easy thing to do. It was pleasant at Maple Lane. Mr. Johnston paid us ten dollars a month, plus our food and the cabin. There was a small bit of iron work to be done—maybe a half-day's worth—and there was only eight draft animals and horses to care for. Charles and Titus worked them well, so I was back to field work.

There was two kinds of livin' we did at Maple Lane. When there was no traffic—that is, no fugitives to hide—the place was a regular farm with work from dawn to dusk and an occasional evenin' social with all of us together sharin' a meal and talkin'. Mr. Evans would stroke out some tunes on the fiddle he played so well, and we'd all sing. Miss Rose would start us out with hymns. I got along real well with the Roses, especially Titus, who loved horses as much as me. We'd talk and joke a lot, and I took to eatin' most meals at Miss Rose's little house.

One time not long after we was there Cleveland introduced me to some other Negro families in the area. Those folks, nice as they was, was settlement folks—as Ned Saunders would say—and they was glad to be that. They took no interest or carin' in the frontier, and thought me a mite strange for likin' it so. After a few meetin's I got tired of bein' stared at or giggled over, and I didn't go visitin' at all.

"I knew you wouldn't last long with them," Titus said one evenin'. He didn't go out much neither, and so we took

181

to spendin' the evenin's at the stable or ridin' in the woods.

Of course, visitin' was out of the question when our other life of slave runnin' was on. Even the Negro families was left out of that, 'cause—surprisin' as it seemed—some free Negroes couldn't be trusted not to give us away.

Tolin was happier than I'd ever seen him. He was finally on the kind of farm he'd always dreamed of, and got a chance to teach, too. Myself, I was a bit edgy most times we was runnin' slaves, but I did enjoy seein' the folks and knowin' we was bein' of some help to them.

My readin' was gettin' better and I was learnin' script writin' from Mr. Evans, too. But with field work and smugglin' work I never got time to heat up iron and work much at the forge.

Tolin enjoyed bein' a farmer and he got out his old twill britches for workin'. He saved his newer clothes and fine ridin' boots for Sundays when he would escort Miss Samantha to church. Mr. Johnston would go, too, but I don't know that Tolin noticed he was around. I stayed in my leather most of the time, although I did make a trip into town with Titus one afternoon and bought some cotton pants and a few new shirts.

"Well, look at you," Tolin commented that evenin'. "You actually bought some settlement clothes."

"Yep. They've got a pocket already made, too, so I don't have to sew one for my money," I joked.

"What's this? Work boots." Tolin tapped my new shoes with his toe.

"Umm. My moccasins are wearin' a mite thin, so I figured these would do till I got them resoled." I had actually been thinkin' on how I should head out to to the Territory and get myself some more.

"Well, I never thought I'd see you out of buckskins."

"And I never thought I'd see you in them again," I said as he slid into his fringed shirt.

"Miss Samantha sorta likes the way I look in rustic clothes." He pinched his face up to hide the smile that was always there when he started talkin' about Miss Samantha.

"That lady's got a lot of power with you, Tolin. Supposin' she says she likes you wearin' a skunk-skin hat?"

He threw a towel at me and started talkin' somethin' about common dedication to a cause. I just laughed and went over to the Roses.

One day not long after my trip to town I heard chickens squawkin' and the sound of horses' hooves ridin' fast. It was early August and I was repairin' a twiner at the barn. Tolin was at our cabin, and other than Titus and us there wasn't no other menfolks at the farm. There was no traffic at all. By the time I got to the stable door there was a rush of dust through the garden, and I saw six horsemen up by the back of the house. I recognized Fannin's gray mare and got cold to my toes.

"Check under those cabins! Break open that toolshed, too," Fannin was orderin'.

I took up a scythe—the handiest weapon I could find— and walked over from the barn just as two of his roughnecks dismounted and started tearin' at the base of Miss Rose's house. Miss Rose stopped her needlework and started rockin' in her chair real calm. Tolin stepped onto the porch of our cabin about the time I got there. His rifle made a terrible crack as it splintered the wooden slat one man was pullin' on. The man drew back his fist and sucked where the wood had spiked into his skin.

"I've seen more than enough of you, Mr. Fannin," Tolin said real harsh. He reloaded. "What do you want here?"

"Well, well. I wondered what had become of you." Fannin grinned and his eyes rested on me. I hefted the scythe a bit and he looked back to Tolin. "I'm lookin' for runaways."

"Runaways! Have you seen any stray horses, Jason?" Tolin asked with a smile.

"No. Can't say that I have, but I know where there's a few jackasses," I ventured.

Fannin's mouth got hard. The corners turned down and his eyes was icy. "I plan to search this place, and Percy Fannin won't be denied!" He nodded to his man to continue workin' on the slats, and Tolin fired another shot.

That thin man of Fannin's reached for a pistol in his belt and I heard a huge roar of a gun. The horses started buckin' and pitchin', and I saw why. Miss Samantha was standin' at the corner of the house holdin' a big shotgun. She had fired it into the dirt right in the center of where Fannin's horsemen was standin'.

"We won't ask you again to leave," she said in a steady voice. "You are trespassing, you know. And then there's the fact of my honor being jeopardized."

Tolin had reloaded and he was sightin' right down on Fannin's fancy vest pocket. Fannin started an evil chuckle. "Come on, boys. We'll get what we want eventually."

" 'He that walks upright walks surely; but he that perverts his ways shall be known,' " Miss Rose called as they rode off.

"*Phew!* Does that happen often?" Tolin asked. Miss Rose went back to her needlepoint. We walked over to Miss Samantha.

"It's been a while since he's tried anything," Miss Samantha said. Her arms drooped with the weight of the shotgun. "He used to bring the constable out with him, but they were never able to find anyone, so the constable stopped coming."

I suddenly realized how Miss Samantha had come out of the house, and Tolin must have seen it, too. We stopped right where we was. It was obvious she had been restin'. Her high-collared dress was open at the throat, exposin' a lot of pale skin, and her dark hair was loose and all long over her shoulders and bodice. Her toes—kinda pink— rested in the grass under her dress hem. I turned away and studied the clapboard on the house, but Tolin moved closer.

Mrs. Evans called up the hill from her house. "All in order up there?"

"Yes, Mrs. Evans. Thank you!" Miss Samantha called back. "That's a handsome rifle you have," she said to Tolin. "I'm quite glad you were here. Mr. Fannin does frighten me terribly."

"I would have never guessed it. How did they get here without warning? That worries me."

"Oh, dear!" she exclaimed, and I figured she remembered her appearance. "Titus might be hurt. They didn't come by the lane, so they passed him at the gristmill!"

We found Titus gagged and trussed up from a buildin' beam like a carcass ready for quarterin'. He wasn't hurt none, 'cept for his pride. The whole affair seemed commonplace to Maple Lane folks, but I didn't like it none at all, and I started thinkin' of the mountains and those rollin' prairies along the Platte. I even missed the wind.

In mid-September Titus and me was cuttin' dried corn out of the fields when Tolin came out and stood beside me lookin' real serious. "Mr. Johnston has word that there will be two Negro men hiding out near Carthage, and they'll need help getting through to their next station." I stopped my work and waited for him to say more. "He wants me to go down to get them past the slavers in Barton County and to their next station. He said that with my Southern accent and all, I could pass them off as my bondsmen and bring them through."

"What happened to the regular conductors down there?"

"One man is in custody for supposed thievery to keep his station closed. Another is ill." He looked at me real steady. "I want you to go with me."

"Me? I don't know about that."

"It would be better, because you don't sound like you're from Missouri either. Besides, when I'm traveling back with three men and the vigilantes are only looking for two, we'd get through more easily."

My heart was poundin'. It all sounded simple as he told me the plans, but I didn't like the idea of headin' into trouble. I swallowed hard and said all right. I wondered why I was goin'. I sure enough was bored with farm work, but this wasn't the kind of change I had been thinkin' of. I finally admitted to myself that I was doin' it for Tolin. I knew he would go by himself if needs be, and after so many years of our goin' to trouble together, I guess I just couldn't say no.

The next mornin' I was sittin' on the seat of a flatbed wagon with Tolin. His horse, Rogue, was tied to the back for him to ride later. Mr. Johnston gave Tolin money to buy farm equipment which would be our cover story comin' back—that we had gone to buy those tools. Mr. Evans wrote out some fine papers that looked like bills of sale for those two men we was goin' to help, and one for me, too, so everythin' would be slave legal. I took some dusty linsey pants and an old shirt. The pants were too small and I had a beat-up pair of brogans that somebody left behind at Maple Lane. I was to wear those clothes when we got close to Carthage. Mr. Evans made Tolin carry a long, round piece of wood with rubber around it.

"What's this for?" Tolin asked.

"To keep your slaves in line. With you bein' so young you're goin' to have to act mean so folks will believe you. This here is what planters whip their field hands with—it don't leave no marks on the body and so their sale value isn't hurt."

"I'll be glad when this is over with," I muttered.

"It's a good thing you're doing, Jason," Miss Samantha said, and squeezed my wrist.

"It'll be mighty strange with me holding a beating stick and Jason wearing those miserable clothes," Tolin stated.

"It's all just pretend for you and Jason," Mr. Johnston

said. "But they'll hang those two men if they're caught; you know that."

"We'll make it," Tolin said firmly. I forced a smile.

"Take care, Mr. Cobb," Miss Samantha said in a half-whisper to Tolin.

"God's speed, gentlemen," Miss Rose called as we pulled out the lane. " 'The Lord is our refuge and strength; and very present help in trouble,' " she quoted.

It was eerie, and I was cold scared like I was ridin' off to do battle with a whole camp of Blackfeet—alone! But things went real smooth. Tolin bought the farm equipment to load on the wagon, and made contact with the people who were hidin' the runaways.

On the sixth day we got our "cargo" and Tolin trussed them like they was in bondage. There was no talkin' between us, and at night—the times when most runaways was travelin'—Tolin tied together the legs of his "slaves." We were passed in the night a few times by riders, but no one questioned us.

The next day I saw the bounty hunters comin' before anyone, 'cause I was drivin' the wagon. Tolin was ridin' behind on Rogue as a rear guard. I started whistlin' "Soldier's Joy," which was the signal that someone was comin,' and Tolin started actin' mean.

"You keep on your feet, damn you!" he rumbled at the man who was walkin'. "You've cost me half a day already!"

"Ho up there, mister!" a rough voice called. I kept the team movin' real slow.

"Pull up, you fool! Can't you hear the man?" Tolin growled at me. "They got nothin' between their ears but sawdust," he said turnin' back to the man.

Tolin was puttin' on a good act and he talked with the men about dumb slaves and lazy workers, and how he was walkin' the fat off his new buck.

"We're lookin' for two runaways," the leader of the

hunters finally cut in. "Bucks. Brothers, I think. One's gonna hang for layin' with a white woman."

"Well, that's the damndest thing!" Tolin fished for the bills of sale Mr. Evans had done up. "Bought these boys in Arkansas."

After starin' at me, one of the men rode to the back and stared hard at the other two. I shifted sideways to watch him. I knew they was lookin' most for the man in the wagon. He was layin' there in a coat that made him seem smaller than he was, and he started whimperin'. I suspect it was from fear.

"What's the matter with him? Stand him up!" the snooper said.

"Fever," Tolin said. "Took with it in the swamps two days after I bought him. I'll be lucky if he lasts out the week. I'm sick of hearin' him." Tolin rode back in a fake rage and moved between the hunter and the wagon. He raised up that rubber-wrapped stick like he was gonna strike the fugitive. "Shut up that mumblin'!" That seemed to satisfy the hunter.

The bounty-hunter leader handed back the papers and rode around us again. "Well, travel on. Send word to the authorities if ya hear tell of those two I was talkin' about. Texas boys, they are. Their master wants them back bad."

"Good luck to your huntin'," Tolin said in his heaviest Alabama drawl. "There should be harsher dealin's with nigras that run off, and jail for the white folks that help them!"

It was a good thing I was as scared as I was or I would have laughed instead of shiverin' over the reins. It wasn't time to rejoice. We kept to the act, with Tolin yellin' orders at me. I clucked up the team and the run-off men kept their eyes down and was real quiet. We got through the worst part.

The next mornin' early, we pulled up beside a dryin' cornfield near a church. There was a man scythin' the stalks. He looked up.

"Do you ever find weevils in the corn silk?" Tolin asked.

"Yep," was the reply. "I found two just this mornin'."

Tolin cut our passengers loose and they slipped away just as quiet as they had come.

"We did it, Jason. Very successfully, too," Tolin said quietly when we stopped at midday to eat. "It was wonderful. I feel really good about it. I guess it's the first good thing I've done since I got the courage to tell you about your freedom." He took off the planter's coat he was wearin' and slipped into his plaid wool jacket. "I hope it wasn't too much of a torment for you. Thanks for coming."

"I'll admit, Tolin, I'll not do it again. I'm mighty glad it went so well." I changed out of the raggedy clothes and back into my weather-dark, slightly stiff, cool-to-the-touch buckskins and moccasins. They sure felt good. I fastened the bear-claw necklace around my throat and rubbed my thigh where my money pocket was.

We rode wary through the afternoon, thinkin' that someone might have figured out our trick, but by the next day we were both relaxed and not feelin' tense anymore. Tolin even took to sayin' poetry.

> Sun, your golden rays embrace
> The leaves and fling them into grace
> And dash them on the earth's sweet face.

"How was that?"

"All right, I guess." We was climbin' a hill between colorful woods filled with sweet gum and oak. The trees were thick and the low branches arched over the road like a roof. The wagon crunched through year-old leaves on the rutted road. Tolin was sittin' beside me with Rogue tied to the wagon. We started over a rise.

> Orange and yellow, red and green.
> More beautiful sights I've never seen.
> Falling to the—

"Hold it right there!" There was a man on the road in front of us. I nearly jumped from fright. He had a big

Hawken gun pointed over the neck of his horse right at us.

Highwaymen! I hoped my money pocket wouldn't make a bulge. Other men walked out from the trees and I suddenly realized that they wasn't stoppin' us for money. One of the men was the tall, thin crittur who had ridden with Fannin each time we seen him. Tolin must have recognized him, too, and he didn't say a word.

"Get off the wagon, boy," that reed of a man said, and he poked me in the ribs with a wooden bar. "Mr. Fannin wants you in one piece, but I'm not agin roughin' ya up a bit."

"What you're doing is wrong!" Tolin cried. "He's a freedman, not a runaway. He can prove it!"

I didn't move. I was so mad and scared it was like I was froze to the seat.

"Ya deef or somethin', boy? Git on off!" The man hit me on the back with that stick.

"Stop it, damn you!" Tolin grabbed the end of the stick and I was on my feet to club the man. The horseman rode over and hit Tolin over the head with his rifle butt. The sound of that wood on Tolin's head stopped me fast. He fell back on the seat.

"Tolin!" I reached for him, and three men grabbed me and pulled me from the wagon.

There wasn't a man there bigger than me, and I sent one flyin' into the mule team. The mules started wigglin' around and brayin'. I put a knee to another man's chest and smashed the jaw of a third with my fist. I kicked and put all my strength into hurtin' those bushwhackers; but there was six of them, and just one of me. Pretty soon I was tied, belly down, half conscious, over the back of a horse and we was ridin' through the woods. Tolin was still slumped on the wagon seat the last I saw, and I kept rememberin' how Taggart had killed that Indian with his rifle butt in the Territory.

The horse was bein' led by one of the riders, and I bounced and jostled with my feet and hands bangin' into tree limbs and bushes. My stomach was achin' from being hit and then slammed against the horse. I started hatin' those men more than I hated anythin'. I hated them so hard I wasn't even scared. All I could think was Jason-the-freed-man-Cobb was bound up again. But I had lived free for over a year, and I wasn't goin' to give in easy.

23

The world was upside down, and the smell of that cream bay horse I was tied onto made me sick. I couldn't make out nothin' except the dark of tree trunks and the nightmare of movin' too fast, and in the wrong direction—south. When they cut me off this horse, I thought, I'll kill them! But when the horses stopped and I was stood upright, my head throbbed; things looked blurry. My legs was numb.

My brain wasn't numb, though, and I learned real quick that the thin man I'd seen too many times went by the name of Pritchard. Pat Jergens was another face I put to memory. It was him that struck Tolin.

They stripped me of my belt and Green River knife, and Pritchard slapped me hard in the face and shoved me to the ground. He cut loose the pouch around my neck.

"Lookee here," he drawled. He held up the bit of money I had in the pouch, then pocketed it. "A money-totin' black is always troublesome. Thinks he's somebody!"

My dinner was brought to me and I began balancin' that tin plate on my knees so I could eat with just one hand free.

"Wal, now, what's this?" Pritchard handed my freedom paper to Pat Jergens.

Jergens squinted at it. "Say's here he's a freedman."

I stopped chewin', wonderin' if they would get the skitters about stealin' me off now they knew I was free.

"Freedman! Haw-haw-haw," Jergens went on.

They passed the paper around. Couldn't none of them read hardly at all and they stumbled with the words. Pritchard snatched it back and walked over to me with a stupid grin on his face.

"He shore don't look too free. Hee-hee! Freedman!" He spit toward me, and if I had been able to get my hands on him he would have been hurt bad.

I didn't refuse no food the next couple days, for I was sure enough goin' to keep up my strength. I had put aside the dream of killin' them 'cause I knew that, one, I couldn't do it, and two, I'd be hunted forever if I did. But I was goin' to fight my way out of there if I got the chance. I'd be fightin' for Tolin, too. The memory of him sprawled in that wagon seat made my skin hot when I thought of it.

"Ho up! We'll make camp here," Pat Jergens said. It was only midday and I got chilled knowin' we must be near the sellin' place. There hadn't been a single chance for escape. "Somebody get that nigger tied to a tree. I'm ridin' ahead to see if the boss is here."

I was hauled off the horse and tied against a rough-barked hickory tree. The black-hulled nuts was all about and they felt like rocks under my backside. Pritchard kept an eye on me while the others was makin' camp. Some food was fixed and I did my balancin' act with the plate. My chin itched 'cause it was gettin' bristly from not shavin', and they hadn't allowed me to wash up. Jergens came back to camp about the time I finished eatin'.

"The boss'll be here this evenin'," he announced as he pulled the saddle off his horse. "Pritchard, you get the nigger cleaned up. Fannin left word he wasn't to have a mark on him, 'cause he's lookin' for nearly twelve hundred dollars off that buck." He settled in with some food.

The sun was hid behind low, gray clouds that promised a drizzly rain before the day was out. Nobody wanted to leave the fire as the day got colder. Pritchard lazed around the camp till Jergens hollered at him.

"Get on that nigger, Pritchard. Fannin'll be in here afore the evenin' meal!"

So Pritchard and one other man (still wearin' a bruise from where I had whacked him three days back) untied me from the tree and cut my feet loose. I felt little prickles all down in my toes where the blood started movin' better. I'd been on my feet very little. They had barely let me upright to relieve myself when I'd a need, and that was only after meals and before they tied up my free hand. I had to be real careful those times, so they wouldn't see my money pocket.

With my feet free I started lookin' for chances to get away. Pritchard and this other one took me to a crick not far off and my feet was tied again as soon as we got there. Pritchard took out a razor and shaved me. He wasn't none too gentle, but he didn't draw any blood. With my feet tied, they cut my hands loose and told me to rub my wrists to get the rope marks out of my skin. Then they made me wash up, and Pritchard pulled leaves and burs out of my hair.

"Like tryin' to clean sheep's wool," he complained.

I swung my elbow hard and caught him real sharp in the stomach. The other man kicked my feet out from under me and I crashed to the ground. But I felt a sight better just seein' Pritchard holdin' his middle.

"Git him back to camp! Damn nigger!" And I was half dragged by the collar of my shirt.

"What the hell do you think you're doin'?" Jergens yelled. "I told you to fix 'im up, not rough 'im up!"

"Whoever buys this buck will have to cage him for a while," Pritchard grumbled as he grabbed my legs and the two men took me back to the tree.

"Leg irons'll tame 'im down."

"How ya gonna keep a blacksmith in leg irons?"

Ain't it so, I thought with a bitter smile.

The clouds swung lower. It got colder. I watched a

woolly worm inch its way up the leg of my moccasin and then fall off into the leaves. Jergens paced back and forth with his Hawken like he was expectin' an Indian attack.

I must have dozed a bit, 'cause the next thing I knew there was a lot of racket and leaves crunchin' all around. I opened my eyes and looked up on Fannin's gray horse. He was sittin' in the saddle and smilin' down at me with a real satisfied look.

"Percy Fannin won't be denied," he said with a chuckle. "A freedman. Ha!"

"He's that," Pritchard said. "Got his paper right here." He handed the pouch to Fannin.

Fannin pulled out the paper. "It's nothin' but a scrap," he said after he read it. He got off his horse and walked to the fire. I watched the flames grow yellow and dance around the paper. My freedom paper! "Get him off that tree and strip him out of his shirt."

I was sort of stunned by seein' my legal freedom go up in smoke like that. With bein' bound up again and that paper gone, I seemed to lose some strength. I barely noticed Pritchard untyin' me and pullin' me out of my shirts. Two men hauled me to my feet and I took a deep breath—tried to think straight. Fannin's hand was movin' over the burn scars on my shoulder, and just him touchin' me nearly brought up my dinner. I had to get away, I thought. I can't live like this. I've *never* lived like this even when I *was* a slave.

"They don't look too bad. They're old burns," Jergens said. "Black skin, black scars; won't nobody notice much."

Fannin grunted and tossed my shirts to me. I put them on and was tied up again.

"The buyer's goin' to meet us in Bentonville. We'll push off in the mornin' and be there by Thursday noon. Have you been carryin' him tied like that?" Fannin asked. Pritchard nodded. "Well, cut his feet loose tomorrow and let him sit the saddle."

I kept my face plain and calm, but I was smilin' inside.

195

"What are you boys eatin'?" Fannin asked as he squatted by the fire.

"Beans and rice. Smoked pork."

"Bah! I want some fresh meat! Take that damn rifle of yours and bring in some venison or something. I saw some turkey when I was ridin' in. Smoked pork and rice! Ugh!"

Jergens hustled to his horse and saddled up. He called another man to go with him, and I started thinkin' on how I could get them to tie my hands in front of me the next mornin'. If I was sittin' in the saddle and could get control of the horse, they'd be hard-pressed to keep me in tow.

The trees started throwin' long shadows, and a shot was heard far off in the woods. Fannin looked pleased, and I figured Jergens would be back with the meat soon. The light was gone, and the rain that had been threatenin' all day started fallin'. The men put up lean-tos and packed off wood to stay dry for the fire. Fannin tossed a blanket over me, and I drew my legs up to keep the chill away. It got dark. Somebody put more wood on the fire. The leaves rustled as the rain got heavier. I hunched my legs up closer to my chest.

"Jergens is comin'!" one of the men said as we heard some sounds. "Hey, what the—!"

The horses snorted loud and I could make out just a shadow of them as they ran off through the woods. The men cussed and tried to go after the horses, but them animals wasn't stayin' around.

I felt the tension on my arms loosen up. The ropes had been cut!

"Are your feet tied?" came a whisper. I nodded and felt the handle of a knife in my hand. Quiet as I could, I slipped my hand under the blanket and cut through the ropes that was around my ankles. My toes tingled and I wiggled them real good to get the feelin' back.

"When the time's right, back off behind this tree, then cut around to the crick. You'll know when," the voice said. The person took back the knife and I put my hands around the tree like I was still tied. Who would be cuttin' me loose? When the time's right, he said.

Fannin came over and stared at me real hard. The rain was drippin' off his hat in a steady stream. "Pritchard! Get this nigger closer into the camp. Somethin's goin' on and I don't like it."

"Boss. Two men disappeared. They went after the horses and I can't raise them!" Pritchard's voice sounded scared.

Fannin pulled a pistol from under his coat. Him and Pritchard and the one other man left at camp stood back from the fire and looked into the woods. Somebody yelled, "Hey, I caught somebody!" Then there was gunshots. Fannin and the man closest to the trees ran toward the noise. Pritchard backed closer to me—movin' real nervous.

I didn't waste no time. I jumped up, crashed my clenched fists down on the base of his skull, and started off like I'd been told. I could hear myself breathin' as I ran through the trees. The rain had wet the leaves real good and I didn't make much noise with my moccasins on. I circled back toward the crick.

"Jason!" came a loud whisper. I headed for it, still wonderin' who it was. It was Titus Rose! He nodded at me with a little smile, and led the way through the trees.

There was more yellin' from the camp, but I didn't dare look back. Next thing I knew, I saw the rumps of two mules. Titus scrambled on one, and I jumped to the saddle of the other. I followed Titus at a fast pace through the dark and the rain, and we was soon on a little trail goin' up a hill. I heard some more shootin' far off, then there was the sound of somethin' behind me. I looked back. My sweat mixed with the rain on my neck. The white face behind me looked eerie in the gray night.

"Tolin?" I couldn't believe it.

"Keep ridin', man," he said as he pulled closer to me. "We're not safe yet."

We kept to the little trail for a bit longer, and then cut off through some thickets and come up to another camp.

Didn't nobody say nothin', and the white man that was there stripped the saddles from the mules as soon as we was off them. He had water in a bucket, and poured it over the mules' backs and rubbed it in so the dry marks from the saddles wouldn't show up. Titus and Tolin hauled the saddles into the trees and were puttin' them up on horses. I grabbed one and followed. Dancer was waitin' there, and he was sure a pretty sight all wet and ready to run.

We were in the saddles before five minutes, Titus, Tolin, and me, and we started off through the trees without even a farewell to the man with the mules. He was huddled in under a canvas lean-to and lookin' like any traveler caught in the rain. We followed a crick a ways, then out the other side, and across a roadway onto another trail. The pace slowed to a trot, and then a walk.

"I don't think they'll pick up our trail," Titus said.

In a clearin' we pulled up to a stop. The rain had quit and the moon was tryin' to peek through the clouds when we got off the horses. I patted Dancer's strong neck, and then looked at Tolin and Titus.

"I don't think I've ever been so glad to see two folks in all my life!" I put my arms around their shoulders. Tolin and me hugged tight. Titus slapped me on my back and smiled. "I thought you was killed, Tolin."

"It takes more than a whack on the head to do in this Cobb."

"When Tolin got to Maple Lane he had quite a lump there, and he was mad aplenty," Titus said. "Him and me headed out that very night."

"There was a powerful lot of shootin' back there. You all didn't kill nobody, did you?"

"I surely wanted to, but I didn't. That man with the Hawken killed a deer. I knocked him out with a stick and tied up the other one at gunpoint. I took some of that fresh-killed meat and tossed it to where the horses were. Titus had already cut the picket line."

"That's when I came around and cut you loose."

"After that it was them shootin' at noises, and catchin' themselves tied up in the woods." Tolin laughed.

"We was ridin' off and they was still blunderin' around."

"I never in my life saw mules cut out like that!" I exclaimed. Titus laughed. "And who was that man?"

"Don't know his name," Titus said. "He's a conductor. Has those mules trained to take off like a shot. It's a fine thing."

"Well, let's head north," Tolin said. "We can talk more as we go."

"Yeah. They're all waitin' for you at Maple Lane," Titus said as we mounted up.

I got a sudden fear in me as I remembered those flames wrappin' around my freedom paper. "I can't go back, Tolin." The moonlight was on his face as I spoke. "Fannin burned my freedom paper."

"He burned it? Ah, to hell with the paper. You're free, Jason. We all know that."

"It ain't so, Tolin. I gotta prove I'm free. Fannin will have the law with him, now that he knows I don't have no proof."

"We'll write to the courthouse in Alabama and have them send proof."

"That'll take time," Titus said. "Ten days to get the letter there at least, another ten days back. Could be a month or more before you heard from them."

Tolin's mouth opened, but he didn't say nothin'.

"Jason's right," Titus continued. "He can't go back up there unless he's gonna live in the false wall behind the fireplace. Maple Lane is the first place Fannin will look, and he'd have Jason sold down to Texas before we could fiddle a tune."

"I'll go into the Territory," I said. "You send for the paper."

"You don't have supplies, and your tools are back at the farm."

"I got money. They didn't find my money pocket, so I

can buy what I need. We can't be too far from the Territory even now. I can make it."

The silence in that clearin' was like my ears had quit. Even the horses weren't movin' or blowin'. I sat and looked at Tolin. He knew I was right. I felt chilled, 'cause we was finally goin' separate ways. I might never see him again.

"There's clothing and your work boots in the pack bags, as well as a bit of trail gear. Your wool coat is in the blanket roll," Tolin said. "Here. You'll need a rifle." He pulled his Hall breechloader from the saddle boot and handed it over to me, leather case and all. He gave me his possibles sack and powder horn.

"Take a knife," Titus said as he gave me his. "The trail here goes into the Territory. There's a big river about a day's ride. When you get there you'll know for sure you're out of the States."

"After you find a place to winter, write Maple Lane and let us know where you are," Tolin said as I shook Titus's hand.

"Write? A letter?" I could see Tolin nod. I smiled a bit as I realized I could do just that, and even in script writin'. "You mind that dun horse for me, Tolin. He's yours till I bring your rifle back." I clasped his hand. "Take care of yourself."

A cloud passed over the moon and threw us into darkness. I backed Dancer around and struck out on the trail west.

IV

A New
Wind

24

I don't know if there's a loneliness that's worse than ridin' through strange land with no company. At first all I heard was the steady pound of Dancer's iron shoes on packed, leaf-covered earth as we let the night hide our journey. In the morning it was an even trot on high grass that was bent over from a heavy rain. We clattered down rocky washes and splashed through cricks. The sun kept movin', too, and it warmed my back and neck, then glared yellow in my eyes. I missed my wide-brimmed hat and planned to buy another as soon as I could.

The land looked as lonely as I felt with its few trees bare of leaves except for brown and yellow fringes holdin' on to the branches. The soft earth was rutted with trickly lines that had probably flowed fast with water when it stormed. The air smelled like springtime, right before plantin', and I heard thunder far off. To the northwest the sky was dark, and I remembered the storm I had survived along the Platte. I wondered how long it would take to get up there —to Fort Laramie. There'd be days and weeks of crossin' cold, lonely land just like this. I couldn't do it.

I wasn't a person used to bein' alone. Maple Lane, the forts, even travel from 'Bama, I had Tolin for company. At Cobb's it had been like a huge family with all of us workin' together: good moments, hard struggles. Me and Jake, Skal-

ley, Bitty . . . I got cold with my thinkin'. They were gone
—forever gone—and Tolin was behind me goin' north
with Titus. I worried that freedom for me would be one big
loneliness.

The storm rolled off behind me somewheres and made
the evenin' sky look greenish. The grasses was so soft I
could hardly hear the sound of Dancer's quiet walkin'. We
had crossed the big river Titus told about, and I started
south lookin' for a settlement. I kept my rifle primed and
ready to fire, and watched the trail for signs of other travelers, hopin' for hints that I wasn't the only person out there
twistin' and wigglin' down the trails beside that river. But
what people might I meet? Indians, most likely. My heart
pounded with the thought. I was in Indian Territory.

On the third day out of the States, Dancer was so weary
his head was hangin', and we was both hungry. I had eaten
nothin' 'cept some smoked turkey that was in Tolin's huntin' bag. I was real pleased to come up on a little three-
buildin' town, and I stopped for some supplies. Nothin' but
Indians in that town. Cherokee, the storekeep told me, and
he wasn't too happy to have me stoppin' by. I bought a bit
of food, a new hat, and went on.

A day's ride more, and I came to a big tradin' post laid
out on the banks where the river broadened. A flat-bot-
tomed boat was tied at the landin' on the river, and horses
and mules was penned in a corral nearby. It was with some
worry that I slipped out of the saddle and tied Dancer to
the hitch rail. If this was the Texas Road, like I thought,
then there could be white folks here—slavin' white folks,
at that. I hefted my rifle and walked through the swarm of
gnats into the dark buildin'. It smelled of green hides,
grain, dust, and dirty people. I crinkled my nose at it and
squinted into the dark room. Long tables propped on barrels was heaped with blankets and other goods. Three men
was talkin' loud about the boat and supplies while they
played cards. Another was swiggin' from a whiskey jar.

"What do you want?" a tired voice asked. The man speak-

---

in' from behind the counter was really fat, with a little beard and bulgy eyes.

"I come for supplies."

"Just pick what you need." He pointed to the rows of traps that was hangin' from the ceilin' beams.

"No. I need a pack mule and sawbuck. Tent canvas and galena."

"Uh!" The man's eyes squinched a bit. The talkin' had stopped and I could feel everybody starin' at me. Even in the dark of that low-ceilinged room there was no way I could hide that I was a Negro. I'd seen some Indians that was as dark as me, but my face wasn't that of no Indian.

"Where you comin' from, boy?" somebody asked from the shadows.

"Missouri."

"And where you gettin' to," another voice said—not soundin' too nice. Sweat started on my neck and I gripped the rifle.

A big man pushed up beside me. "You're that smith from the wagon camp up by Independence, ain't ya?" It was the conductor who had turned Tolin and me away back in June. I nodded to him, but my eyes was wide with fear over what was goin' to happen.

"A smith, huh? You hired on at Fort Gibson to help with the emigrants?" somebody asked more cheerful.

"They're in bad condition. Hear tell the Creeks what came in this spring and summer was the most raggedy of the lot."

"Creeks?" The word pulled me away from scary thoughts of slavers.

"Yup. They been stragglin' in since last year. Miserable bastards. Don't even have an axe to work with."

"Chickasaws got it worse. It's all there in the paper. They had to sell all their belongings to pay their passage out here."

"No different than for Kentucky folks."

And they started arguin' on how settlers was clutterin'

up the Territories. They didn't pay me no more mind since they had decided I was goin' to the fort to work. That wagon conductor still leaned on the counter, but not lookin' at me.

"There's mules outside," the fat man said. He opened a small leather pouch and tucked some snuff under his upper lip. "Cost you forty dollars."

"That's a powerful lot!"

"So buy your mule somewheres else."

I could easy see why that man's stomach was ridin' up under his chin, but I give him my order and went out to study those mules. If I was goin' to spend that much, I wanted to be sure I got the best one out there.

When I got back I saw that the fat man hadn't even started to measure out my coffee or wrap my things, so I laid three American Fur notes out for him to see. He seemed to hurry some after that. I took up a newspaper while I waited and moved closer to the window to read. It was the *Arkansas Gazette*, and only three weeks old. There was news about how Michigan Territory got named a state, and somethin' about a telegraph, but my mind kept goin' back to the headline: LOW WATER SLOWS INDIAN REMOVAL. Indian Removal. Creeks comin' into Indian Territory.

Louisa was saved by Creeks! There was a chance she could be out here. I shook my head against the thought.

The fat man brought me my change and then shoved a bill of sale for the mule at me. "Make your mark." It pleased me a lot to sign my name in rounded script. "Uh!" the man grunted with surprise.

"How far is it to the fort?"

"Oh, two-days-plus by road. One by water."

"When the water's high," a man grumbled, and somebody started complainin' again about the supplies and when they could get their pelts downriver.

I took my things outside and hitched the sawbuck on the mule. Creeks in Indian Territory. The thought kept runnin' through my mind. But even without that fact, goin' to the fort was good sense. I'd probably find work there for sure. I tied my goods in place and started off, wonderin' what Fort Gibson would be like.

When I rode through the stockade gates two days later I knew Fort Gibson was goin' to be nothin' like Laramie or Atkinson. There was soldiers there, all in uniform, and a big munitions center. It wasn't a tradin' fort or a missionary fort, it was set up like there was a war goin' on. A buildin' backed with warehouses had a sign over the door, EMIGRANT OFFICE, and some Indian folks was standin' on the steps arguin' with a white man. He stopped his haranguin' and looked at me ride by. His look reminded me of that bull-whacker I'd seen at the tradin' post, and I commenced to wonderin' if that man still worked for Fannin.

The stage office had a sign out about carryin' mail, but I had nothin' to tell Tolin. No point in writin' about nothin'. Down a ways was a command office, and a post house. Next to that was a dram shop. I headed for it, not so much for a drink, but for information. There was always more news in the gatherin' spots of forts than in any office.

"I got my orders not to sell liquor to the injuns," a man shouted at me when I went in. "Gct on outta here!"

"I ain't no injun." I stood there for a minute to let him get a look at me and then walked on in. "Don't want liquor anyways. I just come in to see what help the emigrants is needin'."

"Emigrants!" somebody grumbled. "Stinkin' wretches don't even have enough to chink a house together. You a supplier?"

"I'm a blacksmith. Is there a need for a smith in the Territory?"

"Thought you was a trapper from your dress," the barkeep said. He squinted at me. "Where you from, boy?"

"Missouri."

"Sounds more like Georgia to me. Fort commander is turning all you Indian-Negroes over to your owners."

"I'm a freedman! I didn't come here with no injuns!" I backed up, tense from his words.

"Ahhhh! You critturs don't know a fat cow from a poor bull!" That was real mountain-man talk, and the man talkin' looked familiar. "Look at them moccasins he's wearin'. When d'ya see a Chickasaw who could work leather like that? Them's Crow boots."

"They are, sure enough. Had a gal make them for me out of Fort Laramie. They're a mite thin on the sole, but shinin' all the same."

The man's face brightened. "Say! I know you, seems like. Ain't too many coloreds dressed like that out here. Yes, sir!"

I looked real hard at the wild whiskers streamin' over the stained leather coat. There was a deep scar on his cheek, and his jaw bulged out with a wad of tobacco. I remembered him just as he called out, "I got it! American Fur! Cap Drewry's train last year."

I could see the barkeep lookin' surprised. "You got a good eye," I said as we shook hands. "I was with that train. Jason Cobb's the name."

"Yes, sir! This child knows what way the stick floats. My name's Wiggins. K. V. Wiggins." He turned to the room. "I don't want to hear no more about half-baked Easterners. This here's a Western man. Yes, sir!" He pounded on my back with a hard hand. "A real mountain beaver if I ever seen one."

"Last I saw of you, you was wearin' a fur cap and a fringe jacket with a lot of beadwork," I said as he steered me to a table.

"Yep. I lost that hat in a shale slide near Raton last fall. Lost my partner there, too. The coat I traded along with all my plews to some ornery Kiowa so's they wouldn't take my hair. I swiped this coat from a corpse they'd left up the trail a day more east. Don't know why they left it. Say! You travelin' alone?" He poured himself a drink. "I thought you was with a white boy?"

"Left him back in Missouri last month."

"Hmm. How is it you left his company?" His eyes narrowed and he moved closer so he couldn't be overheard. "You ain't a runnin' niggur, are you?"

"No. I'm a freedman." I studied that gnarled old face to see if he believed me. He just nodded a bit.

A group of four men came in all loud and laughin'. One was real big and carryin' a whip. I sat back, stared. My breath was comin' hard till I saw their faces.

"Well, you may not be runnin' from that white boy, but—" Wiggins's voice was real low, then he grinned. "That there's a fine-lookin' necklace you're wearin'. Got to be a story in it. Tell you what." He slapped the table with his hand. "I'm runnin' a bit low on grub—lost a side of meat in a card game—but I got some starter if you got flour. Let's get out to where the air's fresh. You tell me the last you seen of ol' Bornston and some of them other Rocky Mountain beavers. Yes, sir!" He took up the jar of whiskey and we went outside. "No better thing than to meet a man you can talk to."

The light was growin' dim with evenin', and I glanced at the emigrant office again. I wondered if that was where I'd find out about a job—and about the Creeks. I wanted somethin' way out in the Territory so's not to worry about Fannin or slavin'.

"I know a place near some trees out on the banks of the Neosho," Wiggins was sayin' as he mounted the old mule he was ridin'. "Real quiet place. Not nothin' to worry you at all."

"Sure," I said, not thinkin' on his words 'cause what I was seein' on the street had my full attention. There was a woman comin' toward me. Not too tall, thin, head wrapped in calico. She was carryin' a baby. But when she passed by I could see she was older than me and all Indian. I let out a long sigh.

Don't think on it, Jason, Tolin had told me. *You'll drive yourself crazy!*

That was sure enough true. And I followed Wiggins out of the fort.

25

I dreamed that night. A pleasant dream at first, come from
good food and yarnin' with Wiggins all about his day in the
shale slide, and me tellin' about the Black Wind and the
fight on the Loup. I dreamed that I was passin' some Indian
planter's field and there was Louisa with our baby tied to
her back. I bought her freedom and we rode away, three
free Negroes. Jason, Louisa, and Marcus—that's what we'd
call the baby if it was a boy. Jason, Louisa, and Marcus
Cobb.

But somewhere near dawn that dream got twisted
around. I was seein' the Creek warriors ridin' off with
Mistuh Cobb's horses. I was even there! Standin' by the
stable door and watchin' it all and not bein' noticed. I
dreamed I was holdin' Louisa and the soldiers was comin'
on us. They was ridin' stocky gray mares, and dressed in
tan suits. One was big and carryin' a whip. Then this Indian rode by and snatched Louisa out of my arms to save
her. The soldiers closed down on me.

I bolted awake from the realness of it. Sweat was on me
even as the cold was bitin' into my neck. The wind was
whippin' through the trees and scatterin' October leaves all
over. Dancer's leg was cocked in sleep, and the sky was a
clear, mornin' shade of pink. It all seemed so peaceful.

I pulled back into the blanket and threw brush onto the

glowin' coals. The dry weeds crumpled, then caught, and flames started easin' up from the pit where we had cooked. I put some more sticks on and laid back. My heartbeat was calmin' some . . .

Next thing I heard was the sound of horses runnin'. I sat up fast and grabbed my rifle.

"You sure are skittish," Wiggins said from where he was wrapped in his blanket. He had the coffee boilin' already. I saw some men in the distance drivin' horses toward the fort.

"Just worried about horse thieves," I said with a laugh. I pulled my blanket around me some more.

"The nose of winter's come down!" Wiggins declared. "Pretty soon it'll howl and bite. A month or so." He took up a canteen and snorted loud after he had drunk. I got a whiff of liquor on the breeze. "My mornin' supply. Want a warm-up?"

I said no.

He took another swig from his canteen.

"So where you been, Jason? This is a long way from American Fur."

"I come down here from Missouri. Been back from Fort Laramie nearly four months."

He just nodded. "Four months in Missouri, huh? You—you got slaver problems?" He poured us both some coffee. "Oh, don't bother about what I might be thinkin'. I say every crittur's got a right to make his own way. Besides, I seen the way you tightened up when them ornery bulls come into the dram shop. Who you runnin' from?"

"I'm a freedman, Wiggins!"

"I believe you, boy, but what are you doin' out here?"

"Missouri's full of slavers. Thought I'd just stay out of their way, that's all."

"Wasn't that white boy makin' trouble for you, was it?"

"Oh, no! I just—" I sighed and figured to risk his trust. "A man stole me off and was fixin' to sell me to Texas. He burned my freedom paper." Wiggins was frownin' at me to tell more, so I spoke about the way Tolin and me was come at on the road, and how I was belly-whupped through the woods on a horse, and about the rescue.

"*Waugh*, that'd be a good yarnin' tale, if it weren't so grim. So what do you aim to do?"

"I'm gonna sit tight here in the Territory, or someplace out of the States, while Tolin writes to Alabama for my papers. I'm hopin' to find a place soon, with the winter settlin' in like it is."

"Yep. It's doin' that, all right. Winters here will come on you like you was camped on a mountain peak with no lodge. Freeze the breath right outta ya."

"Maybe I should go down to Taos."

"Well, the wimmen would warm you some, but they got slavers there, too. Catchin' injuns mostly. Sellin' Pueblo folks off to the Navajo; some to the Mex and Texans. Say! I hear they're lookin' for hunters over at Bent's Fort."

"Where's that?"

"Out the mouth of the Cimarron. Bufflers plenty on those plains. Get good money for them dang hides, too. Of course you got to fight off the Comanche sometimes."

"I don't care for that part of it," I said as I poured some more coffee. "I'm a blacksmith. Hope to find a settlement that would need my work."

"Blacksmith. You did say that. Why sure, you could get somethin' here in the Territory. There's emigrants what moved out toward Camp Mason last spring. They don't hanker none to white folks, but they might let you come in. That's out past my sister's place."

"You got family in these parts?"

"Oh, you can call it that. We ain't close none. My sister started off to Texas five years ago. Lost her man to cholera and just stopped where she was. She's got two no-good boys. They're down in Texas fightin'. I come in here for a visit and she hooked me to stayin' and huntin' for her this winter. Figured I might as well till I find a new partner."

"It must be nice havin' family."

"Aw, hell! It gets worrisome. That's why I come up here to the fort. All these settlement folks is borin', too, and I just kept hopin' for a crittur I could talk to. Winter don't seem right without yarnin' and liquor and a squaw in my blanket. I get the liquor at the camps—got so much liquor out there the injuns is crazy with it. Don't know what to do about the squaws. These emigrant tribes ain't friendly like the mountain folks. Choctaw. Creeks. I never met the likes of them."

"Creeks." The memory of those raggedy people waitin' for the boat at Tampa Bay came to my mind. They'd be out here somewhere now. "Where are the Creeks?"

"Oh, sort of in the middle of the Territory. Half started livin' out here back in '31. Another passel been comin' since last summer."

The sun had melted the thin frost off the grass and I stared at the ground for a while, then started packin' my stuff.

"So what you got in mind, Jason?"

"Find some work. Maybe with those Creeks you was talkin' about."

"That's mean country out the Canadian." He cut off a chaw of tobacco. "You really think those slavers will come out here after you?"

"I don't rightly know, but—"

"But there's somethin' else clawin' at you, too." He scratched at his backside, and rumbled up a big belch. "Well . . . The agency is up the road a piece. Man might be there by now. I'll show you where."

The Creek agent's name was John Campbell, and he was all set to turn me over to the fort commander until Wiggins vouched for who I was.

"There's a public smith here already, and the Choctaws have their towns set up fine," he said, still frownin' at the spot where Wiggins had spat tobacco near the steps of the office.

214

"It's Creeks I was aimin' to serve."

"We've no money to hire on any more, and they've none to pay you with." He hunched his shoulders and started lookin' over some papers as he went inside the building.

"Is there a forge cold? I'll make my way all right. I just want a place to settle in," I said as I followed him inside.

"Oh." He sighed heavy and looked at the big map tacked on the wall behind the desk. His finger started trailin' along the line that marked the Canadian River. "North of Camp Holmes there's small towns. People from Georgia and Alabama." His finger stopped. "Here, I guess. Chimalee."

"Chimalee?"

"Yes. He speaks English and his people are doing better than some. But there's no pay."

"I know. I know." I was smilin' when I said thank you.

Wiggins just shook his head at me, but while we was goin' back to the fort he said, "Well, I might as well ride with you, if you don't mind the company. We can stop at my sister's for my gear and take off from there."

"You'd be doin' that?" I was surprised.

"Yep. I would. Settlements is a bother anyhows." He spat tobacco juice again. "So now what?"

"I write to Tolin and have him send my tools."

"You're puttin' a lot of faith in that boy. Don't lean too hard." He shifted his chaw. "There's a man at the post house who will write a letter for you. He don't charge too much."

"No need. And after I'm done here we might as well start on out."

"Now, whoa up, Jason. It's rough out there. Got to get yourself some meat. Salt it down. Smoke some. No tellin' what the food situation is, and like as not, those folks won't share too much. Besides, no point in goin' till you get your tools."

I could tell by how he said it that he didn't expect the tools to ever come, but I didn't say nothin' about my certainties. If the mail got through and the water got high, I figured to have my things in less than a month.

The rains started that very day and swelled the rivers. I was powerful happy even though I had to put in with Wiggins at his sister's place for five nights. The woman wasn't too glad Wiggins brought me, 'though she did say I was a sight cleaner than the trapper friends he'd brought by before. The house was near the town of North Fork, and there was dram shops and gamblin' all over. Wiggins stayed in liquor a lot, and I paid for my keep by fixin' a ceilin' beam and chinkin' the windows for winter.

When the sun come through next, Wiggins argued a mule out of his sister, and we put our packs together to leave on the wagon road toward Camp Holmes. That was the address I'd given Tolin to send my things, and even though I knew the letter had barely reached Independence, I was anxious to get there. Addie, Wiggins's sister, fussed about him not takin' care of her. "You're wastin' time lookin' for meat out in that wildness!" she hollered. He didn't pay her no mind.

We took off west and I could see the fields that had been worked by the Creeks that year. Corn, mostly, and the cribs was filled in some places. But the farther west we got, the poorer the people looked. Game was hard to find and no one had much livestock. Folks took to dressin' like the tribes of the plains and not in white folks' clothes, and there wasn't too much English spoke.

Wiggins knew a little of the Creek tongue from drinkin' with some of the men in North Fork. I started pickin' up what I could. I also kept noticin' everybody I saw. My brain told me it was crazy to hunt a familiar face, but I did it anyway. There wasn't too many Negroes at all, so it gave me a start each time I saw a face a bit darker than the rest.

When we stopped at Camp Holmes I started thinkin' Addie might have been right about the huntin', 'cause nobody had a good thing to say about game. After buyin' supplies we headed northwest, and it took us twelve days to scare up three deer and four antelope. Wiggins grumbled the whole time we dressed the kill and smoked some of the venison. "Squaw work!" he said. And I had to admit it wasn't anything *I* liked doin'.

November set in with cold bright days. I had thinned out from all the ridin' and hard work, and I let my chin whiskers grow bushy and down to my coat collar. Wiggins and me must have looked to be a grizzly pair when we rode down to the tradin' house near Camp Mason (up the river a ways from Holmes). I asked about how the boats was runnin', and was saddened to learn there hadn't been a boat or supply train into Camp Holmes since Wiggins and me left. Wiggins didn't say nothin', but he sort of nodded like he had figured how things was gonna be.

"Well, tools or no tools, I got my supplies. So I think I'll go on to that village," I said to Wiggins.

But it didn't work out. I made a casual comment that it was November and I was twenty-one years old that month. He took on like I said it was the Fourth of July, and bought some potent whiskey called Taos Lightnin'.

"*Whooo!*" he declared. "This'll put fur on your chest so's you won't need a coat. Yes, sir! Come on around," he called to everyone. "My partner's havin' a birthday. Come on. Have a drink!"

Wiggins poured whiskey down me, and other folks started buyin' and drinkin' with us. We laughed and howled and told awful, awful stories. Pretty soon the darkness in that half-lit tradin' post seemed even darker. My legs felt powerful tired and I finished tellin' about gettin' caught in the blizzard—this time with wolves and a grizzly bear!—and slumped beside the table and went to sleep.

While I lay passed out from the whiskey, Wiggins was gamblin'. And he lost. He lost all the meat we'd took on the hunt. Every bit!

"It's all right," he said groggy the next mornin' after I seen what happened. "Man says there's buffler down by the

217

Washita. I'd take buffler any day over antelope. Wouldn't you?"

"You gambled away my meat!" I shoved hard on his shoulder so he'd look at me.

"Aw hell, Jason. It ain't so bad. And—and I'll make it up to you. One buffler and one hide tanned. I'll get it!"

And he did, too. He loaded me up with a whole hump of a young cow, and he tanned up the hide real nice. That eased me out of some of my mad when I felt that robe all smooth and soft like a horse's nose on one side, and with the hair still on the other. He sure worked hard on that thing, and he never once grumbled about it bein' "squaw work."

But all that was *after* we had rode a whole week south of of the Washita after the buffalo. We had to cold-camp sometimes 'cause there was Kiowa and Pawnee down that way who was fierce over all the invasion of their land. And for me it almost hurt to be gone. We had left Camp Mason and Camp Holmes and the chance of gettin' any word from Tolin. Worse than that, we was out of Creek land.

When we did get back, the river was high and rollin'. We ferried across from a Choctaw landin' to Camp Holmes. It was a-bustlin' with all kinds of folks. There was a freight boat at the dock.

"How long since the boat came in?" I asked right off when I went inside.

"Two days, this trip. Came once last month."

"Did they bring mail?" He nodded. "Anything for Cobb? Jason Cobb?"

"Who's askin'?"

"That be me. Jason Cobb."

The man started searchin' through a pile of envelopes and papers. I used my arm to wipe sweat off my forehead as I watched him. He set aside a slip, and then handed me an envelope. "You got heavy stuff, too."

I opened that envelope quick, hopin' by some miracle my

freedom paper would be inside. But it wasn't. At least there was a letter, I thought.

The man hauled a crate out of the corner. "This here's yours."

I pushed the envelope in my boot and took up the heavy crate with a single swoop. *"Eeeeyaaa!"* I went out to where Wiggins was talkin' with a man. "It's come."

"Your boy come through, did he?" Wiggins sounded sort of somber.

"He did. My tools are here, and a letter, too."

Wiggins nodded, and spit into the pile of leaves that was blown against the porch. "Looks like I'll be losin' myself a partner, I guess." Then he grinned. "Aw, hell. Gives me a good excuse to get away from that ol' sister of mine. Where you gonna be again?"

"In the village of Chimalee. A Creek village!"

"Why, I'll come and visit you sometime. That I will, Jason. That I will."

26

Chimalee owned the store in what was called a town. The store, with a lean-to storage, and the beginnin' of the smithy was all that was there. Off about a mile or so I could see the few, pitiful corn stalks in the fields, and near that was a cluster of little houses. I could tell right off that the town and the village was somethin' separate.

Chimalee, he looked me up and down real hard when I went into his store. I was waitin' for him to ask me about my slave status, but he didn't. I told him why I was there.

"The agency man tell us he would get a blacksmith here last spring. We started a forge, but the man didn't come. Iron come, but no tools, and no smith. Agency man tell us *next* spring." He looked like he could have been a smith himself: wide-fisted and tight-muscled.

"I was hopin' I could put in with you for the winter. Do some work."

"We cannot pay you."

"I know that."

He walked to the door of the store and looked at Dancer and my mule, all laden down with my belongin's. "I will show you the forge."

He locked the store and I followed as he led his mule across the beat-down area that was to be the street.

"How many people live here?" I asked. I wanted to ask

how many slaves they had, but I didn't think it wise.

"Twenty-two families. I have told them all to take to their houses. There is no field work. No shops to run. I will be stayin' home soon. My store will not be needed until spring, or when the supplier brings new goods from Tullahassee."

There wasn't much to the shop: a well-built forge under a side-sloped roof and supported by only two walls. The bellows leaned against one wall. I'd have to make a treadle and rig it, I thought. I smoothed my chin whiskers and looked around the area. There was a whole lot I'd have to do.

"We had much before we came here. Farms, stores. My mother's father fought in the first war against the whites, but we didn't fight this time. The soldiers burned us out anyway. Chained us to boats, brought us here to this place of fighting and no food."

I remembered the ashes and the blackened wood of the Cobb house. Soldiers. It still hurt to think about it.

"My people and my brother's people started here together. We were thirty-eight families. Many children. Now there are few left. Children . . . have died." He sighed and gripped his hands behind his back. "Hunger comes often. Hunting is hard because of the wild tribes to the north. You must provide for yourself."

"I have planned for it."

"Then you stay. Maybe one—two seasons. There will be a Creek smith by then. This is good!"

Chimalee started back to his village, where the trees and houses stood out harsh and black on the smooth, white background. There I was—alone again. I wanted to stop right then and do somethin' to make myself feel better, but Dancer was still packed heavy with my gear and extra supplies Tolin had sent. I had been forced to walk all the way from Camp Holmes 'cause he was so loaded down. When I stripped the burdens from him he seemed to sigh, and I watched him roll in the snow-stiff grass and frisk around like a young colt. My mule was loaded with all my dried meat and hides, and he was pullin' a pony drag like the Plains tribes used when travelin'. That was full of my tools and another rough-cured skin with salt meat in it.

I put all the packs between the two walls, tyin' the food sacks from the roof beam so mice and such wouldn't get to them. The wind started blowin', and the sun was just a round glare through the clouds. There was a soft fuzz of snow on the ground and the promise of more in the air. Dancer and the mule had turned tail to the wind and I knew I'd have to shelter them. There was trees down a draw, maybe fifty yards away, that would have given them cover, but I didn't have no trust to leave them that far off.

I took the animals down to the crick, and while they drank and cropped grass, I set to work cuttin' and strippin' saplin's. When we went back up the hill I used those to fix a shed onto one outside wall of the forge. I laid four other saplin's in a square behind the shop where I would build my quarters. It would take a few days before I got that finished, so I dropped my canvas at a slant off the back openin' of the shop so I could live between the walls for a while.

With basic comforts arranged, I started a little fire, rolled over a piece of log to sit on, and took the letter from Tolin out of my boot. The paper was gettin' pretty smudged from my readin' it so often in the past three days. I unfolded it and started readin' again.

My most admirable friend, Jason. It cheers me greatly to know of your safe repair to the Territory. We have all wondered for your well-being. I have crated your precious tools and sent them overland to Fort Smith, and they shall reach you by flatboat much near the time of this letter. May your fortune be for a warm winter at a glowing forge.

Of the important papers which I know you are in need of, I have sent an urgent request for them by coach, and hope to have a reply before the year's end. You shall be contacted as soon after word is received as is possible.

As for myself and these good people of Maple Lane, we are well and keeping to the business of the day with some success. I shall also say that Miss Samantha and I seem to have the same thoughts of the heart. I intend to greet the summer with garlands and wedding vows, although I have not yet approached the lady with these thoughts. Of course, I expect you to be here by then. To continue the talk of women, I add that Mr. Evans's daughter, Dorothy, has returned from Illinois, and a more gracious young lady you're not likely to meet. I am praying the mail brings what we await soon so you can return here and we can both add to our comforts.

Titus wishes you well, as do Mr. Johnston, the family Evans, and all others. Not a day goes by that Miss Rose doesn't say a prayer for your safe return. A pat for the good steed, Dancer, and until further word I remain your faithful friend.

Tolin Cobb

Two days after I got to the village I had the treadle for the bellows rigged, but I still hadn't seen a soul in town save Chimalee. On the third day the forge was glowin', and heatin' up the high-ceilinged buildin'. I started poundin' iron to make a froe to split shingles for my own house. The village suddenly showed its people. Distant figures I had glimpsed gatherin' wood or gettin' water were right up on me. They looked mighty beat down, those Creek folks, but there was a kind of light to them that they was goin' to make it.

For three days they came to me with split plow blades and chipped axes. Some had a horse or mule in need of shoes, and I was glad I knew the farrier trade. Others brought iron bands and braces from old, broken wagons and I beat the metal down to make tools. The only pay I got was in service. Young boys would cut wild rye for my animals and see that my water skins was filled. I got small sacks of corn, and once, a cup of meal.

A man took up my froe one mornin' and split shingles for my house roof. They was stacked real neat by the horse shed by midafternoon, but the froe was gone. It turned up two days later at the front of the shop along with a fresh-killed rabbit. It was hard for me to take that rabbit when I knew there was people with next to nothin' to eat. The last rations they received had been sour and the flour cut with lime, and the meat partly spoiled from where the brine barrels had split durin' shipment.

"Don't feel bad. You are a good smith," Chimalee said when I told him about the rabbit. He looked around at the way I had fixed things up in my shop. "In three days you have given my people more help than any outsider has offered since we came west."

"I'm—I'm sort of returnin' a favor," I said low.

Chimalee studied me a bit. "You were a smith in Alabama. Southeast of Montgomery, maybe? I hear it in your voice."

"I was raised near Union Springs."

He just nodded. "A few of us had Negroes back there, but we had to sell them."

"All of them?"

"Yes. Very few who came west could bring much of their property. It may be just as well. We have enough trouble trying to feed our own."

"What do you think happened to them?"

"Given off to the white landholders. You were not there during the war?"

"A bit. Came west last year."

He gave me a strong gaze from his brown eyes. I busied myself honin' an adze. "How many other settlements are Creeks from Alabama?"

"Many. All through this area. We chose to move far from the whites. We have seen enough of the whites."

"And not any folks with slaves?"

"Perhaps. A few. I'm not sure."

"Where? North of here? East?"

Chimalee frowned and went to the shop door. "While you are in my town you will not be slaved again."

"That wasn't my worry, Chimalee. Thank you. I'm a freedman."

"Not for always. Not if you're from Alabama. But that is not my concern. You are a skilled smith. You help my people. This is good."

I watched him go back to his store and knew he meant what he said, but I also felt a distance—that my stayin' here was allowed only because they needed my service. That was a mournful thought.

I had kept track of the time by markin' days off of a calendar Tolin sent, so I knew it was four days into the new year, 1838, when I heard a whoop that must've carried clear to the village.

"Hey there, Dancer, you ol' Black Wind, son of a gun! Where's that long-legged crittur what rides you? *Ja-son!*"

"Wiggins? Sure enough! Sure is good to see a friendly face!"

He pounded me on the back and swung off his mule. "I was gonna come earlier, but those nephews of mine came home from Texas and Addie wouldn't let me ride off. Screechin' about family bein' together and all. Well, you know Addie. *Whooo!* I brung you a present." He started untyin' a whole skin of whiskey he brought me. "Looks like you need it, too. Ain't a dram shop within sixty miles of here."

"Well, I thank you, Wiggins. Come on in."

He admired my one-room house I'd built, and how I had laid dry grasses and then pegged the robe he gave me over them and into the bottom logs to form a nice furry floor on one side. I had used my hatchet and axe well durin' the month, and had made myself a chair and a small table. There was a stool in the forge shop with whittled legs, and I had arranged my tools on the wall.

Wiggins made himself to home and started right in on the whiskey. With that and the tobacco, and the fact that he probably hadn't bathed since the first frost, he stunk up my little house somethin' awful in the four days he stayed. But the talkin' to a friend and the pleasure of havin' company made it more than bearable.

When he left I gave him a letter to send to Tolin. He studied the envelope for a while. "A fine thing, I must say, that you can read and write. You tell that boy about meetin' up with me?"

"I sure enough did. And about our buffalo hunt."

"And did you tell him why you was sittin' way out in this barren land without even a friendly soul nearby?"

I just stared at him, rememberin' the words I had put down about the Creeks, and the settlements, and how I hoped to talk with their Negroes—get some news of Louisa. It seemed silly, but Tolin would understand. It was one of those good dreams I had to keep holdin' to so's not to get so down in the mind that I couldn't do nothin'.

"Well, I'll see that this goes out of North Fork with the next carry. I hope all this cold hell is worth it to you." He put the envelope real careful into his possibles sack and mounted his mule. "I think I'll drop back by here come March or so, see how you're doin'. Maybe we can make some plans for the warm season."

"I'd be pleased to see you anytime, Wiggins." I shook his rough old hand.

He let out with a whoop that sent my mule dashin' to the far side of the rope corral I'd put up. Then Wiggins put spurs to his animal and they took off like he was ridin' a startled pronghorn—Wiggins hooplain' and yowlin' all the way. I watched him and his mule get smaller with distance. The gray-white sky seemed to blend into the frosty land as he disappeared, and I felt like a dot on a blank page of paper. Like that whole great overhang of snow clouds was goin' to mash me flat into the ground.

27

The sun beamed strong for a week and melted the snow into a gray mush. Some hunters ventured off from the village and came back with a killed bear. It must not have lasted folks for too long, 'cause two days later I saw three wagons headin' off for the issuin' station. Chimalee opened up his store while they was gone, 'cause other folks was out durin' the thaw, too. The word had passed that there was a smith in Chimalee's village, and people came in from other settlements with work for me to do. One man was real impressive. He ordered a fireplace grate, paid me in gold coin in advance, and—he had a Negro with him.

I hammered away on that rich Creek's order and kept tryin' to figure a way to talk to that man he'd brought with him, but the Negro stayed near the wagon all day. The rich man talked with Chimalee a lot, and when the shadows got long Chimalee took him out to the village. Then the Negro eased over to the shop.

"Hey," I said, real friendly like. I studied him over real good, wonderin' if I had known him back in 'Bama. Nobody I knew would recognize me, what with my bein' taller and havin' a beard. "Think this weather will hold?"

"Maybe. You belong to the head man here?"

"I'm freed. All legal."

"Freed! Mercy me. I'd be off in—Albany! Yes, Lord.

I'd—" He squinted at me. "So why you out here sweatin'
for these folks?"

"I never did like cities much."

"Uh. You's got trouble in the States. That's the only
reason anybody comes out here. Renegade white men.
Trashy kinds! Folks with no money, and niggers with a
rope waitin' for them." He looked at me kinda funny. "Are
you guilty, or are they framin' you for somethin'?"

I didn't feel like tryin' to tell him different. "You ever
hear tell of some Creeks that stole off horses back in 'Bama
from a place near Union Springs?"

"Union Springs? Never heard of it. But there was a lot
of thievin' goin' on back there. I'd hate to say what I saw.
Why, one time—"

"This was kinda different, 'cause the soldiers was chasin'
this group and the soldiers took to killin' the Negroes at the
plantation."

"Sounds like somethin' happened in Georgia. That's
where we's from. Georgia. Some beautiful country back
there. I—"

"It happened in Alabama. Southeast of Montgomery." I
laid down the work I'd been fiddlin' with. "Or maybe you
. . . you met up with a girl while you was comin' west." My
face was feelin' hotter than from the forge fire. I swallowed
hard. "Just a bit of a thing. Named Louisa. Light-skinned.
Seventeen, she'd be now. And has a baby." I was achin' to
hear him say; Oh, yes, I remember her, and to tell me where
she might be.

"Don't sound familiar. Young girls . . . they go first at
sellin' time, and ain't no babies here'bouts, neither colored
or Creek. Ain't hardly no colored out here anyway. Me and
my woman, we been with this man awhile, and so he's good
to us. He got two field hands, too. Other than that . . ." He
scratched his head. "I guess the only other I heard of is east
on that Deep Fork crick. Why you lookin' for this girl? She
a—"

"How's the work goin', blacksmith?" The rich Creek

man was back—eyes lookin' at us hard. His man went off to the wagon real quick.

"The fixin's nearly done. Maybe another hour," I said solemn. I turned my back to him and worked the bellows.

"Good. I'll see that my man don't bother you no more. And—and be sure you don't bother him none, either!"

I looked around at his sharp tone and remembered that my freedom wasn't trusted by slaveholders—white or Indian. I frowned at him, and saw Chimalee watchin' from the steps of the store. I could almost hear him thinkin', Do your job, blacksmith. Do not make trouble in my town.

I sighed heavy and went on with my work.

Two days later all the forge work was done, the visitors was gone, and I was thinkin' of ridin' east to that town the man told me about. But the weather iced us in again. A fierce wind started up just when the wagons got back with rations, and it kept blowin' for days. Sleet glossed the snow, and there wasn't nobody goin' nowhere.

I heard a noise one evenin' and peeked from my door to the horse shed to see that the animals wasn't fussin' about somethin'. A little boy was standin' there. His hair was light and straggly, and he was breakin' the ice on the water bucket with a stick so Dancer could drink. I couldn't tell if he was white or Indian till I went out to him, and then I saw he was a bit of both. He started to run.

"Hey, wait a minute." I pulled him back out of the wind and smiled at him. "What's your name, boy?" He stared at me and I figured he didn't talk English. "You live in the village?" He frowned. "In the village." I pointed to the houses off by the fields. "You live there?" I asked in the bit of Creek I had learned. He shook his head and backed closer to my house. "Where'd you come from?"

He pointed to where the cold, black sky was dotted with stars down to the earth line.

"Along the river? River." I said it again in Creek. He nodded. "They got more folks like me back there, don't they?" I touched my face. He patted my beard and nodded. "No. I mean like this." I stroked my cheek. "With victory skin," I said, even though he couldn't understand.

He wasn't listenin' anyway but starin' at my house, where warm air and good smells was comin' from. I was cookin' up a buffalo meat stew, and it did smell fine.

"I'm Jason," I said in Creek. "This is Dancer." I patted the horse. "What's your name?"

He pointed to himself. "Phillip," he said. His eyes was like two black holes in his skinny face.

There didn't seem to be no one else around, so I took him inside and dished up a plate of food. "That's for tendin' my horse. Go on. Take it."

He smiled real quick, took the plate, and ran out the door.

"Phillip!" I grabbed the capote Tolin had sent me and went after him.

He disappeared around the corner of the store, and when I got back there he was squatted in the lean-to shack eatin' the food and sharin' with a woman. I guess she was his ma, and she jumped up when she saw me. There was a big knife in her hand. I went no farther. She might have been skinny and ragged, but that knife looked to be sharp.

"Away!" she said, sort of funny like. Her face was bad pock-marked, and her shoulders was bony lines under her blanket.

"There's people in the village," I said, and pointed south to the houses. "They can help you." She waved the knife at me, grabbed Phillip close, and shook her head so that her untied hair spread wild around her face. I could tell there was no point in talkin' more.

Phillip handed the plate back to me—food still on it. "No. You eat. You helped with my horse. You eat." And I went home.

I didn't see much of them after that 'ceptin' sometimes at night when the woman was diggin' roots and strippin' bark down by the crick for them to eat. Phillip, he come back a lot—always when the shadows was long. My animals was well cared for, and I gave him meat and flour. I taught him how to set rabbit snares, and then—after several good takes—I made a cape for his scrawny shoulders. He hugged me, and danced around real proud.

The temperature dropped again, and in mid-February it was the coldest it had been all winter. I was glad for my bushy chin growth that kept my face warm when I went out. I didn't see Phillip for four days straight, and I started to worry. Finally I bundled into my capote and struck out across the road to the store. Phillip was huddled in the lean-to with the chalky face of his ma restin' in his lap. Her body was wrapped in a thin blanket, and the little coat I'd made him was over that. I knew soon as I saw her she was dead.

Phillip let me take his hand, and I led him away from the place. His fingers and ears were frosted white, and when I took him into my house the warmth made him cry from the pain it brought to his half-frozen body. I rubbed him all over for a long while, then wrapped him in a blanket and spooned some broth down him. He nearly went to sleep in my arms, and I put him on the buffalo rug to sleep.

I worried about his ma's body layin' in that lean-to, but I didn't know the ways of the Creek with their dead. I built up the fire, bridled Dancer, and rode out to the village to tell Chimalee what had happened.

"Uh. The evil one," he said. "She told hiding places of many people during the war and said a curse would come to anyone who tried to kill her. We have left her alone. She is bad luck."

"She's dead, Chimalee. I have her boy at my place. He was half frozen."

Chimalee sighed and looked at his wife. "The child is too young to be evil," she said.

He nodded. "We'll come for the boy. This is good." He had said his judgment, and I knew he'd stick by his word.

They buried the woman secret so that the other villagers

231

wouldn't find out she had been there, and then they came back and carried Phillip home with them. I wished they had left the boy. He had been good company.

What am I doin' out here? I wondered to myself as the days kept passin'. I rode out a few times. Visited a few settlements east and south. Tried to hunt. "It's cold and lonely," I complained to Dancer. "And one day don't seem no different than the rest." Dancer just plodded on, used to my talkin' to him.

There wasn't no Negroes in the settlements I went to. One group of Creeks was from Alabama, but when I started askin' about a plantation raid they turned away— got hostile.

By accident I went to the place where that rich Creek lived. He met me on the road with a shotgun.

"You keep your freedom talk to yourself, blacksmith," he ordered.

"I'm just ridin' by," I said quiet. And he stood there to make sure I meant it.

I thought about ridin' to Camp Holmes to check for the mail, but one time when I stayed out for two days some of my meat was gone when I got back. I didn't say nothin' to Chimalee about it, 'cause I could understand the need. But I knew strayin' too far from home could leave me mighty poor.

Wiggins came by the third week of March and he was trailin' a pack mule. He was headed for Bent's Fort to hunt buffalo. He stayed one night; finished off the rest of the whiskey he had brought me before, and packed up the next afternoon.

"One thing I'm wonderin', Jason. Did you ever find what you come out here for?" My silence gave him the answer. "Are you sure you won't come with me? Feels mighty strange not havin' a partner, and you'd sure be a damn good one."

"Thank you, Wiggins, but I've hopes of returnin' to the States soon."

"Hmm." He heaved his old frame into the saddle and I wondered how he was goin' to fare out at Bent's. "Oh well, since you won't be goin' with me I guess you'll want this here letter I picked up at Camp Holmes." He handed me the envelope. "That's a mighty fine friend you got there. Yes, sir! A rare thing," he called as he rode off.

I held my breath while I opened the envelope. Only one sheet of paper inside, and the words on it wasn't cheerin'. No news had come from Alabama. Tolin had written there again, this time enlistin' the help of Nathan Caulborne. I sighed heavy and continued readin'.

Although the traffic here has been light the citizens of Jackson County have come on strong against us. The Mormons in Far West are very much in favor of abolition of slavery, and that—coupled with Mr. Johnston's previous assertion for the Mormon rights—has placed Maple Lane on what we have termed the "enemies list." A Howard County farm was burned out not too long ago and three Negroes were captured. One killed. They had passed through here not too many days before. It was a sad thing.

But I tell you I'm not quitting this time. I backed off of the Seminole War, I abandoned the frontier life, but this I shall hold to. Perhaps it has always been the very thing I wanted to do. My mother always spoke strongly against slavery.

On the brighter side. The young women of Maple Lane grow lovelier each day, and I wish you were here to enjoy the beauty. I speak highly of you to Miss Dorothy, and I'm sure that your return will increase her interest in you. Please write to us (a luxury Jason of old could not employ), and tell us of your life in the wilderness. I trust the coming year will bring us a new wind blowing in our favor, and I shall remain at the helm.

Affectionately, Tolin

The letter was dated December 28. I wondered if he had yet received my reply to his first letter. I started readin' parts of it again, distressed 'cause it sounded like Fannin-

233

type people was growin' in number, but I knew Tolin's heart was true to his work.

And him talkin' me up to Mr. Evans's girl, Dorothy. I wondered what she would be like. All dressed out in ruffled skirts just like Miss Samantha, I supposed, and talkin' fancy after goin' to that Quaker school. Tolin probably had it all thought out how I should hitch up with Dorothy Evans, and him marry Miss Samantha. I knew he figured we would live there at Maple Lane—farmin' and sneakin' Negroes north; readin' poetry. I laughed as I thought of it.

If Miss Dorothy Evans could see me now! I thought while scratchin' my beard.

Well, Miss Dorothy might never see me, I decided, with the lack of news from 'Bama. I wondered why Tolin thought Nathan Caulborne would help him prove my freedom. Him with his eighty bondsmen and two hundred bales a season. Probably more, now that he had the Cobb land. I looked to the west where Wiggins had rode off. Maybe I should've . . .

"Blacksmith." It was Chimalee. I looked up at him on his mule. Phillip was with him and lookin' all happy. "The boy wanted to see you. I have to prepare the store for new supplies. He will stay with you for the day."

I took Phillip from Chimalee's arms and hugged him. "That's fine, Chimalee. Sure it is!"

"This is good." He rode off to the store.

Havin' that boy there with me (the two of us tryin' to talk in two different languages and him gigglin' when I put him up on Dancer's back) brought back some hope to me. Phillip's stomach was round, and there was a shine to his hair. The awful gray of his skin was gone, and he was laughin'. I started thinkin' positive like Tolin had wrote. A new wind. It might be that way. I'd keep hopin'.

28

The winds did change. They blew warmer and folks started lookin' forward to spring. Chimalee worked at fixin' up the store, and Phillip stayed with me at those times. He cared for my animals and watched me whittle froe clubs or work at the forge. I showed him how to work the treadle that pumped the bellows, and he set right to it. He was goin' to be a smith, he declared. "Just like you, Jason." I laughed and started teachin' him the names of tools, and all about iron. He listened real good, but what he liked best was the hammer song.

I taught him the words, but when we started singin' it I got a sad feelin' inside. Phillip didn't notice, and kept on singin'. After a while I didn't mind too much, especially seein' him so happy. The days went by more quickly when he was with me, and in the evenin's I didn't notice the loneliness as much.

We got another week of snow, although it wasn't near as cold as before. I was pulled up by my fire one night durin' that spell readin' the book *Rob Roy* when I heard Dancer whicker a bit. It was a low sound, but I knew horses well enough to know it was from worry. Somethin' was out there that he wasn't familiar with. I primed my rifle and slipped into my jacket. The last time he had called a warnin' like that, there'd been a wolf pack movin' along the crick. I'd had to light a fire in the yard to keep them from comin' up to my animals.

The sounds got more insistent, and then the mule started brayin'. I went out the door ready to shoot, and seen a pony take off toward the village. A man was lyin' tight over the back of it. There was shots from the village, and I could just make out eight horsemen ridin' off northwest and drivin' a few cows and a mule before them. A war whoop sounded behind me, and I spun. Got off a shot. The man fell forward on his pony and the animal kept goin'. I reloaded and crouched in the shadow of the shed. All shootin' had stopped, and I waited. A fire flared up in the village, then slowly died down. The night got quiet and calm.

In the mornin' I checked the pony tracks. They were unshod. The fear that hadn't come on me the night before now struck me, and my breathin' came fast. A hatchet was stuck in the post of the horse shed by where I'd been standin'. There was also blood on the snow.

Chimalee rode up on his mule. "I'm glad to see you well," he said.

I found it hard to smile. "And your people?"

"No one hurt." He stared at the snow. "You hit one."

"Seems that way."

He rode back home.

That afternoon nine people came staggerin' in from the south. Chimalee told me later their village had been burned. Eight people killed.

A detachment of soldiers showed up the next mornin', ridin' slouched on their brown horses. I rode with them to the village to introduce Chimalee. He met us on the road, Phillip by his side.

"Got a group of Ponca on the raid," the sergeant announced as he lit a stubby cigar. "Keep an eye out."

I started gettin' mad, wonderin' how long they'd known about that. Chimalee didn't say nothin'. "They hit us two nights ago," I said. "Burned out a village south of here, too. Killed eight."

The sergeant eased around in the saddle and scratched his beard. "Well, guess that's the way of it."

I couldn't believe how uncarin' he was.

"This is the protection the government promised?" Chimalee growled.

"Which way they go from here?" the sergeant drawled.

"Northwest," I said.

"Uh. Can you spare your boy to ride with us and track?" he asked Chimalee.

"My *boy* is only seven. I don't think he'd be much help," Chimalee said. "If you mean the blacksmith, he can ride wherever he pleases."

The sergeant just scowled and rode off. Chimalee went back into the village. I rode back to my cabin—alone.

The next time the hunters were startin' out, Chimalee came and asked me to ride with them. "You have a good rifle, and our ammunition is low after that fight with the savages."

"Can someone keep an eye on my place?"

"I will watch it. You go with my men. This is good."

So I did, and we found a herd of buffalo grazin' their way back north. We also got a bonus of spottin' a wild horse herd. I helped plan the catch, and when we got back to the village we had enough meat for everyone, and nineteen horses. It was a shinin' thing to see the fine smiles on those Creek people.

"The blacksmith brings us luck!" one of the men called.

They let me help portion out the meat, and later on that week Chimalee brought me a smoked loin to go with what I'd took earlier.

The supplier came from Tullahassee and stocked up the store. There was a good-size load of iron in the shipment, and more travelers was comin' along the road. Spring settled on me and I started doin' little things to feel good with the new season. I made a shelf for my tools, whittled another stool for the smithy, burned my name in wood and

237

hung it over the entrance. I was restless, and the warmer it got the less comfortable I seemed. Finally, I shaved off that beard, figurin' that was the whole problem. It felt good to have the wind on my chin for the first time in five months.

I was shakin' out my sleepin' robe when Chimalee and Phillip came in from the village for the day. "Papa! Papa!" Phillip drew away from me when I turned around.

"Ha-ha!" Chimalee laughed at Phillip being afraid. "It is still the blacksmith. Just with no face hairs."

"I ain't changed none, Phillip." His little hands touched my cheeks and he stared. I laughed and tossed him into the air like I always did. Chimalee rode off still chucklin'. Soon Phillip and me was workin' and talkin' like always. My Creek talkin' was gettin' better, and his English was gettin' better. I even showed him how to make the letters of his name. He thought that was a fine thing.

I was gettin' included a bit more in the doin's of the Creeks 'cause they considered me lucky from the first hunt. The men was friendlier when they came to town, and we'd talk about the land. There was another hunt, and while it wasn't as good as the first, it was good. Even so, I felt out of place.

I got up one mornin' and found a young sorrel mare tied by my horse shed. She was from the wild herd we'd took. I walked her over to the store and told Chimalee I didn't need another horse.

"The mare is yours," he said flat.

"I thought the people shared the property?"

He nodded. "Creeks share with Creeks. We pay those who work for us. You keep the mare. This is good!"

It might have been good for him, but it made me feel hollow inside. I wished for the Crow and Arapaho folks of the Rockies where huntin' with the tribe made you one of the people. Wiggins had said the emigrants wasn't too friendly, and while I walked the mare back to the shop I wondered who was leadin' the pack train to the rendezvous this year. I thought about Tolin, too, and the friendly folks at Maple Lane. But I had a feelin' my freedom papers was never to be, and north—into the Western Territory—was the only bright spot. I'd wait till June, I thought, and then I'd pull out.

"Hammer come down," I was singin' on a sunny day. "Hammer come down. Hit that iron make a mighty good soun'. Heat up the iron. Make it glow red. Pound ten froes 'fore I go to bed." Phillip's little voice sang along with my big one. ". . . Take up the tong." I stopped my work and wiped my forehead with an old shirt.

"Iron's my life and I'll hammer it strong."

It wasn't Phillip singin'.

I looked to the door and saw a brown face lookin' at me. She was dressed in old cotton clothes, and had a blanket pulled around her. Her hair was braided over her shoulders like a Crow woman's. But the eyes!

"Louisa?" My voice was hoarse and cracked. She stepped into the shop and stared at me. I dropped all I was holdin' and went toward her. "Louisa!"

"No!" Her voice stopped me from embracin' her and she looked around real quick. Her fingers touched my face. "Jason," she whispered. My heart pounded and I took in everythin' about her.

"*Louisa!*" someone called from the door of the store.

"Don't go. Please!" I squeezed my hands on her arms. "*Louisa!*"

She turned and ran. I started after her, but halted when I saw a man help her onto a cotton cart. He was smilin'. He patted her shoulder, sat beside her; straightened her blanket. It seemed he was more than a master, and I stared. My heart turned to stone. The ox pulled the cart away. She didn't look back.

It was a nightmare havin' her right in front of me and now gone. The cart got smaller as it went out the north

239

road. I should go after her, I thought. Find out his price. Buy her away. But I had only fifty-two dollars.

"Hammer come down," Phillip started singin' again. "Come on, Jason!" he called. "Hammer come down. Hit that—"

I yelled at him so it made him cry, and it took me quite a while to let him know how sorry I was.

"I'm gonna close the shop the rest of the day," I told him. "You go on back to Chimalee." I tried to smile so he wouldn't worry, but I felt weak, and sick. Phillip looked out the north road and then ran off to the store. I went into my little house and tried to figure what to do.

29

I didn't lay no fire in the hearth that night. I slept sittin' in the chair and leanin' on the table. All the ghosts from 'Bama joined me: Skalley, Jake, Horace, Seth all crowded around. Was Louisa a ghost, too? Was she real? The visions floated and twisted into the pain of everything burned. *She was carried off by the Indians,* Mrs. Evans's voice whispered. And then Louisa was standin' there with solemn eyes, braided hair, a blanket around her thin body.

I shivered awake before dawn, dreamin' of Louisa bein' pushed onto a steamboat at Tampa Bay. "Jason! Jason!" she called in my dream, and my eyes shot open with fear. I almost ripped the leather hinges from the door when I opened it and bolted into the darkness.

It had rained durin' the night. The earth smelled fresh. I wanted the sun to come up and show me standin' in the fields of Cobb's place. I wanted to be back there—with no memories of all this. But it didn't happen that way. The sun came up. I was in Chimalee's village. And out that north road . . .

"Where are you going?" Chimalee asked when he brought Phillip over. I was saddlin' Dancer with my bed-roll and travelin' gear.

"I got some business to attend." I could still hear Louisa's voice: *Jason!*

"You have orders to fill. I saw many people stop at your shop yesterday." I kept to my fixin'. "People come because there's a smithy here. It is not good for you to leave it unattended."

I set the "Closed" sign in front of the shop and looked back at Chimalee. Phillip's eyes was big with fright. "I got to go, Chimalee."

I rode out that north road lookin' down it as though I could see that cotton cart still bein' pulled along. The rain had washed away most of the tracks, and I just kept hopin'. Why hadn't I gone north before? I wondered. And when the road forked, I agonized over which branch to take.

I went right. There was deeper ruts that way, and I rode and rode and rode. The sunlight got dim, and Dancer was slowin' down. We came out on a ridge and I could see all the way down the valley and across the Deep Fork. There was no sign of a town. Not a buildin' or a cleared field. I managed not to cry, and made camp.

Before the sun was up good the next mornin' I had started back. I took the left branch of the road, and all the time I was ridin' I kept hearin' Louisa's voice from my dream: *Jason!* Maybe it was all a dream, I started thinkin'. But when I closed my eyes I saw her before me, thin and solemn-eyed. So changed it had to be real.

It was midmornin' when I stopped Dancer at a crick that crossed the road. I was tired, and scared that I'd not find her again. I slumped down against a tree while Dancer drank. I closed my eyes, listenin' to the birds chirpin' above me. *Jason!* I heard Louisa's voice and I damned my brain for tormentin' me so. "Jason." I pressed my hands against the ground and almost screamed.

"Jason?" A hand was on my shoulder. I looked onto a cotton skirt. She knelt beside me with tears in her eyes. "Oh, Jason," she cried. "I didn't never think I'd see you again."

She was in my arms and cryin'. I was holdin' her—I was holdin' Louisa in my arms. We kissed and held each other.

"I was comin' back to you," she said. "I was scared before, but this mornin' I left to come back to you."

I looked up and saw the buckskin mule standin' at the crick. There was bundles tied on its sides. "Did you run away? Will they be lookin' for you?" I stood and stared across the crick.

"No, Jason. I don't got to run here. I ain't slaved. I'm Creek. It's listed that way at the fort."

"Then, that man you was with—he—"

"That was Oneechee. He took me for a daughter."

I looked down at her and touched her tan skin and soft, braided hair. My gettin' taller in two years made her seem even smaller.

"When the Creeks came to the farm in 'Bama they thought I was a Creek who was slaved, and they saved me from the soldier bullets. Oh, Jason! So much has happened!" She cried some more and I kissed her tears. "I fainted when I got snatched up like that, and when I come to I was afraid they'd sell me off, so I pretended I was like Skalley. I didn't talk and I guessed at what they was sayin'. They kept me with them, and soldiers caught us after two weeks."

"Why'd you run away back there when you come to my shop? Why didn't you stay? I've been so miserable—"

"I was afraid. Oh, Jason, I'm Oneechee's daughter, and my whole thinkin' has been in Creek. When I heard you singin' Jake's hammer song, it was like a ghost layin' its hands on me. I had to see if you was real. Then I took fright that if I stayed, things would be like they was before. Workin' for white folks. Never havin' nothin'."

"I'm a freedman, Louisa."

"That's what they said at the store, but all I could think was of 'Bama fields and hoein'. Out here I'm Creek. We work for ourselves. I was afraid to give that up."

I backed away from her and frowned. "I don't work for nobody but me. You act like it was me you were afraid of."

"I'm here, ain't I? I came back to you." Her next words

was almost a whisper. "I love you, Jason."

And I loved her, too. Dear God! How I loved her.

"They said—they said you were carryin' a baby," I said timidly while I held her again. "At Caulborne's—and we got word from Judith—"

"Judith? Where is she?"

"North. In freedom, now. I didn't see her, but I talked to folks that did, and they said—"

"There ain't no baby, Jason." Her face got hard and her eyes narrow, holdin' back tears. "There was, but it never come. The boats was hot; there was sickness when we was in New Orleans. By the time they shipped us to Rock Roe, up in Arkansas, I took sick with the pain, and the baby couldn't stay in me."

I held her closer. It didn't really matter about the baby. We could make another baby.

"Oh, Jason, this is all like a miracle now. Like the special things the preachers talk about at revivals. How did it happen?"

We sat down and I told her about Tolin and me comin' back from Florida and findin' the place burned and everyone gone. I told about Tolin sellin' the land and our headin' west. "He freed me, too, Louisa. All legal and everythin'. I'm Jason Cobb now."

"Masta Tolin did that?"

"He did. And he wouldn't like it none your callin' him *master.* He's in Missouri right now helpin' runaways escape to the North."

She shook her head. "Mattie always say he was different. More like his mama than his daddy. But how come you to be out here?"

I told her about Percy Fannin and why I had come to Chimalee's village. "I was hopin' for word about you."

She started cryin' and poundin' her fist on the ground. "It's white folks! They're all so mean!"

"It ain't that way! There's some good ones. Tolin give me my freedom and helped me get out here. Why, did you know he taught me how to read and write, way back when we was kids! The Johnstons are real good people, and there's other folks. Lots of folks that ain't that way!"

"But there's folks that is. And there's more of them! Slavers! Folks that'll do anythin' to get slaves and to hurt people. I don't want to ever go back to that!" Her anger calmed to a quiet hate. "There was slavers on the road from Rock Roe to Fort Smith. I was so scared! When I was sick they didn't bother me none, but later . . . they'd come around . . . I ain't never again gonna work for no white man!"

"Creek folks have slaves, too," I reminded her. "I don't know how you kept them from bondin' you, even though you do look like one of them. How is it that this Oneechee took you in?"

"They was needin' help, and I helped them."

I could tell it was somethin' hard for her to talk about. I thought about the Creek folks I had seen in chains in Montgomery and wondered if that had happened to her. And there was boats that sunk in New Orleans; and the swamps; and the sickness.

"Oneechee's wife, Zena, fall down next to me one day in Rock Roe, too sick to carry her load. Oneechee, he had saved a lot of things from his farm. He had some money, too, but no mules or cart. This white man came and say he'd give Oneechee a cart and ox for half of all he had. Oneechee was gonna do it, but I say I'd carry for him. That's how come me to be with them."

"Didn't they know when you talked you wasn't Creek?"

"If they knew, they didn't care. I wasn't sick no more, and I took to findin' food. I made herb broth so Zena get better. I stayed with her while Oneechee hunt. I go into towns and beg food. There was never enough food. Never enough." She sort of shuddered from the memories, then sighed deep and kept on.

"This white man came with food once. Not much, but he started takin' all the property for payment. Him's that one that was takin' up Negroes. Oneechee saw me scared and he made me tell him the truth. He never told no one. When we got to Fort Gibson they was settin' down names in the tribe book. He tells them I'm his daughter. Louisa Oneechee, it say."

She leaned against me and shivered, not from cold, but from the memories. I wanted to take all that sufferin' away from her. I wanted her young again and laughin'. To see her eyes shine like happiness was all she'd ever known was what I wished, but the pain and hardness was on her. Her face was tired.

The sun was past midday, and Dancer had strayed up the crick lookin' for grass. I called him, and then had to go after him.

"This is Dancer. He saved my life once when I was caught in a blizzard," I said when I brought him back.

Louisa stroked the soft nose. "He's pretty, Jason."

"I've got a mare, too. A wild one that me and the hunters caught last month. She'll be saddle-broke before too long." I mounted Dancer and took up the reins of the mule.

"This mule is mine. Oneechee got two more from folks on the trail what died. He let me take this mule when I told him I was comin' to you."

"Sounds like Oneechee is a good person."

"He's my father, Jason. He say that nothin's gonna change that."

She started to get on the mule. "No," I said. "Ride with me." I took her hand and pulled her up behind me. "I don't want us to be apart no more."

The sun had dropped to a big orange ball on the trees when we got back to the village. We could see fires south by the fields and there was good smells of food in the air.

"Plantin' feast," Louisa said as I stopped Dancer by the smithy. "Our fields isn't ready yet. I was afraid Oneechee wouldn't want me to come, with so much work to do." I got off the horse and put my arms out to her. She looked at the shop and then at the tiny house behind it. "I didn't know there was a house."

"It's little. I didn't make it thinkin' of no more than me livin' here." I held her to me before settin' her down.

"You did it all yourself?"

I nodded and she walked through the covered passage to the door. I was real proud to have her step into that little room. She touched the table and looked at the fireplace sunk down into the ground.

"It keeps the ground warm," I explained. "Since I didn't put in a floor."

Her fingers moved along the back of the chair. "It's the kind Horace used to make." She turned to me quick. "How many? Who? Who got killed back in 'Bama?"

I hadn't even thought that she wouldn't know, and I hated to tell it. "All except you, Mattie, Judith, and some younguns. I don't know which ones. Mistuh Cobb was killed."

"Didn't nobody kill that strange old man. He fell out from a stroke when he saw the Creeks takin' his horses. Fired one shot from his flintlock, and just keeled over. Seth went to him and saw he was dead." She swallowed hard. "I was watchin' it all from the smokehouse. I seen the soldiers comin' up the top-crick road. They saw Seth bendin' over Masta Cobb and killed him where he stood." She started cryin'. "I saw—I saw Skalley fall."

She wiped her eyes with the edge of her blanket. We was quiet for a while. "They all get killed 'ceptin' who you said?" I nodded. "Well." She put her blanket across the chair. "You better see to that fine horse." She took up the flint box to get a light for the fire, then looked up at me with a wide-eyed stare. "It's Jake's!"

"I got most all his tools."

She nodded and tears started on her cheeks. I left real quick, not knowin' what else to do. All the time I was tendin' to Dancer and the mule I thought about the things she told me. My dangers seemed like nothin' to what she had been through. Her face was so sad and solemn. She hadn't smiled once. Not once!

I went back in with her bundles and the stool from the shop. The fire was cracklin' around the wood, and Louisa was layin' on the buffalo robe with her blanket over her. She looked tired, and she was still grippin' that flint box. I started fixin' a stew. My cookin' was so plain, and I wished I had somethin' extra fancy to give her. I served up a plate and took it to her, but she was asleep. Her face was relaxed and peaceful-lookin'. Her hands was still around the flint box, and for that moment—for one pinch of time —the years slipped back and we was in Skalley's cabin. Louisa and me. That's how it would be from now on: Louisa and me.

30

Mornin' light slipped in under the hide I had tacked over the window hole. I turned a bit and felt Louisa next to me. Her sleep was a deep-breathin' affair like rest had never been with her before. My rollin' in beside her in the night hadn't bothered her, and that mornin', when I touched her soft, dark brown hair, it didn't cause her to stir.

I got up, started the fire, and set the coffee to boil. It was still chilly, and I was lookin' forward to warm weather so I could wash myself good all over. Bathin' and shavin' seemed real important since Louisa was there.

"Jason!" Phillip came through the door all excited. "There's another mule in your corral!"

"Shhh!" I pointed to Louisa.

Phillip's eyes got big, and we went outside. "That's the woman what give you weakness! Why is she here?"

"She's my woman. My wife. Chimalee has a wife, now Jason has a wife."

"You don't want me to come no more? She take care of Dancer now?"

"No! No, I still want you to come like always. Dancer wouldn't stand nobody else combin' him but you and me."

"And the mule, too?"

I nodded.

"Jason?" Louisa opened the door. Phillip stared at her

and then took off through the shop and toward the store. I hugged Louisa and we went back inside.

The mornin' warmed quickly. We ate a small breakfast and I went to the shop. Wagons was already movin' on the road, and I knew I had work to do. Dancer and the mules was still standin' in their night spots. The mare was in the shed. I looked around for Phillip before I tended them.

About midmornin' Louisa came into the shop. Her hair was freshly braided tight and straight over her shoulders. "We should go to the village leader and tell him I'm here. It's good to do, and I can help in the fields."

"I thought you said you was through with that kind of work."

"I won't do it for no white man, is what I said. Here we work for ourselves. All the women work in the fields. It's the way of things."

I took off my apron and Louisa and me walked to the store. Phillip was sittin' just inside the door, braidin' a halter. He gave Louisa a timid smile.

"Chimalee," I said after he finished with a customer. "I have a wife. I wanted that you should know. She wants to help with the village work." I stretched my arm out to Louisa. She came up and the sunlight from the window shone on her. "Her name is Louisa."

Chimalee's face was tight. I felt Louisa grip my hand. "This woman was in here two days ago. Her father is Oneechee from the Cottonwood village."

I nodded.

"Jason and me was together in Alabama before the war," Louisa said. "We was separated in the running." The Creek language was easy on her tongue.

Chimalee squinted real hard at me. "Blacksmith, we don't hold with Negroes takin' Creek wives."

I was shocked. "But I'm a freedman!"

"I know, but—" He looked again at Louisa. "Your father, he knows you are here?" Louisa nodded. "He knows who you are with?" Louisa nodded again. Chimalee sighed.

"Blacksmith, you have brought good fortune to my people, and you gave me a new son by saving Phillip in the winter freeze. For these reasons I accept your wife, but this is not good!"

Phillip didn't come to the forge shop any more.

Louisa helped in the cornfields every day that first week, but then she started puttin' in a garden plot behind the house, and only goin' to the fields sometimes—maybe seekin' out company. Of course, we had each other, and that was a fine thing. Talkin'. Bein' close. Lovin'.

Louisa. In so many of my dreams I'd called to her. All the things I wanted to share: grief and joy. When we talked I left out much of the grief, for she had suffered so much. If Louisa could have counted *coup* she would have had many eagle feathers for the last two years. While I was enjoyin' the scenery on the way to Fort Laramie, Louisa was helpin' Zena and Oneechee haul their belongin's through the swamps of Arkansas. When I was racin' horses and playin' games, she was fightin' off the Delaware and Kiowa from under a cotton cart. My winter in the cozy confines of the fort with fresh meat and apple pies was a pain to mention when she had been diggin' roots and scrapin' bark just to exist.

"People died a lot," she said. "And the only good thing was we got what they left."

She hunted with Oneechee, fought the snows to go the one hundred and ten miles for rations, pulled plows through rough, unbroken soil. Her hands was callused and strong; and she'd killed as many men in Indian fights as Tolin and me put together—includin' one of them Ponca that come through the month before.

One night after two weeks of workin' part-time in the fields, Louisa came home so quiet and solemn I thought she'd taken ill. I couldn't even get her to smile when I told a funny tale, and she usually liked hearin' me spin yarns.

"It ain't friendly here," she said after supper the next

night. I was usin' my axe to make a new chair. "Has it always been like this?"

"Pretty much."

"You don't get asked huntin' with the men no more, and that boy, Phillip, he stands in the door of the store watchin' you, but he don't come to the smithy no more." She put down the mendin' she was doin'. "It's my fault, ain't it? 'Cause they think I'm Creek."

"It ain't you. It's just the way of things. I've been here nearly six months, and nobody but Phillip uses my name. They always call me Blacksmith, that's all."

"You're a good blacksmith, Jason. Real fine. You could set up a shop anyplace. Do we got to stay here?"

"This is where I told Tolin I'd be. We'll be hearin' soon, and can move on."

"Tell me again about the western lands," she said as she bent back to the mendin'.

"The mountains?"

"No. I seen mountains in Arkansas. All rough and covered with trees. Mist hangin' like a curse over the piney ravines."

"It ain't that way out there. Nothin' like it!" And I told her again about the mountains and huntin' trips, and added the times we visited Indian camps. "Those folks are real friendly if they're tradin' with you. I got these moccasins from a Crow woman." I touched the dusty beadwork on the boots and remembered my times with Spring Star. I didn't say no more about Indian women.

"But it was the Cheyenne that call you man of victory skin."

"Yep." I had to grin. "That really amazed Tolin. Me, too."

"Masta Tolin, he really lets you call him just Tolin?"

"That's the way of it." I still hadn't told her the route we took to get to that friendliness. "I didn't have no trouble with most of them western folks, neither. Not that there ain't some who would be troublesome."

"Like that fight you had with that white man. I sure would have liked to see that." There was a hint of a smile from her.

"You see, a man who can pull his share out here is looked on no different 'cause of skin color."

"It's dreamin', Jason. It don't sound quite real."

"Well, it's real enough. Like the folks at Maple Lane. When we get back there you'll see." She was quiet, and I looked over at her worried face. "No need for you to be afraid. Folks at Maple Lane will love you like I do."

"It would be good to be around friendly folks, that's true." But I sensed she didn't believe any of what I'd told her.

I packed off on Dancer the next day and rode the two days to Camp Holmes to see if the letter had come. Louisa stayed to tend her plantin'. She had to haul water up from the crick, 'cause the springtime had given mighty little rain. There was new settlements of Creek people all through the valley, and the wagon road near Camp Holmes was well used.

"What are ya after?" someone greeted when I entered the buildin'.

"I'm hopin' for mail. Has there been a letter for Jason Cobb?"

"Oh, you're the one with the crate last fall. Shaved off your beard, I see. No nothin's comin' up the river. No rains. There's boats stuck on the sand bars near Fort Towson. Looks to be a dry season."

"Nothin' from the winter?"

"I give a letter to that Wiggins character. Didn't ya get it?"

"Yes, but that was in March."

"It had been sittin' here since late January. I was about to figure you lost to the Comanche, or somethin'."

"I fared well in a Creek village. It was a hard winter for them folks, but they got a good plantin' in this year."

253

"Don't know as these people are ever gonna make it. They're sick and poor. Hell, word is the Chickasaw is bringin' in smallpox. Couldn't get them to stay at Fort Towson till the doctors came. They just rode off across the country to try to get land for plantin'. Of course they got to plant so they'll make it through the winter." He shook his head. "They're damned if they do, and damned if they don't. Poor beggars."

Sickness was somethin' these people didn't need, sure enough. I remembered Jake tellin' of the smallpox he saw in Carolina in the first years of the century. Folks was all wasted out and black-marked. He had been given some kind of medicine so as not to get it. Folks died, he said. Folks died plenty.

Louisa's face looked anxious when I got back to Chimalee. "Was there a letter?" she asked.

"Nothin'. The rivers are low. Might be they'll start haulin' mail in wagons, but there's nothin' now."

"Word come here about smallpox. A man came down from the agency sayin' Upper Creeks at North Fork was struck with it. He says doctors is gonna be at the agency with medicine."

"There was mention of it at the tradin' house, too. Man there said it was Chickasaws what had it."

"The village had a meetin' about it last night, and I went. Chimalee say we can't leave the crops long enough to go four days to the agency and four days back."

"It's a long trip, sure enough." I unloaded the meats.

"I'm afraid, Jason. I don't want to see no more dyin'. What if it was to strike you or me? I just couldn't bear it!"

"I know, darlin'. I know." I pulled her to me and comforted her, and we started plannin' the trip to the agency.

"Blacksmith." Chimalee rode up to the horse shed while I was fixin' the travel packs on a mule three days later. Phillip was with him. "I have word that you and your woman are going to the agency for the vaccinations."

"That's right. We're leavin' today."

"My wife and I have lived through the smallpox once in Georgia. Others here, too, have survived it, but—" He sighed heavy. "Here. Take Phillip. He must have the medicine. My three children all died on the trip to this land. Phillip is all we have. Take him with you." He handed me a bundle of clothes and put Phillip down. "You will do it?" he asked. I nodded and drew Phillip against my leg. "This is good."

We left at midday with one pack mule. Louisa and Phillip were ridin' on the sorrel mare, and me on Dancer. We took the north road until evenin', and stopped for the night with Oneechee at the Cottonwood village. It was a day extra of travel, but Louisa wanted it that way. Zena, her adopted mother, cried for joy at seein' her. Oneechee was solemn, but friendly. Louisa explained where we were goin' and begged them to come.

"I have the medicine already," Oneechee said, and he showed us the scar on his arm. "Zena, you do not. You go with them."

So in the mornin' we hitched the mule to Oneechee's ox cart. Phillip and Zena rode in the cart with the supplies. Louisa took the reins and we tied her sorrel to the back. We started east.

31

The agency was quiet when we got there in late afternoon. The next issuin' of annuities wasn't for a few weeks, and so there was only a few folks who come for medicine, and those that was loiterin' or travelin' through. The signs were up by the agency office about vaccinations and an arrow pointed to the side door. The agent, Mr. Campbell, was on the steps of the building. He frowned at me. I nodded to him and he watched while I took Phillip in my arms and we all walked to the side door of the building. I knocked, and a tired-lookin' man in a gray suit and vest opened the door.

"We come for vaccinations," I said.

"What village are you from?" he asked as we walked in.

"Us three are from Chimalee, north of Camp Holmes. This woman is from Cottonwood."

"Good. Western folks. There's hope for you, since you haven't been exposed. Let's have the boy first. You all bare your arm. Up here." He tapped near his shoulder.

Phillip started whimperin' when Louisa rolled up the sleeve of his shirt. Zena went to him and comforted him while I pulled out of my leather shirt and rolled the sleeve of my cotton one.

"Won't hurt much, but you got to hold real still . . . That's it . . . Good boy."

Phillip cried loud and yelled *ow!* My stomach started flippin' over as I watched the doctor scratchin' on that little arm with a needle. I never had no doctor around me before, except Bornston—I don't remember much about that—and my mouth felt pretty dry as I got ready. Louisa was bug-eyed and pale. She huddled against me and we watched as the doctor brushed dust off Zena's arm with the back of his hand, and he started on her.

Wasn't more than a half hour later and we was all vaccinated and outside. My arm smarted a bit, and in a few days it would itch a lot, but it wasn't as bad as I thought it would be.

"That's it!" Campbell was standin' by the cart as Zena and Phillip got in the back. "You're that blacksmith that rode in here last fall lookin' for work."

"I did. You sent me to Chimalee. I wintered there."

"Why, there was a man rode in here askin' directions to Chimalee just a while ago. Said he was lookin' for a blacksmith by the name of Jason Cobb. Is that your name?"

"That's me." I wondered who could be lookin' for me. Wiggins knew where I was. There wasn't no one else out here—unless it was that man of Fannin's I had seen at the tradin' house on the Neosho last fall. I started feelin' hot. "What man was lookin'? A heavy-set cuss—looks like a bull-whacker?"

"Oh, no. A young fellow. Riding a chestnut horse. He might be around someplace. He looked trail-weary and it's likely he's camped back by the river."

"What is it, Jason?" Louisa asked as she climbed onto the cart seat.

"I might be dreamin', but it sounds like Tolin is out here lookin' for me." I grinned as I climbed in Dancer's saddle. Louisa's eyes got wide. "I'll ride out to the camp area. You follow. We have to stay the night here anyway." I rode off as Louisa was slappin' the reins on the mule's flanks.

If Tolin was here it meant he had some word from Alabama. My heart was poundin' as I rode out to the camp area. The news must be bad, or he'd have never come into the Territory.

I think Dancer knew before me where Tolin was. He must have smelled out that horse he'd spent so much time with last year, and I was suddenly only a hundred feet from Tolin's camp.

"Tolin Cobb!" I yelled as I reined up. He was stakin' out his canvas for the night. He had on brown cloth pants tucked in his handsome ridin' boots, and he was wearin' his fringe leather shirt. I was out of the saddle before he turned around good.

"Jason! By God, if it isn't fortune that guides our paths!"

We hugged and pounded each other on the back, then we was wrestlin' and laughin' and fallin' out in the grass like two bitty boys.

"Damn, if you haven't grown some more!" Tolin finally said as we sat studyin' each other.

"It happens," I said. "But what's that yellow stuff on your lip?" I asked about the well-trimmed mustache.

"Ah, yes. Makes me look older—more prosperous. And Samantha likes the way it tickles when I kiss her."

"Ho! You've got to that stage, huh?"

"Maple Lane is waiting for me to come back with you so we can have the wedding," he said boastfully.

"A weddin'! How about that!" I thought about what he said. "I'm to go back with you? That means the paper come."

"Didn't you get my letter? I wrote in February that it had arrived. I said, 'Meet me at Fort Gibson the first week in May.'"

"I didn't get a letter. We're up here for vaccinations against the smallpox. Mail hasn't come to Camp Holmes since January."

"I figured something like that when you didn't show up the past four days. That's why I was coming out to that village to get you." Tolin bolted up and rummaged in his poke bag. "Here it is, Jason. Proof of what we already know. You're a free man." He handed me the paper. "And I went to the Independence courthouse and registered you there, too. That's what I should have done last year. Now, let's see that damn Fannin try something!"

"I wasn't sure the papers would come when you said you were askin' help from Caulborne."

"He did it, he surely did! Wrote me a big long letter when he sent the paper, about how he considered me foolish and headstrong and completely irrational. He said he knew about my freeing you already—I guess it was the talk of Union Springs all that summer. But he sent the papers. The county clerk had ignored the first letter. Caulborne said, 'No matter how ludicrous your request seems to me I shall continue to be a man of my word. I promised you my support for your endeavors, and I hold to that promise by sending you herewith the paper for your blacksmith.' "

"I would have never believed it." I stared at the paper.

"Ha! If he knew of my endeavors with Mr. Johnston he would never have cooperated."

I heard the creak of a cart and went to the road. It was Louisa. I waved the paper and went to the mule and led it off the road.

"Your paper?" She looked breathless, with a hint of a smile. I nodded. Zena and Phillip slipped out of the cart and came around.

Tolin walked over. "What's this? You've got a whole family!"

"Hello, Masta Tolin," Louisa said in a quiet voice.

Tolin stopped like he'd been struck with a club. He looked at Louisa and stepped closer. His eyes blinked; his hand went out—not quite touchin' her face.

"Dear God," he whispered. "Louisa. You've found her, Jason." He smoothed his hand along her hair. She backed away, tight-faced and flushed. "You call me Tolin, please, Louisa. Just as Jason does. I'm master of no one but myself." Louisa nodded and studied his face carefully. I couldn't do nothin' but watch. Proud to have her with me, and to have Tolin for a friend.

Tolin looked at Zena and Phillip.

"This is Louisa's mother, Zena," I said. Tolin's eyes were puzzled. "Louisa is listed on the Creek rolls at Fort Gibson. Zena and her husband, Oneechee, adopted her. This here is Phillip." The boy was leanin' tight against my leg. "He's the son of Chimalee at the village where my shop is. We brought them for the medicine, too."

Tolin was smilin'. "Well! I would be pleased for you and your—your family—to join my camp." He bowed deeply from the waist and spread his arms toward the fire.

Zena and Louisa started right in fixin' a big meal. Phillip helped Tolin and me bed the animals for the night. Tolin took to that little boy right away, and when I swung up my axe to cut more firewood, they were loungin' against a saddle and Tolin was drawin' letters in the dry ground. We ate a fillin' dinner and the sky turned black with night. The fire crackled and snapped around the wood. Tolin and me started talkin' about Indian Territory and my meetin' with Wiggins. Zena and Louisa talked and played with Phillip for a while, and then the boy and Zena rolled into their blankets in the cart. Soon Louisa was wrapped up and leanin' heavily on my shoulder, asleep.

"You're a man of wonder, Jason," Tolin said as he looked at Louisa. "To find your woman in this vast land. I believed her dead. I truly did. There's . . . no baby, I see."

"No. It was never born. She was left in Arkansas with the pain . . . Her troubles make me ache to think of them."

"I'm sure her suffering was horrible." He sighed and shook his head. "Well, there'll be sadness in the Evans household."

"Why is that?"

"Miss Dorothy. Why, from what I'd talked up about you I think she was more than anxious for you to get back."

"Now what would that little lady want with me? I'm a

crittur of the land, Tolin. I'm not refined and polished like I imagine that girl to be. Put me in a broadcloth suit and it would be like casin' me in slats."

"Listen to you! You can be any way you want. But it doesn't matter. You have your own true love."

"That I have, and a fine, free creature she is."

Tolin laughed and leaned back on his elbows. "You are really amazing! I imagined to find you as I would find myself after seven months alone in this untamed country: gaunt for company and proper food; scraping together an existence. Here you are—prosperous. Even stronger, I believe, than when I left you. You have your woman, your own business, fine animals, friends." He shook his head.

"The friends have been few," I admitted. "The Creeks are singular people; they don't hold much with outsiders."

"It seems they took to your Louisa rather well."

"It's only by the luck of her havin' a white mother that they take her for one of them, but in all, I guess I have fared well. Exceptin' for the loneliness, I find this unsettled land favors me. I take to the country like those revival preachers go to sin: it's a challenge to live with it, and maybe to conquer a part of it."

"That's a fine way of saying it, but then you've always been good with words. That letter you sent in January was a real joy."

"Huh. I can't say the same for yours. What's all the problems up there in Missouri?"

"Oh, I swear! It's even worse now. Folk are squabbling among themselves almost to war. The Mormons are the biggest concern now. It seems their leader, Joseph Smith, was forced out of the East. He got to Missouri in March, and there's been a big increase of Mormon emigrants ever since. Missourians are carrying guns against them. Actually doing battle!"

"What about Maple Lane?"

"Mr. Johnston isn't taking a vocal position just yet. He's planning to run for the State senate now that I'll be there to help Mr. Evans run the farm. He's playing his cards close to his vest, so to speak."

"Politics! Next you'll be runnin' for some office," I laughed.

"You know, Jason. That's a very effective position to be in these days. Henry Clay and Daniel Webster are strong leaders of the new Whig Party, and they are bound to have a positive effect on the slavery issue."

A goatsucker whistled in the woods; frogs croaked from the riverbanks. "You've finally found your place, haven't you, Tolin?"

"I have, Jason. It won't be easy, but I'm committed to it from my very soul."

Louisa stirred a bit and I kissed her forehead. "Well, best we turn in so we can pack out early tomorrow. Will you ride with us to Chimalee?"

"That's right. You do have to go back there."

"We have to deliver Zena and Phillip home, and pack up our house. Come with us."

"I'd like to, but four days there and four days return, then another ten days back to Independence . . . No. I think not. I've my own true love expecting to see me by the end of this week. I'd gray her hair with worry if I was three weeks late and she thought me lost in the wilderness."

"I'm sorry we'll miss the wedding," I said as I leaned back against the saddle. I pulled Louisa closer to me and tucked the blanket around us both.

"The wedding was just waiting for you to get back; it can keep another three weeks. Be sure of that!"

I stared up at the sky that was sparklin' with stars in the clear blackness. The goatsucker was still whistlin' and flyin' off in the distance. Louisa snuggled her head on my shoulder and her hand lay light on my chest. My heart was rested, my head calm with Louisa against me and my friend at my side. It filled the emptiness that I had from Chimalee's cold village.

Somewhere on the agency grounds a dog started barkin'.

———

It was a sharp, runnin' bark that ended in a half howl, then started hard again. A warnin' bark, I was always told. Lettin' the woods know somethin' wasn't right. Another dog joined in across the river, and another farther off. They barked and rippled their message into the darkness. The frogs quit croakin', the nighthawks was quiet. Then the dogs stopped, except for the last one. I could hear him real faint. *Yap! Yap! Yap-yap-yap-yap-yap.* I must have drifted off to sleep after that.

The mornin' started with a warm breeze. Zena was up early and she fixed corn mush with meal she had brought. It tasted good with hot coffee and smoked ham from Tolin's pack. Phillip gathered in the animals, and we started off on the trails. Tolin left us at the agency road and headed northeast to Fort Gibson and eventually the States. We headed southwest, back into the valley of the Canadian.

"Three weeks!" Tolin called. "I'll be looking for you no later than mid-June!"

"Mid-June? What happens then?" Louisa asked as I waved good-bye to Tolin.

"That's when we're to be at Maple Lane. He's gonna marry Miss Samantha then, too."

She nodded and urged the mule ahead. I looked down at her from Dancer's saddle. She was watchin' the road—starin' down it like she could see through it—and her face was plain with no expression.

32

"We're movin' back to the States," Louisa told her parents when we got to Cottonwood. Zena gasped and started cryin', but Louisa hardly changed her expression.

"We can come back," I said quickly. "I could move the smithy here to Cottonwood."

Louisa shook her head no. "I knew we'd have to go. I thought it would be after my plantin's came in, and I didn't know if it would be the States for sure ... And there's other reasons. Talk I heard in the fields last time I was there. There's gonna be laws; laws for Negroes like the Choctaw have."

"Is that true?" Zena asked her husband.

"It's true," he said. "I have heard the talk, too. Last year the Choctaw made laws that Negroes aren't to own property—"

"That's for their slaves!" I said.

"For slave and free; and there's other laws for freedmen. Some places don't even want them in their towns. Creek people are thinkin' those might be good laws," Louisa said.

"They have talked of it here, too," Oneechee said. "I worried. I worried for my daughter and—and the Negro she loves." Oneechee didn't look at me when he spoke, and I knew I hurt him by takin' away his daughter. "It's good that you have a place to go. The Seminole will be sent out here soon and they will have to share this land. They have many Negroes with them. It's better you go before there is anger in our people and they do things unwisely."

Phillip was sittin' big-eyed under the table and listenin' to everythin' we said. Louisa took him to a cot and covered him with a blanket. Oneechee and Zena held Louisa tenderly and then went into a little sleepin' room where they had their rope bed.

"It's all right, Jason. Really," Louisa said.

I was still slumped by the window—unbelievin' at what I'd heard. "That's what made you so sad that last day you came from the fields," I said. She nodded. "You're listed as Creek. You have family here. Those laws wouldn't mean nothin' to you."

"But I ain't Creek, Jason. Just 'cause it's listed on the rolls don't make it so. I know who I am—what I am; and most of all, I want to be with you."

I held her to me, knowin' somethin' wasn't right, but not able to figure it out. I should be happy, I thought. I've got my legal freedom back, I found the woman I love, I'm on my way to friends. But a little jumpin' started in my brain —sort of like that dog barkin' at the agency camp. It drummed to a headache by mornin'.

We made good time back to Chimalee 'cause we were without the cart. The trees were heavy with new leaves, but that was the only green around. The ground was rock hard and dry; the cricks were shallow. When we got to the village Phillip squirmed away from Louisa as we passed the store. He slid from the horse and took off at a run.

"Chimalee! Papa!" he hollered.

It wasn't five minutes before Chimalee's long, steady strides brought him to where we were unsaddlin' the horses. Phillip's hand was tight in his, and his eyes were tear-filled.

"Phillip tells me you're leaving," Chimalee said in an even tone.

265

"We are. I'll finish any work that is here, and we'll leave right away. We have friends in the States who are waitin' for us." Chimalee was silent, just starin' at me. "When I came you said one or two seasons." Chimalee still stared. "We know of the laws, Chimalee, like the Choctaw have. Creeks will have them soon."

"Papa, Papa, don't let him go. Please!" Phillip cried.

Chimalee picked him up and held his head to his shoulder. "The boy loves you," he said.

"I will miss him." I smoothed Phillip's hair, and he reached for me. I held him and tried to comfort him. He was full of sobs and tight hugs when I stood him on the ground. I took off my bear-claw necklace and put it around his neck. "You keep this for me, and I can always feel good about who's got it." I wiped his tears and hugged him one last time. Chimalee said nothing. He made no judgment this time.

"I wish we could take that boy." I sighed as I watched him and Chimalee go toward the village. "I don't want to leave him."

"He has to stay here," Louisa said quietly. "He's Creek, not Negro. We know who we are, and he has to know for hisself, too."

I felt the pain of tears inside me, and I brushed Dancer to a bright shine.

When we left Chimalee, we had barely enough packs for both mules. We left the furniture in the house, but I did take the buffalo hide Wiggins had give me.

It was before sunrise and the sky was gray. I filled the water skins at the crick and tied them on the buckskin mule. Louisa came out of the house, the flint box clutched in her hand. I let my eyes take in every corner and log of that little house.

"I'll never worry none about my comfort. You build a fine house, Jason. It'll make somebody a real good

266

home," Louisa said after she mounted the mare.

"When I lived there I found you again. That place will always be special to me."

"The prairie looks real pretty even with the dryness," Louisa said to me as we rode on the sixth day from Chimalee. "I'm glad we came this way, and not on the wagon road."

"Water on that Texas Road wouldn't be too good with all the travelers," I said. The part I didn't say was that I didn't want to go back on the trail that had slavin' travelers. Some might know Fannin, or men like him. I didn't want to meet that kind of trouble.

Of course, I took the chance of runnin' into some unfriendly Delaware or Osage by goin' north. I watched our trail real good, and turned us into the brush once 'cause I thought I had seen some men on horseback. We stayed low for a while, and there was no sight or sound of anybody. I rode us out of the brush and again saw the dark figures on the rise off to the left. I checked my rifle as we moved up the trail, and then the sunlight showed the forms for what they were—outcroppin's of brown rocks.

Louisa pointed to the rocks. "There's them wild injuns you been hidin' us from," she teased.

"Careful is the only way to be in this land," I defended. I felt mad and a trifle silly.

"Sure enough, Jason Cobb." Louisa smiled a bit, and I started laughin' at myself.

The Verdigris branched west. I filled the water skins and we headed northeast across land that was flat and rollin' with grasses. We camped beside a little crick. A spring bubbled from some rocks nearby and the water was fresh. Louisa kept the cookin' fire small and under the trees so the smoke wouldn't be sighted by hostiles. The evenin' air was warm and we slept without any fire at all.

"Jason, look!" Louisa's anxious whisper made me wake

with a start. She kept her hand on my chest so I wouldn't move, and I stared across the crick. There was three deer steppin' careful toward the water. The buck kept his head high and his nose was twitchin'. A breeze waved the grass and must have pushed our scent to them. They stared at us, then bolted almost silently back into the trees.

"Wasn't they just the loveliest creatures?" Louisa sighed.

"You nearly scared me witless. That's no way to wake a man!"

"I'm sorry, but I wanted you to see them." She snuggled back against me. "Wouldn't it be nice to have a little house right here? Look at that sky! And can you smell the grass? I love this land, Jason. Don't you?"

"I do, but I love my hair a sight better. There's a lot of injun folks wouldn't take to us plunkin' down in their huntin' grounds."

"Well, not right here; but somewheres out in the open. Somewheres so you could see the deer and smell the grass, and not be bothered with nobody if that's how you want it." Her voice was gentle, and I turned to look at her. There was a slight glimmer in her eyes and a softness to her mouth. I kissed her.

"After what you been through these last two years I'd never have thought the land would call to you," I said quietly. "It's been mean to you."

"It ain't the land what's been mean. It's the people. Wasn't the land what burned out the Cobbs or chained me to a riverboat. Remember what Seth would say: Land is all you can count on. If you love it, it loves you back." She stretched and got up to make a fire. " 'Twas the land what saved me when the white people passed me by in Arkansas. I love the land."

I put my hands around that bitty little waist and kissed her cheek. "You wait till you see Maple Lane. It's land to love. There's a huge pond all filled with ducks and geese in this meadow in front of the house. The maple trees in the fall have so much color it's crazy to see."

268

"How many more days, Jason, before we're there?"

"Not too many. Maybe six or seven."

Four more days and we crossed into Missouri near But-
ler to save ridin' through Kickapoo and Pawnee country.
We rode along the wagon roads leadin' to Independence,
through the woods and hills. The evenin' brought smells of
burnin' wood from the farmhouses, and nearly every mornin' we heard a cock someplace greetin' the sun. Cow bells
clanked, and dogs chased after us down the road. Sometimes there were little barefoot children on their way to
fish or hunt birds.

The wagon road got wider, and was well traveled durin'
the day. We passed cornfields and cotton fields. Negroes
was slavin' with hoes and bent backs. Louisa turned her
head away.

Second day in Missouri, we started passin' wagon camps.
Independence was close. "Look at all the people!" Louisa
exclaimed. "And those big wagons. Why are they stopped
here?"

There were more than fifteen wagons, and it made quite
a sight with younguns runnin' and yellin', chickens
floppin', dogs arguin' and yappin', women washin' or cookin'. A knot of men was standin' by the tongue of one wagon
smokin' pipes and spittin' tobacco. I pulled up next to
them.

"Where are you bound for?" I asked.

"Oregon!" a slender man answered. He looked like he
should be a store clerk someplace, and he smiled friendly.

"That's a powerful rough road for wagons this size."

The other men suddenly took interest. "You been out
there?"

"Been beyond Fort Laramie a bit. Two winters ago. The
trails west of that are narrow and rough. Wagons could
have some trouble."

"There's them that done it," a fat man called. "Trappers
is leadin' them through. We're meetin' up with a man at

Council Bluffs who says he knows the way."

"How far to Council Bluffs, friend?" another asked.

"Ten days by wagon, and with good weather."

"They got soldiers at Fort Atkinson now. Does that mean injun trouble?"

"There shouldn't be any between here and there." They all smiled and seemed to take my word for gospel. *Mangeurs du lard*, I thought. "I hope your trails are smooth." I backed Dancer away and joined up with Louisa on the road. "They're headed for Oregon."

"Is that out where you was?"

"No. It's farther west. Out over the Rocky Mountains. They'll have to leave a lot of the things they're carryin'. The wagons will be too heavy for the sand along the Platte, and it's uphill most of the way."

"What will they do when they get to that Oregon place if they don't have anything?"

"If they make it out there they'll be livin' well. The land is said to be rich and the weather mild, and there's trees aplenty."

Thinkin' of that land west of the Rockies felt good, but now I was seein' familiar things around me. We were close to Maple Lane. I urged Dancer into a quicker pace and smiled at Louisa. "Almost there."

33

Maple Lane. The leaves arched over the road and the green-
ness let the sun through in little bright patches. The pond
wasn't quite as big as I remembered, and the lane not quite
as long, but the people . . .

"It's Jason!" Ben Evans called as he took to runnin' to his
place down the hill.

By the time we reached the house Mr. Johnston and Miss
Samantha were on the porch. Mr. Evans, Cleveland, and
Tolin came from the barn before we were out of the saddle.
We had such a reception it was frightenin'. There was hugs
from everyone, and talk so much you couldn't understand
a thing. Titus even carried his ma around to set with us.

Miss Dorothy was there, standin' off to one side. She was
pretty, too, just like Tolin said. She was wearin' a flower-
print dress like Miss Samantha usually wore. She talked
real fine like Tolin and Mr. Johnston. Her hair was braided
tight and hardly showed under her bonnet. Louisa was
studyin' her. They was almost the same age, but Miss Dorothy looked young—like a child, not a woman. Louisa
brushed some of the dust from her brown cotton skirt and
smoothed her hair.

"All right! Come now. Everyone!" Mr. Johnston called.
"These two young people have had a very long journey."
He stood between us with his hand on each of our shoul-

ders. "Let's help them to get settled and give them time to rest. Lend a hand, everyone."

"Did we miss the wedding?" I asked Tolin as he hoisted my bedroll.

"I told you we'd wait. Samantha planned it for Saturday. That's her daddy's birthday, and she hoped you'd be here by then."

And I was there. Feelin' the joy almost like comin' home. Almost . . .

I helped Titus settle Miss Rose on her porch while Miss Samantha and Mrs. Evans showed Louisa the big house and what would be our place to stay.

"Jason?" Miss Rose put her soft hand on my arm. Titus had started for the stable. I sat on the porch beside her rocker. "It's good to have you back. Yes. I'm gettin' to be an old lady, and I wasn't too sure I'd see you here again."

"You've plenty of years left, Miss Rose."

She chuckled in that wise way of old folks. "You're the one with the years, Jason. A multitude of years before you, and I want to see that you start on them right." Her rocker creaked as she talked. "We've got a weddin' to do."

"Yes, ma'am. Tolin's real excited."

"No. Not Miss Samantha's weddin'. Yours, boy. You and Louisa. I've been thinkin' on it since Tolin said you had found your girl."

"Miss Rose, that's right kind of you, but Louisa and me are hitched up. It's for life, with no papers needed."

"Oh, yes. You're hitched up all right, slave style, where there was no point in bringin' in a preacher 'cause never could tell when someone would get sold off. It ain't that way now. You two ain't slave folks no more. And there's legal things—babies to think about. How are they gonna carry your name if you don't give your name to Louisa? I have everything planned, so you just send the little girl down here tomorrow so I can get her all dressed out proper. I'll be able to sew somethin' up for her in no time."

"Miss Rose—"

272

"Now don't argue with me, boy. I give you a gift of my age, and a gift is as a store of grace in the eyes of him that hath it." She was speakin' in her Scriptures voice. "You go ask Louisa to marry you, and then send her down here tomorrow. The weddin' will be on Wednesday. That's all I have to say."

I felt real strange when I left. I had never thought about a weddin' for us.

Louisa came onto the porch of our cabin when I got there. "I wondered for you," she said. Everyone else had drifted away.

"I was talkin' with Miss Rose. Louisa—well—"

We went into the cabin. It was neat and already swept. Frilly curtains hung at the window. Louisa touched them and then the windowpane. "Real glass at the windows. I haven't seen real glass for so long. One day I want us a house like this."

"You saw the sleepin' room back here?" I walked to it. "Got a mirror, a rug on the floor, and even a quilt on the bed." I picked her up and swung her around. "I told you you'd like it here."

She frowned and pushed me away. "You know, Jason, that Dorothy Evans is sure a fine-lookin' girl. Bet she can read and write like you, huh?"

"Could be, but I'm sure she don't sit a horse as well as you do, or speak the Creek language."

"I used to wish I could dress in soft cotton and bonnets. You like that kind of thing on a woman, Jason?"

"Don't take no notions in your head to go changin' yourself! Besides, if you took to ruffles and petticoats, I'd have to start wearin' broadcloth pants and vest. That don't settle well with me."

"Um. Well, I sure don't see many hide clothes around here." She touched the fringe of my shirt, then turned away. "I'll bet these folks was plannin' on your hitchin' up with that Miss Dorothy." She looked at herself in the little mirror over the washstand.

"I never even met the girl till today, and it don't matter what plannin' other folks were doin'. I make my own decisions. I'm a free man, remember?"

"If you was to choose all over again . . ."

"Hush that foolish talk. Lord, girl, I know what I want." I turned her away from the mirror and hugged her close.

"Are you sure, Jason?"

"That's what I was talkin' to Miss Rose about. She said I was to ask you to marry me."

"To *marry* you?"

"She's got it all worked out and there's to be a weddin' on Wednesday."

"A weddin'? Is that what you want?"

"Why, sure it is. It sounds real fine."

"I guess it could be good. It would make a new start for us. If we got married we'd really be free folks. It wouldn't never be like it was before."

"We'll be Jason and Louisa Cobb, and we'll have our own life to live and plans to make."

A glimmer was growin' in her eyes as we talked. "You won't be ashamed of me none, will you? I don't read, but I'll learn. Really!"

"Miss Rose said for you to go to her tomorrow and she'd get you dressed out right."

"Did she say that?" She smiled and hugged me tight. It was the most happiness I'd seen in her since I found her. If marryin' up before a preacher would make that difference, I'd do it every day.

"I'm goin' to be married this week, too," I bragged to Tolin when I saw him the next mornin'.

He was smilin' bright. "I know! At that new Negro church up the road. I teach there three afternoons a week. Let's ride into town and get you a fine suit to wear."

"No need. I've some twill pants here, and my beaded shirt. I found my ermine-tail necklace all safe in the drawer."

"Ermine tails and beaded shirts for a wedding! You'd think you were still in the Territory."

We both laughed and Tolin took up a hoe and headed for the fields. Work had slowed down with the upcomin' weddin', but the weeds didn't ever seem to notice things like that. Tolin, even with his refined talkin', had hands heavy-boned and rough from work. I was glad to see that.

"It's gonna be good to have you back here. Traffic has been light this spring," Cleveland said as I helped him repair slats on a storage bin. "We count a lot on them to hoe and lay crops. It'll be good to have another two pair of hands in the fields. That's a right fine-lookin' woman you got, too."

I took up the hammer and drove a nail in on the next board, suddenly wishin' for the heft of the heavy, broad hammer I used when bendin' adze blades. "I couldn't ask for no better woman than Louisa," I said.

"Do you, Jason Cobb, take this here woman, Louisa, to be your wife, wedded in the laws of the Lord?" Reverend McDade's voice boomed in the little wooden hall that served as the Negro church. "That means you're gonna have to love her, son, as you do your own body. See to her happiness, provide for her in the way of free folks for the rest of your lives." He was a freedman, and a pulley worker at the landin'. His thick-knuckled hands gripped his closed Bible. I felt power in the way he talked.

"I do." My heart beat fast as he asked Louisa the question.

Titus and Cleveland were there, and Miss Rose had made a rare trip off Maple Lane to be there, too. Mr. Evans and Ben came. Mrs. Evans had sent flowers out of her yard and they smelled sweet. Tolin came, too.

"In the sight of God, and by the righteous laws of this here state of Missouri, and the powers vested in me by the African Methodist Episcopal Zion Church, I do hereby call you husband and wife."

Louisa, in a soft yellow cotton dress Miss Rose had fixed up for her, looked scared, and her skin was damp and flushed. She had loosed her hair and pulled it back on her neck with a yellow ribbon, the long dark strands fallin' softly on her back.

"Let us pray," said Reverend McDade. We bowed our heads, and more words was spoke.

There were amens from everyone; and like I always figured, the words took on a new meanin' when I heard them from a Negro preacher. When I walked from that church into the warm evenin', Louisa's hand in mine, I kept hearin' Reverend McDade's words: see to her happiness; provide for her in the way of free folks . . . It was a responsibility. One I'd always felt, but now it was spelled out. Promised by me before everyone who was important in my life.

34

The weddin' on Saturday was held in the Johnstons' house. Everyone from Maple Lane was there, and some friends of the Johnstons, Negro and white, from Independence and other little towns nearby. Even the constable came. I heard Louisa draw a deep breath of awe when she saw the gown Miss Samantha wore. Tolin was donned in a suit like I'd seen only in catalogues. The coat was blue and pinched in at the waist with a rounded tail back and a wide collar that made his fine white shirt seem even whiter. His blue eyes sparkled like sunlight off a lake.

Mrs. Evans smiled and cried the whole time the words was said. And Mr. Evans played his fiddle at the beginnin' and the end. After the weddin' everyone went to the lawn, where the summer flowers were bloomin' in all colors of yellow and pink. The fiddlin' took on a different sound of fast-movin' reels and little waltzes.

"Didn't I tell you Maple Lane folks was something different?" I said to Louisa. She just stood back and watched.

There was laughin' and good times. Titus and Charles set up tables and they was covered in lacy cloths. The food was brought out. I hooked my arm around Louisa's waist and pulled her over to the tables. We all ate together. Later, when the dishes was cleared away and there wasn't nothin' left on the table but a big cake, Mrs. Evans came out of the house with a tray of glasses and Mr. Johnston and Mr. Evans brought out big bottles of wine Mr. Johnston had had shipped in from St. Louis. All the grown folks took a cup of wine.

"To the bride and groom!" the constable said. "May their life be long and fruitful."

"Wait!" Tolin said before anyone drank. "There were two weddings this week. Jason and Louisa were married on Wednesday." He turned to us. "To the bride and groom." His glass was raised high and his arm around Samantha. Everyone cheered and we all drank the sweet-tastin' wine.

Tolin and Samantha came over to us. Their faces were so happy you had to smile to see them.

"Jason," Tolin said. He acted like he didn't want anyone to hear him, but Samantha and Louisa heard him quite well. "If we work it right we can give Maple Lane two fine babies by next spring."

"Oh, Mr. Cobb!" Samantha got a deep flush. Tolin leaned back and laughed. He slapped my back and laughed some more.

Louisa didn't laugh or flush. She was gone. She had run off toward the stable. I turned quickly and went after her.

"What's wrong with you, runnin' off like that?" I said when I caught up to her. She walked fast down the path and didn't answer. "Louisa! Don't you think it would be a fine thing to have us a baby?"

"Yes, Jason," she said solemnly.

I was backin' down the road in front of her so's to study her face. "You don't sound too sure!" I stopped her with my hands on her shoulders.

"I want a baby, Jason, but I don't want—I don't want it here." Her voice was stiff and hard like it had been when I first found her. Her eyes glared at me. "You didn't tell me we was comin' to Maple Lane for good and ever, and now you got me married to you. Ohhh!" She pushed my arms away and started runnin' toward the pasture.

"Louisa, what are you sayin'?"

278

She was leanin' on the fence rail. Tears glistened from her angry eyes. "I'm sayin' what I said before! What I said when I come to you from Oneechee. I ain't slavin' for no white man, no more! That's what you got us doin' if we stay here. It won't be our own life like you said. We'll be slavin'!"

"What do you mean? We're free folks! We work here for wages!"

"And we hoe the field what ain't ours, and tote the crops and tend the pigs what ain't ours? For what? For some bits of money? So your Mistuh Tolin can still live in a fine house while we live in a cabin? And even that ain't ours! I'd rather be back with the Creeks diggin' roots and half starved!"

My breath was comin' fast and I felt that yappin' start up again in my brain so bad that my head was throbbin'.

"When we was at Chimalee we had the forge, and our own little house. You made it all yourself, too. And workin' the fields was for common benefit. Didn't no one person get rich off of the work of the others."

"You sayin' you want to go back to the Creeks? Even with the laws they might be havin'?"

"No, Jason, I don't want to go back there, but there's got to be other places. Places where we can work our own crops, be with the land. Where we can be however we want to be. I thought when you said we was to be married you was thinkin' that way, too." She leaned her head into her arms and her shoulders sloped heavy.

I propped my arm on the fence rail and looked over Maple Lane land. The sound of music floated to me and people was laughin' and dancin' at the house again. Dancer came over and nudged my arm. I patted his nose and watched the sorrel mare race around the pasture toward the barn fence. She skidded to a halt and tossed her head defiantly, then charged off again.

I suddenly saw myself two years back: a slumped-over slave boy sittin' on a cot in a small stable room. I heard my own voice—not a forceful voice like I had now—but a dreamin' voice: *There was land so big you could ride for days and never see another soul . . . I'd have to go out there—where I could stay free and not have to be bound up again.* And I had. I had gone into that big land, and I got along. I had made my own way, my own decisions. I had survived the weather, the Indians, the loneliness. There wouldn't be no loneliness no more with Louisa by my side.

"If we was to find that kind of place—where we can be our own folks—it's gonna mean struggle, Louisa. It's gonna mean bad weather, injun fights, and all kinds of problems."

She looked up at me and snuffed back tears. "I been through it all and worse, Jason. I'm strong for it."

"We don't have much, and by the time we work out to the Territory we'll have even less. We'd need a wagon."

"No, we wouldn't! We got two fine horses, and three mules with the one you left here. They carried us here from Chimalee. A wagon on the trail is too cumbersome; you even said that." Her eyes started brightenin'.

"That wagon train for Oregon—it'll pass through some right fine land." Louisa's face cheered to my words. She started smilin'. "They've left already, but we could catch them easy in two, three days."

"I'll bet they don't got no blacksmith, neither! You could hunt—"

"Tolin told me to keep the Hall rifle, and I've got the muzzleloader, too."

"And Zena taught me a lot about wild roots and berries. We'll live better than any of them!" Her arms were around my waist. "Oh, Jason! You mean it, don't you? We'll really do it?"

"We'll find a valley on the other side of the Rockies, and I'll build us a house."

"A valley where folks will want to settle in. You'll have a fine smithy, and I'll plant a big garden behind the house."

"And we'll have horses. Handsome horses that folks will take envy to see." Louisa laughed and clapped her hands together with joy. She was young and beautiful and laughin' again. I swooped her up in my arms and started toward the music. "We'll get along fine with the injun folks 'cause they'll think my wife is one of them," I teased.

"And we'll have a baby. A baby that'll stay with me."

"A boy baby! We'll name him Marcus for my pa." We was near the house.

"You-all still talkin' babies?" Tolin said with a grin as he came down the path.

When I looked at Tolin I was burstin' inside with joy from seein' Louisa laugh and smile. The bother was out of my brain, and I knew I was goin' to live out a dream. But seein' Tolin brought a stab of sadness. I put Louisa down and she ran to the cabin to start packin'.

"Tolin. It was a mighty fine weddin'. I'm happy for you."

"Happy for both of us, my friend. I never would have dreamed this two years ago when we left Alabama."

"We've had some times, Tolin, you and me, but— But it's comin' to an end." His smile faded. "We have to leave. Louisa and me are goin' to catch the wagon train and go to Oregon."

"Oregon! That's crazy! We've a place for you here at Maple Lane . . ."

"I know. With broadcloth pants and field work. No offense, Tolin, but I'm a blacksmith; and one who loves the frontier. I need a place where I can be my own man." There was a long silence between us with only the fiddlin' and laughin' in the background.

"And not be bound up again." He said the words I'd thought a few minutes before. He drew a deep breath and let it out slow. "You're leaving soon?"

"In the mornin'. The train is three days up the trail." He nodded solemn. "Don't make a big thing about it with the others. There's been tears enough as it is."

He took a kerchief from his pocket and blew his nose. "Damn, Jason. You're hard on a person." He wiped his eyes, and I kept my feelin's in check.

"You keep in touch. I'm gettin' to be real good at letter writin'. I'll need to keep in practice." I felt my throat tighten.

He looked at me with a sad smile. I clasped his hand and held it tight, and then we hugged for all the years gone by.

"I'll do it, Jason. By God! I will."

I left him then and went to help Louisa.

There is a wagon train camped in a tight circle by the windy Platte. Early evening throws purple mirages across the brown land. The fires, like orange glitters in the coming darkness, show shadows and figures of the people. People with dreams bound together on the road for Oregon.

The young store clerk and his family are from Ohio, traveling with one wagon, four oxen, a milk cow. All they had when they left the bankrupt store in Chillicothe. An older man, with a drawn, tired face, and with a bride half his age, left a Pennsylvania farm that yielded only death to his first wife and two of his sons. A third son traveled by boat to the Northwest in '35 and is waiting for his father to help him with the fertile land on the Pacific.

There is a Boston man seeking to enlighten the illiterate of the West; adventurers who are looking for a thrill on the frontier; three lumberjacks from Michigan who heard that the pines were bigger in Oregon; and a merchant who sees the chance to establish himself early in the new land.

A blacksmith travels with them. In the firelight the others often sit and listen to the ring of his hammer as he mends a tire or tightens a chain. He sings a song in a young, strong voice, and his wife works the bellows.

"Stoke up the fire," he sings. "Take up the tong. Iron's my life and I'll hammer it strong.

> *Hammer come down.*
> *Hammer come down.*
> *Hit that iron make a mighty fine soun'.*

July, 1838.

Historical
Notes

26 *The Appeal* was one of the most notable abolitionist papers and was established in the 1820s by David Walker. It was banned in most of the Cotton Belt after 1831, as were most publications of similar views.

31 Until the late 1850s a blacksmith's work did not include shoeing horses. That separate occupation was attended by a farrier.

65 *Freedom's Journal* was a popular paper among the black communities, established in 1828 by John Russwurm, a black 1826 graduate of Bowdoin College. Henry Blair and the Wilberforce colony (page 68) were real entities, although probably not recorded together in one issue of the paper.

129 All characters at Fort Laramie are fictitious except for Captain William Drummond Stewart and Alfred Jacob Miller. Miller's sketches and paintings can be found in many museums across the country, including the Smithsonian Institution. The situations described with these people are true, including the armor taken to trapper Jim Bridger.

131 The trapper Black Harris, a historical figure, was not a black man, but there were black men on the frontier at

that time. Edward Rose was a contemporary of Harris's, and James Beckwourth (for whom Beckwourth Pass in California is named) was born of a Negro mother, and lived in the West most of his life. In 1836 he was a sub-chief of a Crow tribe, and his autobiography, first published in 1856, is a fine example of mountain yarning. It also contains some rather derogatory remarks about Negroes. Beckwourth would probably not appreciate the acclaim he now receives as being one of the first black adventurers of the West.

147   The Panic of 1837 caused a deep depression in the nation's economy; many banks closed and people were forced off their land. The panic was a major factor in the western migration of the 1840s, and also resulted in a partial reform of the U.S. banking system and the establishment of the Federal Treasury.

167   Conflict with the Mormons in Missouri started in 1833 when the Mormons first settled in Independence. In 1837 Governor Boggs set aside an entire county in the northern part of the state which was known as Far West. Conflicts mounted in the following year, and the Mormons were forced to move farther west.

207   There was no formal postal service in the western states or territories, and delivery of mail was a chancy thing. The Overland Stage Company, which was an essential part of western communication, was not formed until the mid-1840s, and the Pony Express (which lasted only a year and a half) was begun in 1860.

214   John Campbell is the true name of the western Creek Indian agent in 1837, although the circumstances in which I have used his character are fictitious. The Creek Agency was located near what is now Muskogee, Oklahoma. Camp Mason and Camp Holmes were actual points along the Canadian River, as was North Fork (later called North Fork Town).

253   The year 1838 was a very damaging year for the western Creeks. Smallpox, brought in by the Chickasaws, reduced

their population by one-third, and a drought during the spring and summer of that year ruined most of the crops put in by the newest emigrants.

264 In 1837 the Choctaw people set up a form of government and established rules for their slaves and any free Negroes. Similar rules were adopted by the Cherokees in 1838, and by 1842 the Creeks and Chickasaws had some form of restriction for the Negro population. The Creeks became embroiled in ownership rights regarding many of the Negroes who moved west with the Seminoles. Seminole-Negroes were allowed to set up their own towns, and many Creek leaders attempted to end this policy by raiding and burning the towns and enslaving the inhabitants. This conflict continued through the War Between the States.

275 The African Methodist Episcopal Zion Church was founded in New York City in 1796, and was one of the most influential Negro organizations in the first half of the nineteenth century.

Throughout the book, all fort names, locations, and descriptions are correct for the years 1837 to 1840, and any literature mentioned is accurate for the time.

Selected
Bibliography

Blevins, Winfred. *Give Your Heart to the Hawks.* New York: Avon, 1976.

Bonner, T. D., ed. *The Life and Adventures of James P. Beckwourth, Mountaineer, Scout and Pioneer and Chief of the Crow Nation of Indians.* Reprint of the 1856 edition. New York: Arno Press, 1969.

Burt, Jesse Clifton, and Ferguson, Robert B. *Indians of the Southeast—Then and Now.* Nashville: Abingdon, 1973.

Debo, Angie. *The Road to Disappearance: A History of the Creek Indians.* Norman: University of Oklahoma Press, 1979.

Foreman, Grant. *The Five Civilized Tribes.* Norman: University of Oklahoma Press, 1971.

————. *Indian Removal: The Emigration of the Five Civilized Tribes of Indians.* Norman: University of Oklahoma Press, 1976.

Franklin, John Hope. *From Slavery to Freedom: A History of American Negroes.* 5th ed. New York: Alfred Knopf, 1978.

McDermott, John Francis. *The Frontier Re-examined.* Champaign: University of Illinois Press, 1967.

McReynolds, Edwin C. *Missouri: A History of the Crossroads State.* Norman: University of Oklahoma Press, 1975.

————. *Oklahoma: A History of the Sooner State.* Rev. ed. Norman: University of Oklahoma Press, 1977.

Mahon, John K. *The History of the Second Seminole War: 1835–1842.* Gainesville: University Presses of Florida, 1967.

Moody, Ralph. *The Old Trails West.* New York: T. Y. Crowell, 1963.

Parkman, Francis. *The Oregon Trail.* New York: New American Library (Signet Classics).

Phillips, Ulrich B. *Life and Labor in the Old South.* New York: Little, Brown, 1929.

Quarles, Benjamin. *The Negro in the Making of America.* Rev. ed. New York: Macmillan, 1969.